THE WAY OF THE WORLD

The Making of a True Warrior

B. Burgess Junek

Images of the World

Published by Images of the World
Rapid City, South Dakota
www.imagesoftheworld.com
iow@hills.net

ISBN-13: 978-0-9630448-6-0

Cover art by: Atula Siriwardane
Cover design: B. Burgess Junek

Library of Congress Control Number: 2022910443
Printed in the United States of America

ACKNOWLEGMENTS

Thanks to beta readers Kathy Trotter, Jaff Auchterlonie, Ron Yahne, Paul Beckett, Luther Busching, and Chris Van Ness for all their comments, encouragements, and insights. Special thanks to my sister, Bobbi Looney, for the final proof read and corrections.

Thanks also to Atula Siriwardane for his fantastic artwork on the book covers and the maps.

I could not have written *A Bright One Chronicles* without the lifetime of exotic traveling adventures, bicycling expeditions, and spiritual quests that I have shared with my wife, Tass Thacker. Nor could I have written it without her red pen and brutally honest editorial skills and sharp critiques throughout the entire process to make the story better. For years, Tass has heroically managed our business and household to give me extra time to write. For all of her humor, strength, inspiration and love, this book is dedicated to my soul mate, Tass Thacker.

LUNAR CALENDAR

The appendix at the back of the book has a **Cast of Characters** list and a **Glossary** for unfamiliar words.

Each moon or month has 29-30 days and is divided into 4 weeks:

Dark Moonday or Divine Night begins the first day of the first week of each month.

Bright Moonday starts the second week of each month and begins evening socializing and travel by moonlight.

Full Moonday starts the third week with a culmination of evening festivities, celebrations and travel by moonlight.

Dim Moonday starts the fourth and last week of each month with moonlight socializing or travel in the early morning before dawn.

Each week has 7 days except bright Moonday with 8. Luckdays are added every other dark Moonday to adjust the lunar calendar to the appearance of the new crescent moon.

1 moon = one month = 29-30 days
10 moons = one decade

Lunar Calendar Conversion To Solar Years:

12 moons = 1 solar year
50 moons = 4 solar years
75 moons = 6 solar years
100 moons (1 century or centurion) = 8 solar years
150 moons = 12 solar years
   (start of tween moons, beginning of adulthood)
200 moons (2 centuries) = 16 solar years, full adulthood
300 moons (3 centuries) = 24 solar years
400 moons (4 centuries) = 32 solar years
500 moons (5 centuries) = 40 solar years
600 moons (6 centuries) = 48 solar years
700 moons (7 centuries) = 57 solar years
800 moons (8 centuries) = 65 solar years
900 moons (9 centuries) = 73 solar years
1,000 moons (1 millennium) = 81 solar years
5,000 moons (5 millennium) = 404 solar years
10,000 moons (10 millennium) = 808 solar years

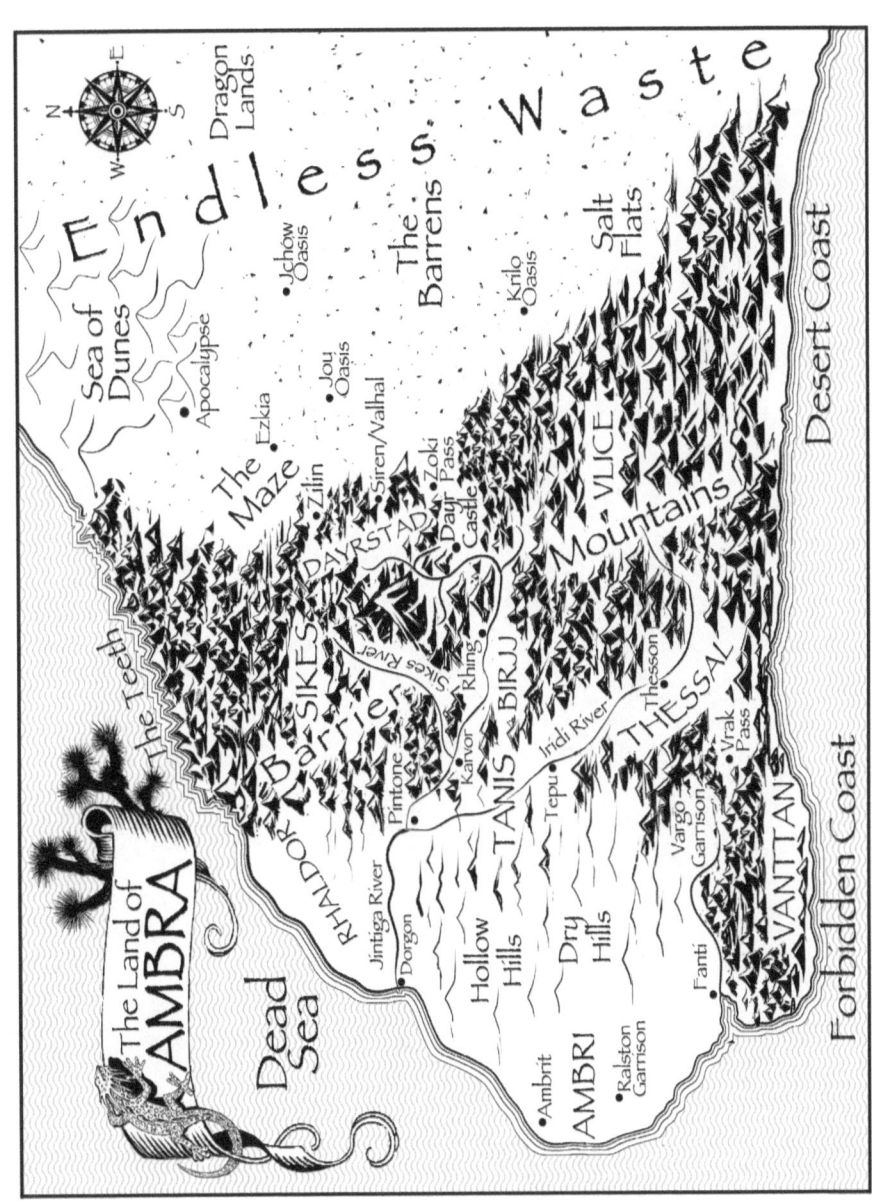

PART I

Her gaze pierces all souls,
Her sword a fiery truth.
Morning Star of Heaven,
Whose dagger slays the Beast.

Kabaal Prophecies

Her warrior heart feared no battle, nor sacrifice.

Hope the Proclaimer

THE YOKE

Riin Ruel sat cross-legged on the floor before a simple altar in her prison cell and fingered her Yoke as she began to pray. Thirteen bones on a string she used for demon hunting. The older bones at the beginning were darker in color than the two newer bones on the end. They were from the little fingers of the sword hands of the two killers who had tried to ambush her on the way to Dayr Castle.

The last bone came from the biggest fighter, whom Lightning had kicked and she had ritually slain, looking into his eyes while putting a dagger through his heart. That had created the Yoke, giving her access to the demon who controlled the man. Riin Ruel was now preparing to battle the demon with a second surprise attack.

Riin Ruel had been trained at the Ambrit Military Academy to be a Blade, the order that protected and served the Czarzina as her personal guard. She had also been covertly schooled as a Dagger, a secret group of warriors instructed in arcane and mystical fighting arts known only to a few, with abilities and expertise unimaginable. She had risen to become the Point of the Dagger, and had been sent in search of the Bright One of prophecy, the Bright One to become Empress and bring a return of the Ambri Empire. That quest had sent her to Dayr Castle and also to Ezkia Nunnery in the Endless Waste.

That quest had also landed her in prison when she had returned to find that the woman who was Will of the Blades, and secretly Hilt of the Daggers, and her mentor and leader, Anna Nana, had died. The new Will of the Blades arrested her.

The new Czarzina censured Riin Ruel as a heretic and excommunicated her in a religious court--and sent her to the Box. The Czarzina had been outraged by the insolence of Riin Ruel's quest to find a prophesized Empress in a Barbarian Kingdom. She considered the idea absurd!

Riin Ruel had been held captive for two centuries in the Box at Ralston Garrison, the most secure prison in the history of the Ambri Empire. Now, once again, she was invoking the *Prayers for the Dead*.

She did not recite any of the first 19 prayers, also known as the *Prayers for the Mortal Body*, which were read at the Womb for a week after a woman died, and again on the following dark Moonday. The prayers helped the bereaved in their mourning process to reach an acceptance of a woman's death and guide her departed spirit to heaven. Priests throughout Ambra recited the prayers at funerals. Only a few knew that there were additional *Prayers for the Dead*.

Riin Ruel recited the 20th prayer, *Flee the Mortal Body*. But she did not follow the normal sequence of the Bridge, which served as a doorway into the spirit worlds and other realms of consciousness. She did not recite *The Path of Clouds*, nor *The Gates of Heaven*, which were prayer maps guiding the highly initiated on a sacred journey to the upper heavens. Her destination was not among the 30 prayers of *The Glories of Divine on Her Throne*.

Instead, she recited portions of *Flee the Mortal Body* backward, to open a trap door for the Yoke. Her body sat in the prison cell while her spirit, attached to the Yoke, took her beyond the Underbridge, past the *Path of Sorrow* and the *Path of Pain*, to arrive at *Wail! Before the Gates of Hell*! Standing at the fiery portal, she did not begin the *Prayers for the Damned* as normal, which locks, binds and blocks evil from entering the world and helps protect women from the influence of the Beast. She recited a key lock backwards. Riin Ruel was instantly transported through the barriers into the fifth level of hell where the demon she was hunting had its lair.

Riin Ruel attacked the demon with an inspired fierceness. She had not returned to battle him since her first attack a century ago. Instead, she had left him to worry about her next move, knowing more assaults were imminent, but not knowing when. Upon her first learning that the demon was in the fifth hell, Riin Ruel knew she needed to better prepare herself for their next conflict. She had eight active demons on her Yoke. One more than normally allowed, and too many to carry while trying to overpower a demon in the 5th hell.

So, she spent decades battling the lesser demons on her Yoke. She had annihilated the demons hiding in the first two hells and killed one of the demons in the third hell. The other was badly weakened. Now she had only two active demons on her Yoke. The demon in the fifth hell would have no idea of her increased power and force.

She easily broke through the demon's protection wards and fell upon the fiend with all her wrath. She fought valiantly, feeling a surge of power flowing through her as she struck again and again, inflicting a multitude of injuries. All the while she felt the tentacles of his lair reaching out to ensnare and hold her spirit fast. The cloud of malice and corruption grew thicker and darker around her. She could feel herself growing weaker. Riin Ruel made a final slash across the demon's throat as she silently recited the words that would allow her to safely escape.

PART II

Only true knowledge can lead to true action.

Kabaal Prophecies

The quest for knowledge can have many ramifications.

Hope the Proclaimer

KARVOR

The Ambri built the enchanting and multi-colored city of Karvor on the precipitous, terraced hillsides near the rim of a deep canyon, with steep twisting streets and tunnels, public squares, and small parks. The Mother Womb was the architectural highlight of course, but there were also a number of other beautiful and brightly painted Womb temples with their high arching domes. The city also boasted a colorful Stadium for theater and music that held three thousand people, a Library, University and Voice, along with an elaborate system of aqueducts, water lines and sewer drainage.

When people in Karvor said they wanted to *go up the hill*, it meant they were looking for an entertaining and exciting time. For wealthier travelers *up the hill* meant visiting the fancy and polychromatic casinos, saloons, and dance halls along Skyline Street, with dramatic views looking out over Jintiga Canyon and the far western horizon. For soldiers and common folk *up the hill* meant going higher to the smaller and cheaper taverns and gambling joints along the edge of Old Town, the small original community above the elaborate city laid out by Ambri engineers and architects. Old Town was rougher, cheaper, and wilder. For smugglers, ruffians, and mercenaries, *up the hill* meant the narrow, twisting stairs and exposed pathways of Cracken Street in the very heart of Old Town.

Tyme, Klew, Jyg and Bones had just come into Karvor. They

had left Dayr Castle four days ago, travelling even through the heat, and all moonlit night, chasing after a man with fancy rings whom they believed responsible for Noot's death.

Noot, the simple stable boy who loved animals and would never deliberately hurt anyone. Noot, with his throat slit, left to die in Merryleg's stall. The horrible image of finding him was burned into Tyme's memory.

The killer had a twelve-hour head start and had ridden his horse so hard they had not been able to catch him. But they were close behind and had followed him to Karvor, the artistic, rainbow-hued, party town in the mountains of Tanis.

They had spent much of the day looking through the stables for the palomino daya ridden by the man with flashy rings, and finally found the horse, with an injured knee, in a small, run-down stable in Old Town. After befriending a stable worker, Tyme learned the man had traded for a different horse and left. He was usually gone for two weeks, during which they hoped to find out more about him. They already knew that he presented himself as a well-to-do manser, yet he traveled with the urgent speed of an important messenger, which indicated he might be a spy. His two-week trip was the amount of time required to get to Ambrit and back.

"His last trip was to Dayrstad," Klew paced slowly. "Yet he didn't come to court with any message, nor meet with King Eyrico."

"Whatever he's doing," Tyme said thoughtfully, "He doesn't want King Eyrico to know."

Klew stopped pacing. "Which means 'tis probably illegal." He shook his head. "Or even treasonous."

"Treasonous!" Bones repeated loudly and shook her head as well.

They all gave Bones a startled look. But this time they did not chuckle at the raven speaking, nor remark on the way Bones sounded like Klew when she spoke the word. Instead, they nodded their heads in agreement.

"Whatever he's planning," Jyg vowed, "We're not going to

let him get away with it."

"If his schemes include treason against King Eyrico," Klew declared, "'tis much more important for us to secretly find out his plans, and who is behind him, than confronting him over Noot's death. I'll send a letter to Dayr Castle to inform the King of what we've found. We may be here in Karvor much longer than we imagined."

Klew did not want to stay at a normal inn. He led them down out of Old Town to a hillside art district where there were cheap apartments for rent. He had been given a generous coin pouch by King Eyrico for their journey and had brought some of his own money along as well, just in case something like this might happen. He planned to make that money last.

"No one would think to look for us here," he said. He insisted that Tyme should be the one to make the inquiry. "You're a woman. They would not normally rent to men."

The sky was growing dark when Tyme found a rooftop apartment above the Glazed Woman, a small ceramics shop in a warren of stairs and alleys just a ten-minute walk up the hill from Skyline Street. The apartment had three rooms, two patios, a comfortable condition, and also a small servants' door in the back of the kitchen onto the stairs of an adjoining apartment building.

"Rather than using the front door, I think we should use the servants' door and not come in and out together," Klew said. "If someone's following one of us, they'll probably assume we're going into the apartment building."

The neighborhood was a gathering spot for craft people, artists, musicians, and their followers, with narrow, steep, winding passageways and stairs up the hillsides. Like all of Karvor, the buildings were painted in a riot of bright colors and trim. The ceramic shop was blue with yellow doors, windows, and trim. The second-floor apartment was aqua green on the front and purple on the backside, and orange, yellow, and light blue on the inside.

The apartment inner patio and windows gave easy access

for Bones to fly in, which she did with stealth only after the owner had handed over the key and left. She landed with a whoosh on Jyg's shoulder.

"Manser Jygero!" the raven's voice boomed in greeting, sounding so human that they all chuckled in amazement. 'Twas the first words Bones had learned to say, imitating the voice of a noble manser who had come to Dayr Castle hoping to buy a falcon from Jyg.

"Good to have you with us," Jyg replied happily. After disappearing in the mountains for a day, Bones was now staying much nearer to Jyg. She had followed him closely all through town, perching on roofs, ledges, and balconies as they searched for the palomino daya, up and down the streets, in and out of buildings, and finally to the patio of the apartment.

Bones was too excited to stay on Jyg's shoulder and swooped down to the floor to hop about. The big black bird stood more than knee high. Jyg reached down to let her rub her thick, ridged, three-inch bill across his hand with affection, and gently bite his fingers.

She hopped over to Tyme and rubbed her bill against Tyme's hand. They had known each other since the raven was just a tiny chick with a plaster cast around her neck. Tyme gave Bones a few pieces of date. Bones then cautiously hopped over to Klew, who smiled quietly when the big black raven daintily accepted a piece of date from his hand.

They each took a quick bucket bath, ladling and pouring water over themselves, then wrapping in thin wet towels to lay out on the patio in the cooling night air before going to bed. The sun was long up when they ate breakfast and planned their next move.

"We can't take turns sitting and watching over the stables without drawing attention to ourselves continually loitering in the neighborhood. When the ring man returns," Klew continued, "the stable manser will tell him that someone was asking about a man on a palomino daya. He'll know that a man of my height and bearing has trailed him from Dayrstad. He'll reward the stable manser for lying to me and protecting him. We have to assume he'll reward others for similar protection and warnings should we be asking about him."

Klew raised his eyebrows. "That means the owner of the inn where he's staying, and the owners of the taverns or gambling halls he might frequent, even the bar tenders and waiters, might warn him if we're asking about him. So, we can't question those people directly. But we can ask lesser servants and bystanders, just as Tyme did at the stables. We'll work apart from each other and start on Skyline Street. 'Tis most likely where a man with expensive rings would gamble."

THE DRAGON

Epoh and the grubbers had been searching for dragon bones in the Sea of Dunes for decades when Grinst had alerted them to the danger of an approaching storm. They had raced through the night under a brightly waxing moon only to be caught and pinned down by the storm at sunrise, just minutes from the shelter of their cave at the seep. They had huddled together on the ground, holding on to each other, hardly able to breathe from the dust, nor hear each other shout from the terrible roar of the wind and sand.

After the initial impact of the storm, Grinst led them with a short, knotted rope. Led them when they could not even open their eyes from the burning sting of the sand, nor see their hands in front of your faces. Led them stumbling and falling from sudden gusts of wind, until miraculously, they all made it back alive to their cave.

The storm lasted four days. When it stopped, they had to dig out the seep for water and spend another four days getting resupplied before they could go back in search of dragon bones.

The landscape of the dunes had completely changed. More of the Dragon Perch was exposed, with still no sign of any door, window, or weakness in the giant tower. They methodically spread out and began scanning the area around the tower in a unified pattern. On the evening of the third day, Harvig climbed a high dune and suddenly dropped down to the ground.

Epoh noticed his unusual movement. Harvig motioned frantically at Epoh to stay quiet then scrambled and ran wildly toward Horton. Epoh and Grinst promptly joined them to see what was about.

Harvig could hardly speak. His eyes were wild. "A dragon!" he gasped. "Bigger than the nunnery." His body shook. "Not bones. Lying sleeping in the sand."

"Sleeping?" Grinst hissed, his eyes bulging out. "What did she look like?"

"Her wings were stretched out." Harvig trembled. "I couldn't see her head."

Grinst motioned for Horton to follow as he sneaked carefully toward the dune viewpoint. Epoh followed with a pounding heart. Harvig nervously behind. As they approached the summit of the dune they crawled slowly on their stomachs.

They peered over the dune to see the enormous body of the dragon, the skin shining like metal, wing's spread, lying just as Harvig had said, with its head buried in the sand.

"Booooo!" Grinst screamed out wildly with an explosive jump into the air.

Harvig shrieked in terror.

Horton and Epoh jolted up out of the sand moaning and trembling, their hearts exploding in their chests.

Grinst howled with laughter. The dragon did not stir. "Dragon bones!" Grinst yelled with rapture as he raced down the dune for a closer look. Only the shiny back and wings of the great animal were exposed from the sand. The head and the tail were still buried in the dunes. The body of the immense dragon was still covered with bright silver skin.

They all climbed onto the top of the long straight back. The skin looked and felt like metal. It grew in great plates with rows of tiny bumps along thin, tight seams. Epoh paced out the length of the smooth back. "Fifty-four long strides," he reported with astonishment. "And there's much more buried in the sand."

The wings were even longer and both sharply swept back,

lying straight with no visible elbow joints. Getting to the wings from the top of the animal's back required a slide down the rounded back and an exciting drop. The protective skin of the wing had smaller plates and the same straight rows of perfectly spaced tiny round bumps along impenetrable seams. The only imperfections were long, straight cracked sections running along most of the back edges of wing.

The dragon looked nothing like Epoh imagined. Nor was it like the dragons described in his book. 'Twas long and rigid, enormously barrel bodied with no neck that he could see, and long, sleek and slender wings more like a falcon but without any apparent joints.

"Why would it die with its body and wings stretched out rigid?" Epoh asked. "Why wouldn't it curl up?" He jumped up and down on the wing. "I think this is metal."

"Dragon skin turns to metal when they die," Horton explained matter-of-factly. "That's why 'tis valuable. Blacksmiths dream of working with it." He smiled at Epoh. "Find a good piece and have it made into a dragon bone sword. Bring that back to your kingdom!"

Epoh smiled and allowed himself to dream a moment. "Yes, that would be a tale to tell."

They scampered all over the beast and camped on a rise of sand where they had a view of the whole dragon. They were all so excited they could not sleep and stayed up most of the night looking at the magnificent silver animal exposed by the sands.

The next morning they had to hike back to the seep to resupply with water and food. Then they would return. "Dragon bones," Grinst cackled the old grubber saying, "means dragon treasure."

After an impatient few days they were back. Again they searched for any weaknesses between the cracks and chinks in the plate metal skin on the top and sides of the dragon's long straight body.

"Dragons swallow their treasure," Grinst explained. "They also keep their treasure in belly pouches. What we want is inside," he pounded on the thick, seemingly impenetrable skin. "We just have to find a weakness to get in."

They started digging where the sand was already the lowest under the wing. Because of the size and angle of the dune, the sand above kept sliding down and refilling the hole. Epoh figured it would take a moon to dig out enough sand to reach the dragon's stomach.

A REGULAR AT
RED PEPPERS

Tyme, Jyg and Klew had no luck finding anything about the killer they were trailing on their first day snooping around Karvor, the bright, artistic, party town in the mountains of Tanis. Nor did they have any luck on the second day. On the third day, Tyme was walking along busy Skyline Street, which was lined with the finest taverns, saloons, and gambling halls in Karvor. She spotted a girl selling pies under a red stairwell. Feeling hungry, Tyme asked for a pie.

"Sorry, ser," the girl replied with embarrassment, thinking Tyme wanted a sweet pastry. "I only have pigeon pies."

"I like pigeon pies," Tyme replied. She was not used to being called ser. "How much for two?"

After receiving her pies, Tyme sat down next to the girl to eat. The girl eyed her with wonder. "Noble born don't never eat my pies before," she said.

"I'm not noble born," Tyme laughed. "I live at a stables. Pigeon pies were a treat for me on Moondays."

The girl smiled but couldn't quite believe it. Tyme was wearing the embroidered blouse that Wiir Waar had given her with ornately detailed stitching. She was not wearing her sword, but she had a finely-made dagger discreetly at her side, which the girl glimpsed when she sat down.

"These are really good," Tyme complimented her. "They remind me of home."

"You're not from Karvor?" the girl asked.

Tyme shook her head but said nothing. Klew had warned her to be careful about saying where she was from.

"Why did you come here?" the girl asked.

Tyme thought if she couldn't tell the girl about her home, she could at least be truthful about her quest. "I came to Karvor looking for a man who wears big fancy rings."

"Why do you look for him?"

"I think he killed someone who was very dear to me," Tyme said solemnly, "and I'd like to find out why."

"I've seen a man who wears fancy rings," the pie seller said. "One of the rings has a big red stone."

"Where have you seen him?" Tyme asked excitedly. She could not believe her luck.

"Walking down the street," the girl pointed across the road to a brightly painted tavern, casino, and dance hall. "He often goes to Red Peppers."

Back at their apartment Tyme shared her exciting news.

"So, he's a regular at Red Peppers," Klew nodded with grim satisfaction. "Now we should be able to learn more about him!"

A WEAK SCALE

Since they didn't need much light, the grubbers often dug at the dragon's stomach in the moonlight, when the air was cool, and it felt good to sweat. One evening during a break as Epoh climbed up the dune to the dragon's back, he noticed a small chink in the skin on the side of the dragon's body well ahead of the wing. The rounded crack had just been revealed where the sand had been sliding down onto their pit. Epoh drew closer and brushed away a few handfuls of sand then yelled down for the others to join him. They all stood watching as Epoh dug away more sand. Part of the crack or seam went horizontal across the animal, and the other part ran straight downward.

"Tis it a pouch?" Harvig wondered.

"Not likely on the side in front of the wing," Horton reasoned. "Mayhaps a weak scale in its armor."

"Tis our way in!" Grinst exclaimed. They all began digging. Because they were able to shovel and push the sand easily down into their former hole near the stomach, the size of the dragon's strange scale was soon apparent—more than six feet wide! The next morning they began digging more away. About five feet down they found a small puncture in the side of the scale.

Grinst was quick to take over and dig the area out further. He cleared out the sand to reveal a small odd-shaped hole. He stuck his hand inside.

"I can feel small bones and pieces of broken metal skin!" Grinst announced. They resumed clearing away sand but did not find another chink in the large and prominent dragon's scale, which took another day to completely dig out. Twas perfectly formed, ten feet high and six feet wide, with rounded corners.

They spent that evening and the next day trying to crack or break off the scale. Grinst repeatedly pried and hammered away at the broken pieces of bone turned to metal inside the small puncture hole without success. The dragon scale did not budge.

SSHH! QUIET!

Klew did not have card skills or coins to spy on the fancy ring man in the gambling halls of Karvor. Especially if the man frequented upscale establishments like Red Peppers. He would have been warned by the stable owner that someone of Klew's description had asked about him and the daya horse. Klew would stand out like a sore thumb posed as a gambler in a casino. He needed to learn about the ring man away from the card tables.

Despite the flashy jewelry, Klew had a hunch that the man had been trained in the military. He had ruined a horse traveling to Dayr Castle, stayed only briefly, then returned to Karvor with great urgency, riding another horse lame, changed mounts, and left again. He had the discipline of a soldier. And the speed of an important messenger who had just visited a Barbarian Kingdom. It seemed unlikely that anyone in Ambrit would have such keen interest in the events, politics, or economics of Dayrstad.

If Klew wanted to figure out what forces might be at play, he needed to get a better idea of the current situation and rumors swirling around the Heart Legion garrison at Karvor. He posed as a mercenary for hire and started visiting the taverns and gambling halls favored by common soldiers. At first the complaints he heard were much the same as those spoken by the male soldiers centuries ago when he had been posted here.

The women offisers looked down at the men. Men could seldom advance, even in the lower ranks. Men were ordered to do all the worst jobs and got the unfavorable postings. Men were the workhorses, while women were the reins. Men were not respected, nor listened too.

"One new thing," Klew told Tyme and Jyg at their apartment, "is all the talk about a men's religious sect called the Fire. Apparently 'tis spreading through the ranks of the Heart Legion soldiers, and also through the mountains of Birjj and Sikes. Even in Dayrstad."

"Have you heard of it before?" Tyme asked.

"Not much," Klew replied. "'Tis not as common at Dayr Castle. Not yet, anyway. But I have seen red wax left by the candles that the followers burn at the altars in the refuge of the keep Womb. Evidently Duke Eddarko at the Siren is a convert and supporter."

Tyme sat at a corner table on the first floor of Red Peppers on Skyline Street, slowly nursing a root beer and watching all the workers, trying to decide whom she might follow and approach to ask about the man with rings. The casino was a popular spot for wealthy sers, nobles and others who had more coin to spend. The ground floor tavern and dance hall had big doors that opened onto shaded street level patios where food was also served. The top two floors were gambling halls with moon decks.

When the heat came, two girls quit work to go home. On impulse Tyme followed them out onto the street, which they crossed so one could buy a pie from the girl under the red stairs. Before Tyme could approach they jumped into the back of a passing wagon to sneak a lift. She followed behind on foot into a crowded back canyon filled with small worn houses and apartments. One of the girls jumped out and went straight into a house. The other stayed longer in the wagon, then jumped out and raced up some stairs between two buildings. When Tyme arrived at the top of the stairs, the second girl was gone from sight.

"I followed two servers," Tyme reported back at their apartment, "but couldn't catch either to talk or even say hello."

"Sounds tricky," Jyg said sympathetically.

"I will have to be faster," Tyme said. "They left Peppers, grabbed a pie, and jumped into a passing wagon to ride home."

"They ate pigeon pie?" Jyg pondered.

"One did. From Dani, the girl I told you about."

"Who said she only sells pies to the servants and workers," Jyg remembered then teased, "not nobles like you."

Tyme stuck out her tongue at him.

"Why are we trying to approach the workers ourselves?" Jyg questioned. "We already have Dani on our side. Let's ask *her* to ask the workers for information about the ring man. Then if someone knows something important, we can talk to them if needed."

"Excellent strategy!" Klew patted Jyg on the back. Jyg beamed, happy to have finally contributed something to their effort.

The afternoon heat was rising. Although Karvor has a cooler climate than Pintone, the capitol of Tanis, the temperature was hotter than the high mountains of Dayrstad. They were all happy to retreat to their small condition to recline on stone couches and give thanks for their lunch: flat bread with goat cheese, cucumbers, olives, dates, and cool, tangy yogurt in small clay pots.

Afterward Tyme did her practice. When she finished Klew asked her more about her devotions.

"When I get up before breakfast, I do contemplative prayers in rhythm to my breathing in and out," Tyme said. "During the afternoon heat I usually do wordless prayer and focus on sitting quietly in the present moment. But now, I'm still reeling from Noot's death, so I've been doing chants, which helps keep my mind from spinning."

"What's contemplative prayer?" Jyg asked. "I thought prayer was when you ask for help from Divine for problems and emergencies."

"There are many different ways to pray," Tyme explained. "Contemplative prayer is beyond talking or asking. Beyond issues and concerns of the mundane world. Contemplative prayer is about building and being in a closer relationship with Divine."

"I say the True Warrior prayer every morning and evening," Klew said, "and make offerings every Moonday at the refuge. That was all the practice I was taught."

"Tao Tau taught me lots of ways to practice," Tyme enthused and raised her thick, black eyebrows. "She also said *real* practice is not just meditation and prayer. Real practice is about how we live our lives. Every moment of every day should be our practice."

Jyg sat listening carefully. Growing up, his aunt Whi went to the Womb most Moondays. His uncle Pio took him to the refuge during large festivals. Jyg had never really thought that much about Divine or having a practice in his life. He figured that was for priests and nuns. However, he always admired Tyme's strength, confidence, and inner calmness. She had an energy about her that was different from anyone he had ever met. "Mayhaps you should teach us some practice techniques," he suggested.

Klew nodded his head.

"Join me tomorrow before breakfast," Tyme agreed with a smile. "'Tis the best way to start the day."

They napped a few hours and then came out to the west patio for a spectacular view of the molten red sunset shimmering far off in the distance. The Barrier Mountains around Dayr Castle prohibited Tyme and Jyg from ever seeing such a sunset before, spread across the horizon and filling the sky with a brilliant reddish haze.

"Karvor has the most beautiful sunsets," Klew declared.

The last few nights Jyg had been training Bones to accept

being in a cage. He realized that sometimes he might need to keep Bones briefly caged and quiet for travel, safety, or emergencies. When 'twas bedtime he again placed Bones in the cage.

Previously, as he shut the cage door, he had leaned in close to say, "Sshh! Quiet." This time before he could say anything, Bones hunched her shoulders, ducked her head and hissed, "Sshh! Quiet!" in a low, conspiratorial tone.

Jyg gasped. "Did you hear that?" he cried out in amazement.

"Sshh! Quiet!" Bones repeated in admonishment.

They all broke out laughing.

"Sshh! Quiet!" Bones said repeatedly, which made them laugh even more. Finally, Jyg put the cover over the cage and blew out the light so they could stop chuckling and fall asleep.

INSIDE THE DRAGON

Early the next morning the grubbers renewed their efforts to pry open the strange scale on the side of the dragon in front of the wing. They had not been working long when Grinst, with his arm again in the one hole, suddenly gave a cry. To everyone's astonishment the big, armored scale popped out and slid sideways a few feet before hitting the sand dune.

"Is it hollow?" Epoh exclaimed in amazement when he saw a hole behind the scale. Did the dragon have a shell like an insect? They dug out more sand to slide the scale open and peer inside.

Epoh looked over Grinst's shoulder into the dragon's body to see oddly formed walls and a dark hallway. The floor was carpeted. There were strange knobs and bumps everywhere. Small drawers and cupboards with unusual handles. Grinst pulled a few open to find each filled with unfamiliar objects. He threw them to the floor. He was looking for treasure.

The others stood in awe, letting Grinst lead. He turned right toward a door. After just a few minutes, he was able to figure out the latch.

"No animal would have this inside the body," Epoh declared as the door swung open. "We are not in an animal. This is *not* a dragon!"

"And your book that got us here is just a story tale!" Grinst answered with glee as he peered into the gloom of the dragon's innards. "'Tis the brain!" he said with astonishment.

'Twas a tight cubbyhole filled with rows of little knobs, bumps, and handles all labeled with writing. Epoh looked closer. Many of the letters were in the Ambri alphabet, although they did not spell any words he could understand. Most of the knobs twisted, while the little handles clicked back and forth between two positions.

There were two strange throne-like chairs. Grinst cackled madly as he sat in one of them, grabbing the big handle of a lever in between, but it would not move. Horton sat in the other chair. They faced two dark eyes encircled with the rows of knobs and levers.

"That's glass," Epoh moved forward and touched the surface, rubbing away the dust. 'Twas the smoothest surface he ever felt. There were no bumps, wrinkles, or imperfections like Ambri glass. "Don't tell me dragon eyes turn to glass when they die," he said before Grinst could even speak. "This has *always* been glass. This is *not* a dragon. I think this was made by the Ancient Ones!"

They left the cubbyhole and went the other direction down a short hallway to a door they had to break to open. Inside was a giant, dark chamber.

"The dragon's stomach!" Grinst said in awe. He opened one of his bags and removed a small oil lamp. The glow of the tiny light spread faintly to reveal a cavern filled with dark shapes. Grinst held the lamp high to dimly see three large mounds, long ago wrapped tightly, one with netting, the others with a strange, thin, light, cocoon-like material, much of it flaked and fallen away to reveal tottering piles of stacked boxes, some fallen from the pile to disintegrate on the floor, leaving strange objects poking through the remains of packing matter and brown and white dust.

The grubbers picked up and examined the incomprehensible gadgetry, much of it made from a light molded material, some with knobs and metal parts. Nearly all had a tightly wrapped wire cords attached, the covering of the wire crumbling and breaking away when the wire was unwound, with two or three short metal prongs at the end.

Grinst reached out and lightly pushed against the pile before them. The touch of his hand crumbled the boxes setting an avalanche in motion as a section of the pile collapsed to the floor in a cloud of fine dust.

They all started sneezing. As the dust cleared, they saw more similarly shaped objects piled on the ground. What the devices might be used for none of them could guess.

Grinst's small light sent flickering shadows dancing in the gloom as they stepped over the objects on the ground and approached the pile on the right, wrapped up and boxed stacks of giant ceramic plates, bowls and cups, some of which had also fallen off the pile to lie broken and spread across the floor. Epoh picked up one of the heavy plates and held it to the light to see a pattern of beautiful color. He brushed away the fragile paper coating on the pile to see other plates with different designs.

The aisle turned around the corner of the pile and ran into the darkness down the length of the dragon's body, a long row of mounds.

"'Tis like a warehouse," Epoh proclaimed in astonishment. "A flying warehouse! Built by the Ancient Ones!"

"What is a warehouse?" asked Harvig.

"'Tis a building where a merchant who has lots of merchandise keeps all her products until they're ready to be sold," Epoh explained.

"Stomach or warehouse!" Grinst shrugged without care. He started down the row into the darkness. "There be treasure here for sure!"

The next mound was totally encased in a thin wrapping like a wasp nest that disintegrated when touched. Underneath were stacks of boxes that also crumbled apart. Inside those were stacks of smaller boxes that broke apart to reveal thin, heavy, rectangle metal objects with black glass on one side. Each had a separate bundle of small folded up wires.

The next three mounds were the same.

The sixth mound in the row looked different. The far corner had crumbled and disintegrated leaving small black boxes lying on the floor in the paper and dust. "Look!" Harvig cried out as he opened one of the long boxes to reveal a woman's bracelet made of beautiful blue stones.

At the same moment Horton opened one of the smaller boxes to find an exquisite woman's ring with a large clear sparkling diamond surrounded by smaller gems. "I've found something as well!" he proudly pulled the ring from the box and held it up to the light of the tiny oil lamp.

Grinst let out a wild whoop. "Now we're finding *real* dragon treasure!"

THE JAWBONE RIDGE GANG

Although Klew, Tyme and Jyg assumed the fancy ring man would not be back for two weeks, they had no certainty that he would be gone his usual length of time. He could come back at any moment. So, each evening Tyme made a quick run up to the hovel of the old woman who worked at the stables in Old Town where the man had kept his horses. She had promised Tyme that she would tie a scarf by her door to signal when the ring man had returned.

One evening as Tyme was returning down a narrow alley in Old Town a stocky older boy blocked her way.

"What are you doing here?" he asked in a menacing voice. He looked mean.

"Why do you care?" Tyme replied with a shrug.

"This is my alley," he informed her.

"Please let me pass," she said respectfully to give no offense, "and I will leave your alley."

"What are you doing here?" he asked again more threateningly as he came closer.

"Just let me pass," Tyme said calmly. "I don't want to hurt you."

The boy sniggered. "You got to pay to pass." He leapt forward and bent to grab her. There was no room to dodge around him.

Tyme jumped straight at him, tucking in her chin to use the front crown of her head to smash into his face, breaking his nose and nearly knocking him out. While his vision was exploding with suns and stars, she slipped past and down the alleyway.

Back at their apartment she shared the news with Klew and Jyg. She felt a little shaky as she told the story. "It happened so fast. The alley was narrow. When he moved to grab me, my reflexes just reacted, without even thinking."

Klew had taught her, if a fight starts, hit hard and fast. He had shown her a variety of ways to head-butt, using the hardest part of the top front of her skull to smash vulnerable areas of an opponent's face or jaw. She had practiced on dried gourds and squash to get the right momentum and power to be effective without hurting herself.

"Your first street fight, and you did well," Klew chuckled and patted her on the back. "Hopefully that will be the end of it--if the boy's smart." He shook his head. "But if he's not smart, he will be out for revenge."

"I won't go near that alley again when I check for the signal," Tyme replied without much concern. "I'll get there from another direction."

"I think you should teach me how to head-butt," Jyg stated with interest. He was already practicing the sword with them. Why not learn a few street-fighting tricks as well?

Kreoko had a major problem.

He had been out in a back alley near the mipes and come across a lone girl who looked like a noble. He had played the tough guy and tried to shake her down for a coin or two when she suddenly knocked him near senseless. She had busted his nose so he could hardly breath until Ma Weeks pushed twigs up each nostril to straighten them. His head was throbbing, and his face was turning black and blue.

What in the seven hells was he going to do now? How could he tell Delgado, the leader of the Jawbone Ridge gang, what really happened? That a girl, smaller than him, smashed her head into his face and damn near knocked him out! He had never heard of such a maneuver. Mayhaps he would just tell everyone that someone--who he never even saw--sucker punched him with a club as he came around a corner.

Two days later, about the same time in the evening, Kreoko saw the girl again. This time in the riffs, heading uphill, but coming from a different direction. He sat waiting quietly, watching the alleyway. Five minutes later she came back down the hill and disappeared around a corner.

Kreoko plotted his revenge with relish. He would get his uncle's sword and be waiting here tomorrow evening and ambush her if she passed by again. He would show the girl a thing or two. She would see who was boss.

The next evening Kreoko was ready with the sword. His uncle did not know he had taken it. He had been allowed to swing it a few times, enough for Kreoko to feel the weight of the blade and imagine the destruction it could unleash. With such a weapon in his hands he would be invincible against the girl.

He was in position when she came up the hill. Kreoko jumped out to block the alley. He swung his sword in menacing arcs. "Now you're going pay!" he cried angrily at the girl.

Tyme looked at the boy with the sword. His nose was swollen purple, and his face was black and blue. He was wildly swinging the sword almost like Noot. 'Twas obvious he had no experience at all. The blade was dinged and worn, like it had not been used in centuries.

"I don't want to hurt you," she told the boy, "Just let me pass."

"You are not passing till you pay for what you done!" Kreoko announced angrily brandishing the sword.

Tyme feinted a few times to watch him clumsily wield

the sword--waiting for an opening. It did not take long before she leapt forward and pulled out her dagger, which appeared suddenly at his throat.

"Drop the sword," she commanded. It clattered useless to the ground. "Put your hands behind your back." She bound him quickly with the wrist restraints she carried in case the lad had not learned his lesson on their first encounter. She retrieved the sword and pushed him into a darkened corner.

"Why do you keep bothering me?" Tyme asked him with consternation. "I stayed away from your alley. I tried to stay out of your business." Tyme shook her head and knitted her thick black eyebrows. "Now you come over here to the riffs and try to put the jump on me."

"That's because you're still in my territory!" Kreoko snapped with rage. "The riffs. The mipes. That's all Jawbone Ridge territory."

"What's Jawbone Ridge?" Tyme asked.

"The Jawbone Ridge gang rules the alleys and protects the people who live in the alleys. Protects the people from nobles who abuse them," he said accusingly.

"Why does everyone think I'm a noble?" Tyme asked with annoyance. "Look. I'm not here to abuse or oppress anyone. I just need to pass quickly through your territory for awhile and then I'll be gone from your city."

"That not how it works," Kreoko seethed with anger. "I didn't tell no one who broke my nose before. But now I'm going to tell the brothers. Everyone will know what you look like. The brothers are going to be after you!" he threatened.

Tyme looked at him in frustration. This was not going to work. She needed to resolve things now. "So, if all your brothers catch me," she asked, "what are you going to do with me?"

"We'll drag your ass before Delgado," he said menacingly, "and have *him* decide."

She grabbed him by the collar and gave him a shake. "Then let's go see Delgado right now and get this all straightened out."

"You can't just go see Delgado," the boy said incredulously.

"Why not?" Tyme declared. "You were all set to whoop me with your friends and drag me to him." She gave him a push. "You know where he is. Take me to him now!" she demanded. "Then I'll untie you. Not before."

"Don't leave my sword!" he pleaded. "My uncle doesn't know I have it. He'll kill me if I lose it!"

"Then you carry it." She picked it off the ground and put the middle of the blade into his hands to awkwardly hold behind his back. "What's your name?" she asked him.

"Kreoko," he licked his lips.

"Kreoko," she held his jaw in her hand as she advised him sternly, "don't try anything stupid. I don't want to hurt you. Okay?"

"Okay," he said with resignation.

"Good. We'll go fast and quiet and keep to ourselves, so no one sees you."

The leader of the Jawbone Ridge gang was at the Blue Moon, a saloon, music, and dance hall. Inside, a woman with a rich emotive voice was singing a languid song. A small but appreciative crowd faced the stage. Tyme discreetly followed Kreoko away from the bar along the back and far side of the room. He approached a screened wall with lights and ducked into a hidden doorway. Three men around a table watched their approach. They appeared surprised at Kreoko's bruised face. And more startled when they saw the girl was holding him tied and hostage.

One of the young men stood and motioned to a back room. "Let's talk where we have more privacy," he gallantly motioned for Tyme and Kreoko to enter first. "Would you like something to drink?" he asked pleasantly as she passed by.

She did not answer his question but went straight to the point. "Your man here," she did not call him a boy, which in Kreoko's humiliated state he greatly appreciated, "keeps trying to stop me on my business." She looked at the leader intently. "I would like your permission to pass unbothered through your

THE WAY OF THE WORLD

territory every now and then," she paused, "only for a short time, a few moons. Then I will leave, and you won't see me again."

"Dear ser," he told her with a smile, "we would be happy to have you do your business in our territory, but you must pay a toll."

"And why should I pay you a toll?" Tyme asked in consternation.

"Because Jawbone Ridge rules the alleys west of Cracken Street and protects the people who live in those alleys," he recited the same creed as Kreoko. "Your toll helps protect the people from the nobles who abuse them." He smiled pleasantly, bluffing. His main enforcer, Vorcono, was not even in the room. The two others with him were okay fighters. But then so was Kreoko, and he was standing with his arms bound behind his back and a busted face. "The toll need not be odious," Delgado offered, trying to maintain some dignity. "A small fee should be ample for a few moons."

Suddenly there was a warning shout from the doorway. "Rocozo's coming."

"Blood and guts!" Delgado swore. He turned to Tyme. "Just stay quiet and out of the way!"

"Trenilo," he ordered one of the men, "Stand by my right hand and hopefully he'll think you're Vorcono."

"He's alone," a whispered shout warned at the last moment from the doorway.

A large, grizzled fighter came into the room with a sword at his belt, a dagger at his side and another on his leg. He scanned the room with a sneer and strode forward toward Delgado. He looked straight at Trenilo and snorted. "This is your enforcer?" he mocked. "This is the famous Vorcono of Jawbone Ridge gang?"

Tyme eyed the big man critically. He was sizeable and intimidating, at first glance. On close inspection he appeared to be out of fighting shape, well liquored, and overly confident.

"I'm here to tell you," the intruder informed them, "that I'm taking over Dowd Street. People are going to pay *me* for their protection. Any of your sorry ass gang comes that way, you'll be on *my* territory, and treated as such. Dowd Street is paying to a new manser. And that manser ain't taking any of your whiny shit!"

Everything about the man fueled a growing rage within Tyme that was fed also by her anger over Noot's killing, and her frustrations in chasing the perpetrator. She could feel all that outrage now being channeled toward the thuggish gang leader. Tyme did not try to stop her growing wrath. This was finally an opportunity to release some of that fury.

"You trying to prove that you're some tough guy?" Tyme challenged the man with disdain, "walking in here by yourself?"

"Who the hell is this?" the big man laughed incredulously, looking from Delgado to the others.

Tyme turned to Kreoko. "Give me your sword," she commanded as she snatched it from his hands still tied behind his back. She swung it to feel the adequate balance. The blade was beyond dull, which meant a hard blow would not cut off a limb, but rather bruise and savage the muscles and tissue. At worst break the bone. The perfect tool for the job.

"Your bully days are over," she announced to the big man. She was ready for a fight and did not even offer him the chance to back down. Not that he would have taken it anyway. "You are not taking over Dowd Street," she informed him. "You are not taking over *anything*. Jawbone Ridge rules those streets and alleys and protects the people who live there," she repeated the creed they had just told her, "from nobles and predators that abuse them."

"You're going to have a girl fight for you?" Rocozo said with disbelief.

"You go first, big boy," she taunted him to pull out his sword, which he angrily did.

He swung and thrust his sword a few times. She easily dodged each move without even having to block his blade.

She had guessed right about his skills and speed. She attacked suddenly with a series of rapid blows, which he was able to defend only for a moment until she broke through his guard, solidly hitting and injuring his sword arm, then quickly bruising and cracking a few ribs.

She dropped back to give him a moment to feel the pain of his injuries, feinted and taunted him a few times, then attacked again with a furious rain of blows, hitting his arm and neck, ending with a serious whack with the flat of the blade to the side of his head that sent him reeling. She danced around him for a few moments, feinting attacks to mock him, and then struck again with a rapid shower of deadly blows all across his body, and a hit to the knee that nearly dropped him to the ground.

"Enough," he groaned and staggered, "I yield."

"Yield?" She taunted him. "A big tough guy like you? That's all you can take?" She shook her head. "You haven't finished your lesson yet."

He made a desperate lunge for her, but she was far too quick. He was covered with ugly bruises and abrasions. She swung hard and took him in the side of his chest, cracking more of his ribs. She bludgeoned his sword arm again, busted out a number of his teeth, and broke a bone in his leg. He dropped in a daze to his knees.

She walked over to him and held up his bloodied jaw so that he was looking at her. "Best you just forget about me," she advised him. "Don't tell anyone about me. Otherwise, we'll have another lesson." She hoped he would not be that stupid. "Do you want another lesson?"

He shook his head.

"Leave us, and don't ever come back." She steered him, stumbling with his sword as a cane as he hobbled toward the door.

Kreoko stood with his mouth open. He could not believe what he just witnessed. She was like some True Warrior out of a storybook who just saved the Jawbone Ridge gang in a desperate moment! Had not he also intended to hurt her? What had he been thinking? He was filled with gratefulness that she gave him only a broken nose, which now felt like a mark of pride. She had been merciful to him!

Trenilo was astonished that anyone, much less a tween girl, could so thoroughly beat Rocozo without taking a single hit herself. He looked ready to bow down before the girl.

Delgado looked equally stunned. "I guess we didn't need Vorcono tonight after all," he joked about his missing enforcer. "Not with our new friend and lifetime honorary member of the Jawbone Ridge gang." He bowed respectfully. "We are all quite in your debt, and yet we do not even know your name."

She looked thoughtfully at Delgado and made a quick decision. There was something about him she felt she could trust, at least in this.

"My name is Tyme," she answered, still breathing and sweating heavily. "I am trying to go unnoticed in town," she shook her head at the irony, "so do not spread word of this, or my name."

"You have our oath," Delgado vowed. "If there is any way we can help in your business dealings in Old Town, we would be honored to be at your service," Delgado spoke with utmost seriousness. "Please do not hesitate to ask. We are here to help."

He smiled broadly. "Now could I get you a drink?" he offered again.

"Would someone untie me?" Kreoko interrupted with embarrassment.

"Sorry," Tyme took off his wristbands. She ignored Delgado's offer of a drink. But she was interested in his volunteering to help. Mayhaps it would take a rogue to help catch a killer. "Do any of you know of a man who wears lots of rings, one with a large red stone, another swirling like a snake?" she asked.

They all shook their heads.

"I'm secretly trailing such a man. He's out of town now but could be back at any time, day or moonlight. He'll be returning a horse to a stable in Old Town." She described the alley and the building.

"The Jawbone Ridge gang will have someone watching around the clock for his return," Delgado promised.

"He will probably be riding a daya, and the horse likely abused," Tyme added. "It would be great if you could follow him and find out where he lives."

"We can also keep an eye on his house," Delgado quickly offered. "See who comes and goes."

"Yes," Tyme nodded with satisfaction. "I will stop by tomorrow evening to hear of any report."

"And have a drink?" Delgado was persistent. He seemed quite smitten with her. He was young, charming and ruggedly handsome.

"Let's start with a report," she replied, and gave him a slight smile.

A POTENTIAL ARMY

Gribono had not reported to Captain Targono in more than a decade (10 moons). During that period he had plenty of opportunity to think and ponder his unusual posting as a spy.

He had originally been sent in search of a Senaser's grandson in the Fire cult. But now Gribono questioned if there was even such a grandson. Mayhaps 'twas just a ruse to find out about the Fire, which was largely soldiers and warriors. A potential army! Why would Captain Targono want information on such a group? What was Targono planning? The intrigue of it all fascinated Gribono.

How strange it felt returning to the remote Hammer Legion outpost in the mountains of Vanttan, taking off his large rings, and putting back on a uniform. He was informed that Captain Targono was with an engineering company building bridges southwest of Vrak Pass. It took a day and a half to reach him.

Captain Targono's command tent was in the shade of a narrow canyon. The Captain had just finished eating and was sitting shirtless at a small table. He had numerous scars on his muscled body.

"Gribono to report," the once-again private saluted and smiled confidently. "I've made a breakthrough!"

Captain Targono smiled in return. "I do believe your talents were wasted as a common soldier." He motioned for the spy to take a seat.

"I met the shaman from Birjj," Gribono began. "He calls himself Shamano."

The gambler told how he had been playing cards for moons with the shaman's brother and overheard a whisper that the shaman would be at Dayr Castle to meet a rebel leader.

"'Twas just last full Moonday. I ruined a horse riding to Dayrstad," Gribono extolled briefly on his efforts. "Then waited at the Womb refuge for him to appear. Luckily he looked like his brother!" Gribono explained how he had approached the man. "My fingers were covered with rings. I implied I would help donate to his cause."

Targono nodded for him to continue.

"When I met up with him the next evening, I told him I felt the Fire, and that I represented a Senaser who seeks to invoke Divine Council to establish the Fire as a Divine Attribute." Gribono had been given the idea during his weekly card game with Tanfaro, the shaman of Karvor, who had told him that he prayed daily for just such an event, which would legitimize the group and bring them into the fold.

"Which would make their shrines legal in the Womb refuge," Captain Targono noted.

"Exactly. But Shamano wasn't so interested," Gribono lamented. "I think he felt that concession as too little, too late. So, I told him I had unusual sources for information, and that I could help his cause by being his spy."

"His spy?" Targono laughed. "Aren't you already *my* spy?"

"Shamano doesn't know that," Gribono grinned with delight.

"And why do you want to be *his* spy?"

"Because I can feed him whatever information you might want him to know or think. I can also find out who he's watching, who he might be fearing, and who he might be talking with." Gribono let his words sink in. "He told me to look into Major Bayn Baya and Captain Wirvimo."

"Interesting," Targono said thoughtfully. "Very clever of

you."

"I also met Bokono, the rebel leader. Bokono knows that Shamano is the heart and soul of the Fire, and the power that brings everyone together. So, he lets Shamano call the shots for now." Gribono shrugged. "How long that would last if any real fighting broke out is hard to say. Bokono's the man most likely to lead the charge if it comes to battle. He's ready to take the struggle to another level."

Gribono smiled confidently relishing the moment. "I also learned Duke Eddarko of Dayrstad, who controls the Siren, fancies himself a potential leader of the Fire and new King of Dayrstad as well." Gribono did not mention the stable boy he had killed after getting that information.

Captain Targono pulled out a bottle of viruna, procured through his spy Lartso, who smuggled liquor for Duke Eddarko and had mentioned his own doubts about the Duke's loyalty to Bokono. But the Captain did not share these details. Instead, he poured two small cups and toasted to Gribono's success. He also gave his spy a generous purse.

The next morning when Gribono left the bridge-building camp, he thought about the questions that Captain Targono had asked him. Gribono was convinced that the Captain was planning rebellion against the Czarzina and was looking for allies in the Barrier Mountains.

DELGADO

The sky was dark. Klew and Jyg waited with growing concern on the apartment patio for Tyme to return from Old Town.

"I got in another fight," Tyme announced when she finally arrived. She didn't appear to have any bruises.

"The boy tried to get revenge?" Klew guessed.

Tyme had almost forgotten about the earlier skirmish with the boy in the alley. "I got into two fights," she revised her story. "The first wasn't much." She told them about the boy, Kreoko, trying to stop her with his uncle's sword, and how she bound his hands behind his back and forced him to take her to the leader of the Jawbone Ridge gang.

"He doesn't seem like such a bad guy," Tyme recalled her first impression of Delgado. "Although he still said I had to pay to pass through their territory. But then he quickly said I wouldn't have to pay much. He said the amount would not be odious," Tyme smirked to Jyg.

"Xacano would approve," Jyg said favorably, recalling how their philosophy instructor always encouraged them to expand their vocabulary.

"He was bluffing from the start," Tyme stated. "When he learned a rival was coming he had one of his guys pretend to be their enforcer."

"Their champion fighter is missing," Klew noted, "and you have another of their guys still tied up."

"I think I see where this might be going," Jyg guessed with a sly grin. Bones sat quietly on his roost.

"The rival is a big, cruel brute," Tyme continued. "He starts throwing his weight around saying he's going to take over Dowd Street and that all the shopkeepers are going to have to pay him money." Tyme grew serious. "He really started making me mad."

"Uh-oh," Klew shook his head.

"The more I looked at him," Tyme said with disgust, "the more he looked out of shape and slow. I think he had a few drinks." She told how she taunted and insulted the man to fight. How she had used Kreoko's blunt sword to beat him into submission. "He said yield, but I kept going. I think he needed more to learn his lesson."

Tyme shook her head. "I was so full of anger about Noot's death that I wanted something to attack. He made a perfect target."

"How do you feel now?" Klew asked.

"Drained," Tyme replied. "Tired. My anger's gone. Now I just feel sadness."

"What did Delgado say?" Jyg asked.

"I am now a lifetime honorary member of the Jawbone Ridge gang," Tyme told them with satisfaction. "He basically said they are forever in my debt. They set a watch on the stables in Old Town for the fancy ring man. They are going to follow him when he returns and find out where he lives."

She didn't mention about Delgado repeatedly offering her a drink.

The following evening Tyme returned to the Blue Moon saloon and dance hall. She stood examining the front of the blue building for a few moments and then went inside. Tyme went across the back and far side wall to some lights on a screened wall with a door that was hard to see until you approached closely. However, those inside could see out into the rest of the tavern, and had their own private view of the stage. Delgado stood and motioned for her to join him at the table. She pointed to the back room for more privacy. He gestured for her to lead the way and followed behind with two of the men from the previous night and another larger, stronger fellow. The missing enforcer.

"Any word?" she asked.

"Not yet," Delgado's eyes twinkled. "Would you like to have a drink?" He motioned to a chair. "Please have a seat."

"I'll have a drink when you have something to report," she promised. "I don't want to come inside each evening to check. There's a pole next to the end window on the outside of the tavern. If you have anything to report, tie a blue strip of cloth on the pole. I'll come in for a drink when I see the blue cloth."

Four days later a blue cloth appeared around the pole. When Delgado saw her come in, he left his table of friends and motioned for her to join him at a smaller private table in a secluded nook.

"At last we can enjoy a drink together," he said with enthusiasm.

"First your report," she insisted.

"There is not much to tell," Delgado said. "The fancy ring man arrived back at midday on a worn out daya. He lives down by the Mother Womb. Upscale neighborhood. Which makes it trickier to keep an eye on his house, being out of our territory." Delgado smiled to reassure her. "But don't worry. We've got somebody on it. I will put the signal on the pole again when I learn more."

He pulled a little cord for the waiter. "Wine? Mescal? Viruna?" he asked her.

"Watered wine," she answered. "One cup."

"Then you must drink slowly," he grinned. He tried to get her to talk, but she would not tell him any more about the ring man, nor her mission, nor about herself, or where she was from.

"Tell me about you," she asked with a mischievous grin that set his heart pounding. Her golden-green eyes were hypnotizing. Her black hair lustrous.

"I grew up on the streets," he began. "My choice was working the kilns or living in the alleys of Old Town. The kiln work was back breaking. The streets were easier...," he smiled handsomely, "if you are in the right group. The Jawbone Ridge gang saved my ass, fed me, gave me something to be a part of. Now I try to pay that back." He said the words seriously and then laughed at his own pretense. "But mostly I enjoy life and listen to good music."

"Rocozo was going to make the shopkeepers pay him money. Do you do the same?" Tyme asked pointedly.

"No," Delgado shook his head. "Nothing's forced. We only offer protection to those who *ask* for our protection. Only outsiders pay a toll, and that's only in the back alleys where they shouldn't be snooping. We make money in other ways."

"Like how?"

"Like from the liquor you're drinking," he smiled. "We help distribute it." He made a toast and they both took a drink. "Now tell me something about how you grew up," he insisted.

She told him about growing up as a stable apprentice and learning to ride Maaps and Riips. He was easy to talk with. She thought the stories innocent but he was able to glean more than she realized. He guessed she was from one of the Barbarian Kingdoms. Most likely Dayrstad. He could have listened to her all night. She radiated with an entrancing aura. Just sitting beside her was a delight. She took her last sip of wine and set the empty cup on the table.

"My lady," he offered, "may I order you another?"

"No, thank you," she smiled sincerely. "I have enjoyed our evening. One is enough for now."

The words *for now* filled his heart with hope.

She grew serious. "A part of me feels embarrassed about the other night," she searched for the right words, "I feel like I kind of snapped and lost my temper. Like that wasn't really me."

Delgado had been astonished by her strength and fighting skills. Now he was moved by her openness and innocence. "Have you only sparred?" he guessed. Could it be--that was her first real fight?

She did not answer but her eyes betrayed her.

"There is no need for embarrassment," he assured her. "You have only our deepest admiration and gratitude. We hold you in the highest honor."

When she stood to leave he gave her a formal embrace. "I look forward to our next meeting. I would like to become friends," he told her boldly.

"Mayhaps," was all she could say.

As she left the Blue Moon he whispered to his enforcer. "You gave Scoop the signal?" he asked.

The big man nodded. Scoop would follow the girl and find out where she was staying. And whom she was with. Delgado looked forward to a full report.

PLENTY OF WAYS
TO KILL SOMEONE

Rocozo had been beaten up worse. He was still conscious and able to stagger out of the Blue Moon that night on his own two feet, and had no life threatening sword or stab wounds.

But he had never been so humiliated and shamed. It had always taken a group of fighters to beat him before. Now, a lone tween girl had done it.

The traitor in the Jawbone Ridge gang had told him that Vorcono, their main enforcer, was going to be elsewhere that night. It should have been the perfect night to make a bold move into part of the gang's territory. He had known all along that the bodyguard with Delgado was not Vorcono. He had been told what Vorcono looked like. Rocozo had pretended not to know in order to hide his own schemes.

But then the tween girl appeared and ruined everything.

Rocozo vowed that he would kill her. Not that he would go against the girl with a sword ever again. That would be suicide. But there were plenty of ways to kill someone besides a swordfight. He just wanted to get his hands around her throat. Let her kick and scratch all she wanted. It would be too late. He flexed his fingers dreaming of choking her to death. He just needed some moons to recuperate, mend his broken bones, and put together a plan.

THE CARGO BIRD

"**D**ragon treasure!" Grinst cried with excitement as he grabbed the diamond ring from Horton's hand for a closer look. The grubbers were inside the dragon's stomach, working from the small light of a single oil lamp. The top layer of the mound before them was filled with small, velvety black cases with hidden hinges—a few still snapped closed. They were perfectly packed and stacked tightly together in piles and rows. Inside the cases they found a jackpot of women's silver jewelry and quickly filled a whole bag with exquisite rings, ornate bracelets and necklaces of the finest, most intricate and precise silverwork they had ever seen.

They were soon knee-deep in discarded refuse from the strange packaging. Grinst worked like a frantic gopher, rapidly throwing unwanted items into a heap behind him. The narrow aisle way was filling with litter.

"We need to pile all the scraps and junk out of the way so we have room to keep working," Epoh suggested. They used cook pots and baking sheets from the mound of kitchen supplies as scoops and shovels to clear the aisle and pile the waste on a mound of the thin, heavy, hand-sized objects with black glass on one side.

Next they found a layer of boxes filled with tightly packed rows of milky and partially see-through pod-like containers with flattened sides and bottom. Grinst carefully lifted one up and gave it a light squeeze. The shell fractured and broke into shards. Inside was an unusual lightweight bracelet with an oval disc of gray glass and small round knobs on the sides. The strap broke when Grinst pulled it from the encasement.

He cracked open another pod. An identical bracelet. Grinst let the other grubbers break apart all the pods while he opened one of the larger boxes. At first they found similar bracelets in casings. Then they found small, finely made wristbands of perfectly linked metal with small-hinged clasps that tightened as they snapped shut. Many of them had round glass dials outlined with twelve little marks, and thin, tiny needles of different lengths radiating from the center pointing in different directions.

Half way through the mound they came to much larger men's strap bracelets. Many were made of heavy, linked metal with giant dials, some with elaborate designs, center pointers, and little knobs protruding out the sides. When the grubbers finally reached the bottom, they found a framework of wooden boards.

"We can use the wood to make torches when our lamp oil runs out!" Grinst said with satisfaction. They had been in the dragon's stomach all night and had bags full of loot. "Should be daylight now," he said. "We've just enough water to get back to camp."

They loaded up the treasure and spent the day hiking back to their base cave. Although Grinst agreed with Epoh that the dragon did in fact appear to be a flying warehouse built by the Ancient Ones, he still refused to call it such. "Flying warehouse is no grubber name," Grinst shook his head in horror.

"We can call it a dragon or whatever you like," Epoh conceded. "But I think 'tis a cargo bird built by the Ancient Ones."

During the three days it took to refill water from the seep and trap more lizards and rodents for food, they fondled and inspected the jewelry they had collected. The fine crafting of each item amazed the grubbers. They all wore one of the big metal bracelets with round disks on their wrists.

As Epoh was examining and picking through the pile of loot, he spun and gently twirled the center knob on one of the largest bracelets. He felt a light vibration in his fingers when the knob moved forward. He gave the knob a tug and it popped out a little. He twirled it again. The largest of the pointer arms moved halfway around the dial. When he twisted the button back, the big pointer swung the opposite direction.

"Look at this!" Epoh called out in astonishment. The grubbers all watched in awe as the large pointer went around the circle. "The little pointer is moving as well!" he exclaimed, "but much more slowly." As he fiddled with it, the others began turning the buttons on other bracelets. "Pull the knob out first," he told them, "and then twirl it to make the pointers move." Epoh pulled on the knob again and it popped out a little further. This time when he spun it, a number in a little window changed. He continued experimenting with the device as the others began making the pointers move on their own bracelets, or tried different bracelets if they could not get one to work.

"Every time the long pointer goes around the circle, the little pointer moves one of the sections or numbers on the dial," Epoh reported. He pushed the button all the way back in. When he turned it nothing moved, but he felt the little vibration again. He held the bracelet up to his ear and turned the knob to hear a faint ratchet noise. He did it a few more times.

"'Tis moving by itself!" Epoh cried out when he noticed the thinnest pointer was jerking its way around the dial.

The others all crowded around to see what the strange device was doing. "These must be clocks," Epoh guessed with sudden insight as he watched the exact rhythm of the pointer.

"What is a clock?" Harvig was always the quickest to ask questions.

Epoh explained 'twas a device used to keep track of time. "Astronomers have elaborate clocks to help understand the cycles of the moon and the sun and the planets." He shook his head in wonder. "But they are giant clocks as big as a house run by water."

"Water?" Grinst was incredulous whenever Epoh talked of the liquid being in abundance. "To run a clock?" he held up one of the bracelets, "as big as a house?"

"There used to be a water clock in all the old cities across the Ambri Empire," Epoh replied. "Only a few of them still work today." Suddenly he had an idea.

"Roll the knob forward on your bracelets a bunch of times and see if the thin long pointer starts moving around the dial," he told them. When they all had the thin pointers moving he had them pull the knob out a little and set the big and little pointers straight down at the bottom. The thin little pointer just kept going on its own jerky circle. "Now push the knobs in." They all did it. "Now we'll see if the pointers all stay synchronized together."

"What's synchronized?" asked Harvig.

"Go the same speed," Epoh explained. They checked throughout the day to find the clocks all moved and pointed the same new direction!

The next day Grinst insisted that they hide the treasure they brought from the dragon to their base camp.

"If someone finds our camp while we be at the dragon," he told the other grubbers, "they would steal everything!" He organized the treasure into three piles and buried them in caves in nearby gullies.

For Epoh the biggest thrill was the awareness that he would soon be going to Jchow Oasis. He could be back home in just a handful of moons! When he had agreed to go with the grubbers, Horton had said they could be out in the desert for as long as 70 moons (6 years) searching for treasure. Now they had already found it. Jewelry and gems from the Ancient Ones! Epoh was thrilled that he would be able to make his way to Jchow Oasis and leave the desert earlier than he ever expected.

SPIES REPORT

Scoop was a skinny little kid who blended well into dark corners and lookouts. He had been a part of the Jawbone Ridge gang since he ran away from the Milk. He was born fafor, a boy trapped in a girl's body. He had no interest in growing up having to care for the crying babies at the orphanage.

When he joined the gang he didn't tell anyone, since girls weren't allowed. He just made sure he never peed or bathed around the others.

He had been sent to follow someone important. Scoop reckoned she was the girl who beat up Rocozo, their former archenemy who had been completely pummeled and broken. Scoop marveled that a young tween girl could have such abilities! He had always enjoyed tales about the Blades and other famous woman warriors. Now he was following one!

The tween fighter went down the hill from Old Town into a neighborhood of narrow and winding streets filled with workshops, arts and crafts stores, and pottery shops. She went into the back entrance of an apartment building. Scoop climbed up into the corner of a recessed and shuttered alley window across the street, bundled up his cloak to stay warm in the cold night air, and settled in to watch the apartment door.

Scoop liked to sit quietly. For him, time was to be savored. Each moment to be experienced, unhurried. He watched through the night and all through the next day. That evening he returned to Delgado to give his report.

"Only a few people from the apartment building use the back door. There was one other interesting person," Scoop noted. "A mercenary. Looked like a True Warrior type. Not a normal renter in an art district."

"But you have not seen them together?" Delgado asked with interest.

"No," Scoop shook his head.

"Keep watching," the gang leader ordered. "Her name is Tyme. The more we know about her, the better."

Three days later Tyme saw the blue cloth around the pole by the window outside the Blue Moon. Inside the tavern behind the screened area, Delgado quickly escorted her to the same private table.

"The red ring man's name is Gribono," Delgado informed Tyme with great satisfaction. His spies had been following the man all over town. "His nickname is the Gambler. He bought out his Legion contract after winning a card game with some offisers. He often plays cards at Red Peppers with a sergeant named Etna Nate."

"Gribono," Tyme intoned his name.

Delgado sat quietly. His report was over and Tyme still had a full cup of watered wine in front of her. "I will put the signal up when we know more." He innocently changed the subject. "Tell me about growing up in the stables."

Before she knew it, Tyme was recounting tales of riding Spike. When she finished her wine, he offered her another cup, but she refused. He grew serious.

"Because I want to help you in any way I can," Delgado began, "there's something you should know." He lowered his voice and leaned in closer to Tyme. "The night you fought Rocozo. He staggered out bloody and beaten. A number of people in the tavern saw him leave and the shape he was in."

Delgado shrugged his shoulders helplessly. "Even though all of us in the back room swore not to tell anyone about what happened, people know *something* happened." He gave her a not-my-fault look. "And that *you* were a part of it. A few people saw you escorting Kreoko with his arms bound behind his back holding a sword." Delgado shook his head." Kreoko left with the sword, but few believe he was the one to use it."

Tyme didn't know what to say.

"You had said you wanted to be discreet," Delgado continued. "So, right away that night, we started spreading false stories everywhere." Delgado smiled ironically. "In some versions you're a big white-skinned woman. In others you have red hair. Or, you're a group of fighters who entered through a back window." He shrugged his shoulders apologetically. ""Twas the only way I could figure to hide what really happened."

Tyme chuckled at his resourcefulness. "Thanks for such quick thinking."

"That is not to say the true story is not still out there," he reminded her. "But only a few will know it. Be warned. Some who know the true story," he said ominously, "may seek revenge."

She took little notice of his caution. "Let the true story be a warning to *them*," she replied without concern as she rose from the table, and walked out the door.

FOLLOW THE LEADER

"The fancy ring man is back in town again," Tyme informed Dani, the pie girl on Skyline Street. "His name is Gribono."

Tyme was tucked into a corner under the red stairs, out of sight from the street, eating a hot pigeon pie. The sun had not yet come up, the sky was yellow-orange, and the early morning air was crisp and cold.

"I have new information as well," Dani replied. "I heard that some boy who works at the Plumed Bird told a story about a man with rings. I don't know the boy's name but he lives on Cergi Rim."

"What's the story?" Tyme asked with interest.

"Something about the ring man paying him to signal something."

"Gribono paying the boy?"

"Yeah."

Tyme quickly made her way back to the apartment to inform Klew and Jyg.

"The boy is a young tween. Dani thinks he works in the Plumed Bird stables."

"Sounds like a good job for me," Jyg volunteered quickly. "I'll just follow the tween workers when they go home for the heat, and find out which one lives on Cergi Rim," Jyg said with confidence, and then laughed. "As soon as Klew shows me where to find Cergi Rim."

"Cergi Rim runs the width of the upper bank. There's lots of ways to get to it. Even through the warren." Klew shook his head. "Pretty much everyone working in the stables, or with labor jobs at the Plumed Bird, lives up that direction. I hope you pick the right boy quick, or you could be following workers for a week."

Klew and Jyg left the apartment separately then met up to go to Cergi Rim, walked the length of it, and then went back and forth to the Plumed Bird a variety of ways. "Those are just the main routes," Klew reminded Jyg. "There are another ten more routes through the Warren."

Jyg began that afternoon. As he followed the first worker from the back alley of the stables, Bones flew along nearby, landing on roofs, sun palms and shop awnings to watch and keep up along the route. Halfway up the hill the worker went into a dilapidated house.

On the third day as Jyg was following a worker through the alleys of the warren, he noticed that Bones was keeping ahead of him.

"Grawk!" Bones croaked in a deep resonate call. "Grawk."

Jyg had heard ravens make a similar relaxed call, but he had never heard Bones call like that before.

The boy went into an apartment building.

The next day as Jyg followed a different worker, Bones began flying ahead again calling out a low, relaxed "grawk."

Was Bones helping him to follow the person ahead?

"Grawk," Bones croaked.

The boy disappeared into a house. A moment later Bones swooped in and landed on the roof directly above the door.

"Grawk," the big black bird dipped her head and stretched her wings, then stood quietly on the roof watching Jyg.

Jyg could not wait to tell the others. "You're not going to believe this!" he announced with excitement to Klew and Tyme. "Bones is helping me follow people!" He told them what had happened the last few days, and how the raven had started saying grawk. "I finally remember where I've heard ravens make that call before. 'Tis when a group of ravens fly in a line. The ravens in the back of the line sometimes say grawk, like a low squawking laugh.

"What does it mean?" Tyme asked.

"Mayhaps 'tis like follow the leader," Jyg guessed. "A game. That is what we were doing, we were both trailing behind someone together."

Jyg already knew some other raven words. He could call Bones in close using the soft kaah of a raven parent announcing the arrival of food for the chicks. If he repeated it a few times, Bones would actually land on his arm or shoulder.

If the inquisitive bird was being a pest, or in the way, and Jyg said shoo, or get away, and waved his hands, Bones always thought he was playing and responded by flapping her large black wings and loudly snapping her thick bill. Jyg learned if he called out a single quork, the territorial cry used by ravens to establish boundaries, Bones would quickly move away. Two quorks and Bones would fly out the window.

Jyg began pointing at the worker he wanted to follow and saying grawk, so that Bones quickly knew whom to follow. Jyg then used hand signals along with other commands, to see if Bones could learn to follow his directions without hearing him speak. Jyg marveled at how attentively the bird watched everything he did, and how Bones was even learning to understand and read his facial expressions.

The big raven also began bringing and presenting gifts. It started with a blue glass bead, which Bones held proudly in her beak as she paraded in front of Tyme and Klew before hopping over to Jyg. She marched back and forth importantly before carefully depositing the bead next to Jyg's hand. The raven gently nudged the bead toward Jyg to make sure he understood whom 'twas for.

"For me?" Jyg asked the bird as he picked up the bead. "Thanks!"

"What about me?" Klew asked the bird. "Aren't I your newest friend?"

Bones hopped over to the food tray, grabbed an olive in her bill, hopped back to Klew, and dropped the olive by his hand.

"Why thank you," Klew praised the bird with an amused laugh.

"And how about me?" Tyme looked at the bird with pretend shock. "Don't I get anything?"

The raven hopped back to the food tray for another olive.

"What a good bird!" Tyme stroked the raven's feathers as she ate the olive. Bones loved to push the top of her head into the palm of Tyme's hand.

The next morning Bones flew in with a woman's hair ribbon in her beak. "Brronk!" The raven cried out as it grandly paraded in front of them with the ribbon, then set the ribbon in front of Tyme and used her bill to push the ribbon into Tyme's hand.

"A gift for me?" Tyme was quite pleased. She tied the ribbon around one of the small braids in her black hair.

That evening Bones flew in with a brass button in her beak. "Brronk!" she hopped about displaying her prize to everyone and then dropped the button in front of Klew. Bones insistently prodded it toward him with her bill.

"Everyone gets a present!" Klew nodded with a grin. "A very diplomatic bird." He examined the button and exclaimed with a laugh, "A soldier's button no less! Thanks Bones!"

"Bones!" the raven replied with a shout.

Everyone jumped in surprise.

"You can say your name!" Tyme gasped.

"Bones!" the big black bird exclaimed proudly.

They all chuckled in amazement.

"Bones gives you a girl's ribbon," Jyg mused to Tyme, "and Klew gets a soldier's button. And I get a glass bead. Interesting." He strung the bead on a cord and tied it around his neck.

SOME EXCITEMENT

"**H**ad some excitement up in Old Town while you were away," Sergeant Etna Nate informed Gribono as she was dealing cards. They were at their favorite table at Red Peppers.

"Mmm?" Gribono gave a low hum of idle curiosity.

"Some big white warrior woman with red hair beat up a gang leader with an old rusted sword. They say she had the Fire in her! She was so fierce his whole gang just stood and watched stunned, and couldn't even help him!"

"The Fire in her?" Gribono inquired casually without showing his true interest.

"Like she was a flaming angel, from what I hear! Some say 'tis a sign that women can be Fire touched as well as men!"

"Mmm-huh," Gribono agreed. He listened as Etna Nate gave yet another lengthy diatribe about how women were discriminated against in the Fire. "Mmm," Gribono shook his head in sympathy.

'Twas not until later that the sergeant happened to mention Major Bayn Baya.

"What's her story?" Gribono yawned as if he was only vaguely interested. She was one of the people that Shamano at Dayr Castle had asked him to investigate and give report.

"She was schooled at the Military Academy in Pintone. Her family lives there. A noble house. Major Bayn Baya is the liaison between the Heart Legion and the Queen of Tanis, and also between the Legion and the Mayor of Karvor." Etna Nate leaned in close. "They say she has spies everywhere."

"Spies?" Gribono snorted with a bit of skepticism, hoping his lightheartedness would compel Etna Nate to say more in defense of her statement. The tactic worked perfectly.

"Listen, 'tis not funny," the Sergeant said. "Everyone at the guard house is careful about what they say. Even words said in private have a way of later getting people into trouble."

"Mmm" Gribono was suitably sympathetic.

"Not just at the toll station," Etna Nate continued in a low tone. "People also get in trouble for things said off-duty while drinking and playing cards! They say she has spies even in the Fire."

"Hhmm," Gribono said. He would need to be extra careful in gathering information about the Major.

"And spies in all the noble houses as well," the big black Sergeant shook her head. "People like Major Bayn Baya are born into power, but 'tis never enough for them. They're always seeking ever more power, through their whole lives."

GOLD

When the grubbers returned to the dragon, Grinst decided on taking a full survey of the inside of the beast. "We need an idea of what's where," he explained as he lit their tiny lamp.

This time they went down the left aisle. The first pile on the corner contained boxes full of hundreds of small bottles. Not clay. Not glass. Some thin, light material. The lids screwed off. Inside were a variety of powders and pellets.

Around the corner they found another long row of mounds. The first two were stacks of sturdy box like objects built with four little bumps to sit on a shelf or table, made of a molded material with little knobs and buttons on what appeared to be the front, and in back strange patterns of holes marked with writing and tightly bound up wire cords with three metal prongs on the end.

The next two mounds were piles of the heavy, hand size objects with a black mirror on one side.

Then a pile of former manuscripts that were now just mounds of papers blobbed with muted colors. Epoh thought he saw something that almost looked like a face, but Grinst was already moving the light on. Epoh rubbed his hand across the bottom layer of the mound and through a hole thought he felt a stack of books.

Then a mound of women's shoes.

At the eighth mound, they found more of the wrist clocks

they now wore, which true to Epoh's prediction, all continued to move their pointers in the same positions. Instead of digging into the pile, Grinst took one of the bracelets and put it in a small bag as a token to remember the mound. When they found a pile of boxes with large hunting knives, Grinst allowed time for them all to break a few packages open and each pick out a knife for themself. From another mound of perfectly made metal cook pots and fry pans, Grinst grabbed a large, thin, deep round skillet with two small handles and tied it over his shoulder.

In a few places the mounds had fallen and blocked the narrow aisle. They had to clamor over a heap of the giant, black rectangle objects, as tall as Harvig, with huge pieces of black glass on one side. Some were cracked but others were flawlessly smooth.

Onward they went all the way down the long, narrow aisle. In a back corner of the dragon's stomach, they found an assortment of long, round metal cylinders with rounded and elongated metal protrusions on top.

They moved on to the next pile, went across the end, and back up the right side aisle, making a complete circuit of the dragon's stomach. When they finished, Grinst opened his bag to reveal ten items he had collected. Adding the thin skillet on his back and the knife at his side, it represented the 12 mounds he wanted to go back and dig through.

"That don't include anything from the center row yet," Grinst said. "Bound to be something of interest there as well!" He looked at his lamp. "We got a bit of oil yet. Let's look into this mound first," he said with relish as he picked up the bracelet taken from a mound at the very back.

They found hundreds of the wrist clocks for men and women. But no other jewelry. Still they collected two bags full of the biggest metal clocks with the fancy knobs and dials.

The next mound to which they returned had boxes of simply made necklaces and bracelets, nice but hardly convincing if claimed to be made by the Ancient Ones. They hoped to find higher quality jewelry but the whole mound was the same.

The next day they found the gold.

The top of the mound started with fancy glass bowls and goblets, a number of which had fallen into the aisle. Then they found much heavier and exquisitely cut glass bowls. About half way down the mound changed to silver rings. At the bottom, rings of gold.

Pure gold.

They took two days and used up the rest of the lamp oil making sure they got every last bit of the gold from the pile, which was difficult at the end because the surrounding mounds kept collapsing and covering the area they were excavating. And they only had the one light to share.

The grubbers returned to their base camp loaded with two heavy sacks of gold jewelry and rings, and two sacks of the cut glass bowls and goblets. Combined with their earlier finds, they already had much more than they could carry. But when Epoh expressed hope that they might soon be leaving for Jchow Oasis, Grinst looked shocked.

"Jchow?" the old grubber barked a laugh. "Not for a long while." He shook his head. "We be wanting a good long snoop here." He looked critically at Epoh. "You think I came all this way just to leave after collecting a few bags of treasure?"

"Well, there is only so much you can carry," Epoh reasoned. "And we already have a great selection of valuables. Gems are worth the most for the weight, but you have to find someone to buy them, someone that you can trust not to rob and kill you for it. Gold jewelry we can melt down and sell in small amounts as we need it, without attracting much attention. And the silver as well."

"I'll take plenty of gems and gold," Grinst cackled, "Don't you fret!" He rubbed his hands with delight. "But I want a few other things besides." He held up his arm with his wrist clock. "I want to take a good look around." He tilted his head at Epoh. "Don't you have any curiosity, boy?"

When they returned to the cargo bird, as Epoh called it, Grinst brought out the thin, large, round and deep skillet he had found earlier, with two small handles on opposite sides of the rim. They had already collected the wood from the racks at the bottom of the mounds they dug out and broke into kindling. Now Grinst arranged a handful of the sticks in the bottom of the skillet to make tiny fire.

"Trying to make a torch is too dangerous with all the packing paper," he said. "One stray spark will set the whole thing on fire." He used a flint to carefully spark a few scraps of the paper in the skillet, which flared instantly into a flame and started the little splinters of wood burning. Grinst hooked a smaller pot filled with neatly arranged kindling to one of the little handles of the big skillet, and gave it all to Harvig.

"Your job is to keep a small flame going for us to see," he explained with an admonishment. "Use as little wood as you can!"

Harvig kept the fire toward the front and tilted the rim of the deep skillet low for the light to shine on the floor. He set the tilted skillet against the kindling pot in a position that best illuminated the area in which they worked. That way he could still continue to search for treasure as well as keep the fire lit and shining the right direction.

As the grubbers worked their way through the chosen mounds, they found two more groups of gold jewelry along with many sacks full of other prized objects. Each time they journeyed back to their basecamp, they carried and unloaded more treasure, which Grinst kept buried and hidden in many different caves and crevices. Epoh was amazed at the old grubber's ability to find and relocate buried items, and his memory for what was cached where.

Grinst had each of them chisel off and collect a bag full of the wrapped up wire cords from one of the mounds and bring them to their base camp. Now he used the chisel to cut off the three-prong ends and broke away the brittle black casing to get the wire inside.

"We need to make bags strong enough to carry the weight of our treasure," he told the others. He unwound the wire cord into tiny strands and then showed them how to begin weaving the wire with cactus twine into a bag. "Be careful not to make the bag too big or awkward for you to lift and carry. Better to have three or four smaller bags than one large one."

From that day on whenever they were at the seep they would work on weaving their bags and baskets to carry everything. Epoh was impressed by the dexterity Grinst displayed with his thick calloused fingers as he rapidly intertwined the wire together. Although he was much slower, Epoh found the weaving relaxing and enjoyable.

It took a moon for them to go through the twelve mounds they had scouted out earlier around the aisles of the cargo bird. When they finished Grinst brought them together.

"Now we can have a look at the inside row of mounds," he said.

"Are we going to climb over the top?" Harvig asked with excitement.

"No other way to find what is there," Grinst nodded. "But with that fire you have to go extra slow and careful where you won't slip." The old grubber waved his finger in warning. "Not as much grubbing for you."

When Epoh saw Harvig's disappointment he patted his shoulder. "I can handle the fire," he told the boy. "You can search full time." After the discovery of the second cache of gold, Epoh had grown tired of the hunt for treasure. He did not see the point. They already had more gold and gems than they could carry.

THE CARRIAGE

Bones and Jyg were following another Plumed Bird stable worker to see if he lived on Cergi Rim. But he led them to a house in the warren district and went inside. Jyg hung around a short time then meandered through the warren toward their apartment. Bones flew along from roof to roof.

They passed a ramshackle tavern and dirty alley where two drunken men were fighting and pushing each other.

"Blood and Guts!" one roared. "Don't you listen?" He smacked the other along the side of his head.

"I'm listening," the other whined as he put his arms up trying to deflect further blows.

"Blood and guts!" a voice imitated the first man from over Jyg's shoulder. *Bones.*

The man in the alley looked up from his cowering adversary to see Jyg standing alone.

"You say something?" the man bellowed. He stumbled threateningly toward Jyg, who turned and ran leaving the drunkard behind.

"Real funny, Bones," Jyg admonished the raven once he stopped, trying not to snicker himself.

When they returned to the apartment, Bones was eager to use her new words.

"Blood and guts!" Bones swore loudly after flying in through the window at a high rate of speed. The big black raven hopped across the table as Jyg took a seat.

"Bones!" Tyme said with false modesty. "Where did you learn such language?" She looked at Jyg for support. "Those are not words to be used in polite society."

Bones dropped her bill and pushed her head against the palm of Tyme's hand.

"That's right," Jyg affirmed and gave the bird a stern look. "I told you that is not funny." He tried again not to smirk. "Although it would bring about free drinks at most any bar," he chuckled.

"Careful with that idea," Klew advised. "I think Bones is much more valuable undercover."

"Of course," Jyg said sheepishly. "I was just having a fun thought."

After a moment of silence, Klew changed the subject. "I met with my friend, Sergeant Cira Raci," he reported. "I waited until I could speak with her off duty." They had been sergeants together during Klew's last decade in the Legion. She had had an obvious attraction to him. He had evaded her by explaining his plans to buy out his contract and leave the Legion. He had told her he was not interested in brief romances. Since he was departing soon, he wanted to remain just friends.

Cira Raci had accepted his convictions without question. But as the moons passed, and she got to know Klew better, she guessed there could be something more. She sensed that he might be fofor, and did not want his superiors to know. Fofors were often discriminated against and not trusted by some offisers in the military. There were suspicions about their loyalties under pressure. Whether they might abandon orders to protect or save a fellow soldier who was a mate.

Everything was different in Ambri society for men who were fofar, who embraced all things feminine. The Ambri viewed fofars very favorably. Men who wanted to be like women. That better fit their narrative and prejudices of female superiority. Fofars were celebrated in all the arts, music and dance.

"I told her about Noot's death," Klew continued, "and our

following of the suspected killer to Karvor. When I described his rings and told her we had found that his name was Gribono, she said she had heard of him, and confirmed that he often played cards with Sergeant Etna Nate. She also said the sergeant was a recent convert to the Fire, and was quite upset to find that most Fire devotees were less than thrilled about including women as followers."

The next afternoon Jyg and Bones' luck finally changed when they followed a boy working at the Plumed Bird who went all the way up through the warren to Cergi Rim. He entered a tottering house of rough, dry stacked stone built at the very edge of a band of fractured rock.

The next morning Jyg returned at first light, just as the boy came out the door on his way to work. Jyg moved quickly to walk beside him down the pathway. He wore a low hat to hide the color of his red hair.

"Do you work at the Plumed Bird?" Jyg asked in a friendly tone.

"Yes," the boy replied. "In the carriage house."

"Are you the one who got tipped to signal somebody or something?" Jyg said with a snigger.

The boy smiled. "How did you hear about that?"

"A friend told me," Jyg said truthfully. "But it didn't make sense the way she said it."

"'Tis simple," the boy was happy to explain. "I work where the nobles park their coaches. A manser pays me to make a signal when a certain carriage arrives. Then later he gives me a tip."

"Whose carriage?" Jyg asked.

"I don't know," the boy shrugged. "The owner gets dropped off at the front door. The coach is black lacquer with silver trim and golden wheels. The horses all palomino."

Jyg whistled in awe. "What's your signal?"

"There's something near the back entry," the boy replied slyly. He wasn't going to give away his secret. "I just move it a little." He held his hands a foot apart. "The next morning," he smiled like he couldn't believe it himself, "there's a ten-copper underneath it and I slide it back again."

"A ten-copper!" Jyg acted suitably impressed. "The manser who pays you, what's his carriage like?"

"I don't think he comes in one," the boy replied.

"Does he wear jewelry?" Jyg asked.

"Lots of rings. One's big and red. Another is like a snake."

FOLLOW A TRAIL

"**I** miss not riding," Tyme said one morning over breakfast. She visited the stables regularly to help walk the horses around the corrals and was ready to saddle up again.

"Yes," Klew agreed. "The horses have had plenty of rest from the chase we did to get here. We need to start exercising them more to be ready for another chase. The next time Gribono leaves, we want to follow him and find out to whom he is reporting."

The stable woman in Old Town said Gribono usually went a decade between his trips. Normally he gave the stable manser a day warning to make sure a horse was ready. But not always.

Delgado, the leader of the Jawbone Ridge gang, had arranged for Kreoko, the young man whom Tyme head-butted and who was now one of her biggest fans, to organize the watch on the stable and put up a yellow flag to signal if Gribono was getting ready to leave. When Gribono did leave, the flag was to be red. From their apartment balcony they could see the small flagpole high above the hillside along a ridgeline rooftop. The signal flag was also visible from numerous points throughout the town, and even from some of the hills overlooking above the city.

"Most likely Gribono will leave early in the morning or on a cool moonlit night," Klew continued. "That's when we need to keep extra watch for the flags and be ready to get our horses."

"If we are getting our horses," Tyme wondered, "how will we know which way Gribono's heading?"

"Kreoko will have a runner follow him with a paint tracker to show which way he leaves town. Then we can pick up his trail."

"What's a paint tracker?" Jyg asked.

"A gourd that leaks drops of colored powder or paint, and leaves small marks at intersections or changes of direction," Klew explained. "All we need to know is which way he leaves town. Then we will catch him on the road."

"Bones can help," Jyg volunteered.

"Bones!" the big black raven agreed.

"Even with Bones' help we would not have caught up with Gribono when he left Dayr Castle," Tyme said grimly. "Not without hurting our horses."

"That's because he had a twelve-hour head start," Klew reminded her. "This time we will leave right behind."

"Sounds like a plan," Jyg nodded approvingly.

"However, if Gribono leaves unexpected, in the middle of the day, or while one of us is out exercising a horse, or preoccupied and unaware, then whoever is ready will need to take up the chase immediately and not wait. That person can leave a faint paint trail at intersections and turns for the others to catch up."

Jyg looked worried. If he started out from behind, Bones would not know who was ahead to be following. Jyg did not think that his paint tracking skills would be adequate to get them started going in the right direction.

Tyme also looked concerned. "I think we will need some practice," she said.

"Yes. You will." Klew chuckled in agreement. "I will leave town and ride through the hills today and leave a trail. Tomorrow one of you can try to follow it. The day after the other tries."

They moved their horses to stables closer to their

apartment. Jyg was happy to let Tyme go first. He had been painfully saddle sore after their long, hard ride from Dayr Castle to Karvor and was not that eager to get back on a saddle.

Even though Klew started with a large drip and bright color on the paint tracker, it often took Tyme or Jyg twice as long to follow his marks correctly through the hills and back into town.

Tyme loved the wonderful, liberating feeling of riding a horse through narrow back mountain trails. She could see why Cadie was Utuno's favorite horse. The daya had a smooth gait and incredible quickness. She was also a very affectionate horse and a joy to be around. While Utuno spoiled her with daily treats and rubs, he did not get much chance to ride her. Now Tyme was taking her out three times a week. Cadie loved the increase in exercise.

After adapting to sitting in a saddle and learning to follow a paint trail, Jyg was also happy to ride Zill through the hills. And Bones always enjoyed a chance to spread her wings and fly across the countryside.

EPOH'S IDEA

As the grubbers made their traverse across the top of the middle row of the cargo bird, or dragon's stomach, as they had resumed calling it, they found more mounds of jewelry to excavate. One evening Epoh went alone to the dragon's brain, the cramped little room at the head of the beast that was filled with knobs and little levers. He sat on one of the two big thrones and gazed with fascination at all the instruments. He liked sitting here by himself trying to imagine the civilization of the Ancient Ones.

He picked up a strange, spindly object with two big puffy rings and held it up for inspection. With a flash of insight, he put it on his head, the puffy parts fitting over his ears. A little wire with a knob at the end was now just in front of his mouth. The device seemed to be made for listening and speaking. Epoh sat until it grew dark and then left the brain to join the others. He had something to tell them.

"I am not helping anymore," he informed a speechless Grinst. "I have plenty enough treasure. Anything more you find, just divide amongst yourselves."

"What do you want to do?" Horton asked.

Epoh looked at Grinst. "When you said I didn't have any curiosity, it got me thinking. I am curious all right. But not about more treasure. I am curious about the Ancient Ones. The people who made all this...and then destroyed everything."

"What does that mean?" Grinst asked.

"I want to look through the mounds that have manuscripts and books."

"Books!" Grinst looked horrified. "We only have wood for one fire," the old grubber threatened, "and that fire we be using to find treasure! Not looking for books."

"I am not asking for any of your firewood," Epoh tried to calm Grinst down. "I have a different idea I would like to try."

Epoh's idea originated with the thin, heavy, metal, hand-size devices made by the Ancient Ones with black glass on one side. The grubbers had found mounds of them in various forms, each with a slightly different size, appearance, and shape. The devices fit so comfortably in his hand.

Holding one at camp one day, he noticed how the sun bounced off the glass reflecting a small beam of light. When he angled the glass to point the light into a shadowed crevice of their cave, it dimly illuminated the darkness. He thought about the amount of light one of the giant, black glass mirrors might reflect. They had climbed over a pile of the strange objects that had fallen and blocked part of the left aisle of the cargo bird. He would use them for his experiment.

Grinst, Horton and Harvig went back to excavating the middle row mounds. Epoh turned down the left aisle, into the darkness by himself. With his hand feeling along the wall, he slowly made his way through the blackness to where the pile of large, black objects had tumbled into the passageway. He pulled a few broken ones from the pile until he felt one with smooth, un-cracked glass, then hoisted the heavy object, nearly as tall as he was, onto his back and slowly carried it through the darkness, using his foot to guide and feel along the base of the wall. He carried the device outside along the dune to where he could angle the black mirror to reflect a large beam of sunlight into the door of the cargo bird. After digging a hole in the sand, he positioned the mirror to stand facing that direction.

Back down the dark aisle way of the flying warehouse, Epoh picked out another large dark mirror. He set the second black mirror in the hallway by the door, angled to reflect the light from the first mirror, and directed the beam down the hallway into the warehouse, immediately illuminating and brightening the center mound inside. He smiled with satisfaction then began stabilizing the device with wire cord.

By now the sun had long ago moved so that the angle of light off the screen in the dunes no longer reflected into the doorway. Epoh trudged across the warming sand to readjust the tilt of the first glass. Then he readjusted the second glass. Once again the light beamed down the aisle into the front of the warehouse, creating a patch of light, illuminating everything in detail, and casting a radiant glow throughout the surrounding area.

"Wahoo!" Epoh yelled in enthusiasm.

By the time the grubbers came out for a break to eat their lunch, Epoh was just finishing the placement of the fourth glass in the dark front corner of the left aisle.

"Be careful not to touch or shift any of the big black mirrors," Epoh told the grubbers. The sun had moved enough that the light no longer reflected down the aisle.

Grinst looked with incomprehension at the stack of objects Epoh had piled up to hold, balance, and position the big black glass mirror at the front of the center mound.

"What are you doing?" Harvig asked, as if Epoh had gone mad.

"Just watch!" Epoh said with excitement, "It will only take a minute. Don't move."

He raced up the hallway, out the door, stepping fast in his double-soled yucca sandals across the now broiling dune. He burned his hand adjusting the angle when he touched a corner of the black mirror that had been facing the sun. As the light aligned and the reflection shot into the warehouse, he heard the grubbers all yell out in surprise.

Epoh dashed back inside where grubbers stood in awe looking at the beam of light reflecting off the black glass mirrors before them.

"By positioning this fourth mirror," Epoh demonstrated as he moved the left corner glass into alignment, "the light reflects down the aisle to the mound of manuscripts and books." He held out one of the hand-sized glass screens into the shaft of light to reflect a smaller beam onto the mounds before them, and then jokingly reflected the light onto Harvig's chest. "Anywhere along the way I can redirect the light to see whatever I want."

Grinst stuck his hand into the shaft of light in wonder. Harvig leaned forward to look up the aisle way toward the source of the light but Epoh stopped him. "Don't look into it," he warned, "'Tis the sun reflected from a glass mirror in a dune, to a second black mirror in the hall by the door."

Epoh gave each of them one of the hand-sized black glass screens so they could reflect a small shaft of light, to illuminate whatever they wanted.

Grinst chuckled with admiration. "A clever trick to be sure!" He nodded approvingly at Epoh. "You might make a grubber after all!"

SULTRY NIGHTS
SECURITY

Tyme was up the hill at the Blue Moon saloon and music hall at the edge of Old Town getting the latest report from the Jawbone Ridge gang.

"Gribono's into the Fire cult," Delgado informed Tyme, "and advocates having Fire shrines in the refuge."

Klew had told Tyme a little about the Fire, and how Divine Council had outlawed it long ago. She had seen small offerings left in the refuge of the Womb at Dayr Castle by devotees of the Fire. She had also seen the remains of red wax from their candles even at the Mother Womb in Karvor, when she occasionally covered up to sneak into the men's refuge to sit before the statues of Tatano, the first True Warrior.

"Gribono played cards last night with the shaman from the Mother Womb," Delgado continued. "Just the two of them, on Gribono's patio."

Tyme listened thoughtfully. "What do you think of the Fire?" she asked.

"Lots of soldiers in the Fire," Delgado stated matter-of-factly, "and some of our gang as well." He shook his head. "Don't know much about it myself." He perked up. "But I'll keep an ear out."

When she did not ask anything more he smiled widely. His

report was over. She had taken only a few sips of wine. He liked that she drank slowly. That way she stayed longer. "Tell me more of your trips on Spike into the mountains," he asked with genuine interest.

She told him about Tao Tau. Of learning to meditate and having a practice.

"So first thing every morning you do prayer meditations and use finger beads to make sure you don't run late and miss your breakfast," he marveled. "Every day you do that?"

"Most days," she remembered the days and nights tracking Gribono to Karvor where she did her prayers in the saddle.

"And you do more prayers during the heat?"

"Sometimes wordless prayer," she acknowledged with a smile. "Sometimes chanting. And then I nap like everyone else."

He appeared speechless.

"And I always take a moment to say thanks before every meal," Tyme teased him with a prim voice and expression. She laughed and grew serious. "Tao Tau said that was fundamental to a healthy practice. Stopping to acknowledge the gift of food and life before you eat."

"Yes," he said, happy to show some similarity at last. "I also give thanks before I eat."

"Then mayhaps you might grow in your practice as well," she replied.

"If you would teach me," he said innocently. She had walked perfectly into his trap. He would do anything to spend more time with her.

She laughed at his obvious ploy. "I will give you an assignment. You can start with a breathing meditation." She explained how to sit on the ground or in a chair with his back straight and eyes closed. Hands on his knees or lap.

"Focusing on your breath is very calming and healthy for your body, mind and spirit. To focus correctly you must be attentive to each breath. Think only of your breath as it flows in and out naturally. When another thought enters your mind, acknowledge it, then bring your focus straight back to your breath." She gave him a smile. "Try it for a few breaths."

He closed his eyes and tried to breathe normally. All he could think about was her watching him as he sat there. Did he look a fool?

"Sometimes 'tis easier by yourself or in a quieter room," Tyme sensed his struggle. "You can also think of calmness, love, or Divine Spirit flowing in and out of your body as you breath."

He took another few awkward breaths and opened his eyes. She grinned at him with her adorable, off-kilter smile.

"Meditation teaches you to have a singular focus, which is important in life, and in prayer." She looked at him thoughtfully. "Practice requires practice," she chuckled. "Now 'tis your turn to talk."

None of his normal pick up lines seemed adequate. "What would you like to know?"

"How did you become leader of the Jawbone Ridge gang?" she asked.

"I was apprentice to the former leader. He died unexpectedly, and I was chosen to be the new leader."

"Do you have an apprentice?"

"I am not old enough yet," he admitted. "I have not been leader very long."

"You said the gang protects the people who live in the alleys. How do you do that?"

"By keeping the alleys safe. And their businesses safe." He ticked off on his fingers. "No pickpockets. No muggers. No problems. Nice safe streets."

"No muggers?" Tyme was confused. "How come Kreoko tried to shake me down?"

"You were not near any of the businesses whose customers we protect," he apologized. "You were in an unusual part of Old Town."

"So what business do you protect?" she asked, "besides the Blue Moon, where you seem to be drinking all the time."

"This is our headquarters," he told her truthfully, "because above us is the Sultry Nights. We are security," he said, as if that should explain everything.

"Why does the Sultry Nights need security?" she asked innocently.

"Sultry Nights is the home of escorts, courtesans and prostitutes." He saw the puzzled look in her eye. "Actually, it is kind of like the flaunts at the cavort," he informed her with a chuckle, "but not hooked to the Womb or run by the temple. The bottom line at the cavort is really all about making more babies. Sultry Nights is all about pleasure. Enjoying one another's company and having fun. 'Tis different in a way that clients like. We make sure everything at Sultry Nights stays safe and relaxed."

When Tyme returned to their apartment she told Klew and Jyg what she had learned about Delgado.

Klew nodded his head in agreement. He had done a little checking into the Blue Moon and the Jawbone Ridge gang himself. "Some of the escorts and courtesans at Sultry Nights are men hired by wealthy sers as companions, lovers and bodyguards," he said.

"Delgado called them trophy moonboys," Tyme nodded.

"The other Sultry Nights workers are prostitutes," Klew continued. "More of them are women. And fifirs who prefer their own gender or gender mix."

"So the gang protects prostitutes," Jyg pondered. "Isn't that protecting the weak and the innocent?" he alluded to the motto of the True Warrior. "Or is that protecting the formerly innocent?" he joked.

Klew did not smile but simply nodded his head thoughtfully saying nothing.

"They may protect prostitutes," Tyme reminded Jyg, "But the Jawbone Ridge gang rules also allowed them to try and rob me in a different part of Old Town."

"'Tis true that the path of a True Warrior is ever braided and hard to discern," Klew noted with lament. "'Tis also true that there can be honor among thieves and hooligans."

"There is an honorableness in Delgado," Tyme agreed thoughtfully. She had not previously talked much about the young gang leader to Klew or Jyg, only telling them of the information he gave to her.

"I drink with him," she impulsively shared, no longer embarrassed, and feeling 'twas the time to let them know. "One cup of watered wine with each report he gives me." She thought for a moment. "He wants to kiss me," she only now allowed herself to admit to the fact. "But so far he's only given me a formal hug."

"Do you want to kiss him?" Jyg asked in surprise.

Tyme struggled to answer. "I'm not totally against the idea," she decided. "I kind of like him, but I'm not sure 'tis in that way."

Unlike Jyg, Klew had noticed the wine on Tyme's breath after her last few visits to the Blue Moon to meet Delgado. Klew had decided to respect her privacy and not say anything, or ask questions, unless she said something first. Now he was glad to hear her explain what had been happening. And he was especially glad to hear she was limiting herself to one cup of watered wine.

"The most effective leaders often have a very persuasive charisma," he warned her. "You are wise to be careful around him."

"He asked me to teach him about having a practice," she smiled innocently. "That's the kind of things we talk about."

"Ho, ho!" Klew confirmed with laughter as he nodded his head, "He *definitely* wants to kiss you!"

SULTAN AND EMPEROR

The next morning it took Epoh only a few hours to wire the last black glass mirror into position, part way down the left aisle, to angle the shaft of light directly onto the stack of manuscripts and books.

Earlier when Grinst had briefly examined each pile with his small oil lamp, Epoh had thought he saw something that looked like a face. But as he slowly moved the reflected beam of light across the top of the mound, the blobs of muted colors resembled nothing at all. He used a thin spatula from the cooking pile to gently pry through the layers, but everything shifted to dust at the slightest touch.

He repeatedly had to go back outside and reset the glass on the dune to catch the correct angle of the sun moving slowly but constantly across the dazzling white sky. He used potholders to safely adjust the scorching hot mirror casing without burning his hands. When he returned inside, it took his eyes so long to adjust back to the darkness he started wearing a hood when he went out. Inside the air stayed cool even during the heat.

Peeling slowly through the layers of manuscripts, he occasionally saw fragments of writing. Some large, some small. Across all parts of the page. Grouped in clusters and formations.

And occasional ghostly images. Mayhaps people, or faces. Patterns like a building. But nothing distinct enough to say for sure. Just a feeling.

Late on the second day, just as the sunlight was beginning to fade, Epoh gently blew away tatters of paper to reveal an intact part of a page with a portion of text. He stared in excitement. Some of the alphabet was like Ambri!

He blew softer.

Words! Some similar to Ambri!

He could feel his heart pounding in his chest as the light faded from the page. In a daze he hurried out to readjust the first black mirror on the dune. Back inside when he could see again, Epoh gently blew another small section of the page clear of paper flakes and dust. With each breath the text grew larger until the middle third of a page was revealed. When the grubbers came out from their work, he showed them what he had discovered.

"What does it mean?" Harvig pointed to the largest writing.

"I am not sure," Epoh answered. "'Tis different from Ambri. Some of those letters are not in our alphabet."

Grinst eyed Epoh with amazement. "You spent all day and this is all you got?"

Epoh ignored the comment. He pointed to another section of page. "I can read part of this sentence. *He lived like a...*" Epoh paused over an unfamiliar word, "*sultan.*"

"That is a Hool word," Harvig said.

"'Hool?" Epoh replied in surprise.

"A sultan is like a king," Harvig explained. He was shocked that Epoh, being a prince, would not know such a thing.

Epoh looked at the strange word the next line down. "Emperor," he pronounced slowly. "Do you know what that means?"

"That is a Hool word as well," Harvig exclaimed. "An emperor is a man who is even greater than a sultan."

"Like a male Empress?" Epoh guessed with astonishment.

Were the Ancient Ones more like the Hool than the Ambri?

THE VISIT

hree days after their last meeting, Tyme saw the blue cloth around the pole by the window outside the Blue Moon. Inside Delgado escorted her to their private table. After brief pleasantries he reported his most recent findings.

"Up the hill off Cracken Street is a gloomy basement bar called the Anvil," Delgado informed her. "There is a secret back room. Gribono plays cards there. The dealer is a Heart Legion soldier named Virga Gavir. Big, tattooed, and bad tempered from what I hear. I don't know any of the other players yet."

"How often do they play?" Tyme asked.

"Once a week. Every Moonday eve," Delgado replied. "All night long and often into the morning. The room is hidden somehow. Probably a trap door."

"Hidden," Tyme mused. "Interesting."

"Indeed. That means 'tis either very high stakes, which seems unlikely given the normal Anvil clientele," Delgado reasoned. "Or, some of the players would rather stay out of sight from the authorities, which seems more likely."

Tyme nodded her head.

"We will watch the place next Moonday eve to find out more," Delgado promised.

She told him about the worker Jyg had talked with from The Plumed Bird stables who signaled Gribono when a certain carriage appeared. "The coach is black lacquer with silver trim and golden wheels. The horses all palomino."

Delgado shook his head. "Don't know who that is but should be able to find out quick enough."

They sat quietly for a moment.

"I was just thinking of my breath, and what you taught me about meditation," he said.

"Did you ask me to teach you about having a practice because you hope I will allow you to kiss me?" Tyme asked.

Delgado laughed nervously at her bluntness. She always managed to keep him off balance. "Yes," he admitted with a smile, "I guess I did." He grew serious. "But I also truly have interest in what you teach."

"And where did this sudden interest come from?" she teased.

"From you," he told her honestly. "I want what you have. I want your focus and power." He told her he had meditated every morning since her instructions. "I think of you sitting beside me," he admitted with his handsome smile. "Thinking of you sitting calmly helps me to be calm as well."

"Meditating with others nearby can be very helpful," she agreed, "and I'm glad you think of me as a calming influence." She was amazed how he could bring everything back around to her. "Basic meditation is all about learning to focus and calm the mind." She raised her thick, black eyebrows. "'Tis the first step toward meditative or contemplative prayer."

"And that is more powerful?" he asked.

"Much more powerful," she answered with a knowing look. "But not power for yourself. The power flows in harmony with Divine Purpose. You don't find yourself in the power, you lose yourself in the power."

You lose yourself in the power. He sat thinking of her words as she took the last sip of her wine. Their time together always flew by much too quickly. He fortified his nerve to speak.

"Before I ask your permission for a kiss, I have a favor to ask," he told her seriously, "and a confession to make." He looked nervous. "The Jawbone Ridge gang is deeply in your debt," he began, "and we take that debt seriously. We believe we can better *help* you if we know more *about* you."

"Okay," Tyme shook her head in wonderment at what he might want next. "What is your request?"

"We can not help you if we don't know where you live," he continued to explain, "in case we need to reach you quickly or something happens."

"Where I live has no…" she started to say.

"I had you followed," he finally said it. "I know about the apartment building, and also about a certain formidable soldier type fellow who also stays there as well."

She was taken by surprise. He had already linked her to Klew. But not yet Jyg. She chastised herself for being so naive. "And your favor?" She could not imagine where this was going.

"I would like to come alone in secret to visit your apartment and meet your companion. Or companions," he guessed.

"And why do you want to meet them?" she asked, admitting there was another.

"If I am to ask you for a kiss, I first want to properly meet your friends, so that they may know of my intentions.

"And what do you care about my friends, or what they might think?" she asked with curiosity.

"This is not a Barbarian Kingdom," he laughed at her naiveté. "We live by Ambri law. A woman's testimony holds much more power in a court of law. Men who overstep their bounds, or place, get castrated. 'Tis wise for men to have witnesses to any developing relationship."

Tyme did not know what to say.

"My lady," he told her in all sincerity, "I stand little chance of winning your heart if your friends counsel against me. I would have them meet me and know that my actions are honorable."

"And why do you wish to meet at our apartment?" she asked. "Why not here, in your lair?"

"Because this is just one side of me," he motioned with

his arm around the room. "In this saloon people can not see past my role as gang leader. Mayhaps in your apartment, in a different light, your friends, and even you yourself, my lady, may see that there is another part of me."

*

He came to the apartment the next evening, wearing an old brown cloak and hood, slipping discreetly through the back door to the stairs of the apartment building when no one was looking. At the top of the stairs he knocked on the small door to the left. Tyme opened the door with a shy smile.

"My lady," he stepped forward, lightly took her hands and raised them together between them at chest level in a formal greeting. He smiled charmingly as he looked into her eyes.

Tyme let go with an embarrassed laugh. She had warned Klew and Jyg that he would probably get all moon-eyes over her. She introduced everyone and they sat at the patio table while Jyg poured mint tea.

"Thank you for having me here," Delgado began. "I wanted to come for two reasons. I am deeply indebted to Tyme and wish to do all I can to help her. Her quest is my quest." He smiled at her, knowing his next words were going to embarrass her. "I am also here because I am smitten by her. I hope to be her friend." He grinned impishly. "And most of all, I hope to court her."

"And if that does not work out, moonboy?" Tyme asked in a serious tone to stop further gushing.

He grew somber. "Should my hope to court you fail, then I would hope to be your friend. Should that honor fail, I would hope to be your servant." He bowed his head.

She was touched by the sincerity of his words. "I also hope that we can be friends," she agreed with a sympathetic smile. But she could not promise him any more than that.

They had agreed earlier to share the truth of their mission with Delgado. Tyme preferred not to tell the story herself so it fell to Klew to explain who Noot was, and how he had been killed and linked to Gribono, the ornate-ringed gambler.

"Who we believe to be in a plot treasonous to King Eyrico of Dayrstad," Klew declared, "and mayhaps the Czarzina herself. "Our plan is to watch him and follow him and find who he's reporting to."

"I will tell you straight up I could care less about the Czarzina," Delgado proclaimed, "but I am with you on seeking justice for Noot's murder and protecting your king. Your enemies are my enemies! I will do all I can to help." He looked at each of them solemnly in the eye.

After an appropriate pause, Delgado changed the subject. He was eager to learn more about Tyme. "How did you meet Tyme?" he asked Klew.

"He is my sword manser!" Tyme exclaimed proudly.

"We've been training together since she was little," Klew smiled fondly. He told the story of her fight with Noot and the wooden swords, how he had helped her with the grip, and advised her not to spar with Noot again.

"Uh-oh," Delgado chuckled, "I can guess where this might be going."

"We fought again," Tyme admitted. "I started it. And Noot hurt my arm. Klew must have felt sorry for me," she sighed. "Because afterword he offered to teach me the sword."

"Did you feel sorry for her?" Delgado innocently asked Klew.

"No," the sword Manser recalled clearly. "I offered to teach her the sword because she said she would protect the weak and the innocent. She remembered the True Warrior vow I had told her earlier. I felt her determination and resolve. I felt her inner spirit." He smiled at the memory. "She is the most amazing pupil a sword manser could ever hope to find."

"So let's hear a few early training stories," Delgado eagerly encouraged. He listened with delight as they talked about working out together.

During a pause in the conversation Delgado, ever the diplomat, brought Jyg into the discussion. "How did you meet Tyme?" he asked, wondering where the boy fit in. He did not

89

appear to be a suitor.

Jyg so briefly told the tale of their meeting at school that Tyme jumped in to help him elaborate. "The reason he started going to school was because he raised and trained a gyrfalcon. The biggest of all falcons." She told of Jyg's climb of the east tower, the highest in the castle, and his climbs in the stable rafters and all around the abandoned castle buildings. 'Twas obvious she was quite proud of her friend's skills.

"Now he has another familiar," Tyme added.

Jyg made a soft call and immediately a raven streaked down to the table and landed with a whoosh of her four-foot wings.

"Manser Jygero!" the big black bird greeted him.

"Hey, Bones!" Jyg replied as the bird began playfully biting and gently mauling his fingers in her large bill.

Delgado was fascinated with the talking bird and insisted that Jyg tell the long version of finding and raising the big raven.

"Bones!" the bird called out and hopped over to greet Tyme by pushing the top of her head into Tyme's palm and then gently biting her fingers. She then visited Klew briefly before turning toward Delgado. The raven did not come closer, but looked him over for a few moments and then hopped off the table into the air and flew to a perch in the corner.

"Tell us of the Jawbone Ridge gang," Klew requested.

Delgado told them about growing up on the streets, and being taken in, sheltered and fed by the gang. He was taught numerous begging tricks and scams, how to appear injured, sick or even missing a limb.

"But once you get a little older, you are not so cute," he explained. "Then people stop giving you money." He smiled. "So I got transferred from begging on the steps of the Womb to unloading wagons and being a busboy at the Blue Moon saloon and dance hall."

His grin widened, a most infectious smile. "My life changed. I was introduced to music and culture. I knew right away that was where I wanted to be. Not on the streets, but inside the Blue Moon." He told them of his rise up through the ranks of workers. "I busted my ass and worked hard."

"Then the leader of the gang, who I idolized, chose me to be his apprentice. He died not long ago. I did not expect to be leader for at least another century."

"Does the gang strong arm and force people to pay for protection?" Klew asked bluntly.

"No. Our customers appreciate and value our security services. The Sultry Nights have their own profession and trade, which they perform on their own premises. What they do is their own business. We are paid to monitor the entrance and provide safety inside and out on the street. That way the workers are safe and protected. And the clients do not have to worry about getting robbed. Everybody is happy."

"So the Jawbone Ridge gang owns the Blue Moon?" Tyme asked with uncertainty.

"Not at all," Delgado shook his head with a snort. "The Jawbone Ridge gang does not own a thing. We do not exist on paper. We are men. They give us a corner of the Blue Moon for our headquarters to make sure we are always there watching out and ready for any problems."

"And you also smuggle liquor?" Klew inquired.

"Who doesn't?" Delgado laughed. "But we do not call it smuggling. We call it free trade. We are small time. Mostly just for the Blue Moon. But sometimes we have a little extra." He got a sly grin. "In fact, I brought all of you a small bottle of most excellent viruna." He pulled it from his bag and set it on the table.

"At the Blue Moon," he said, "Tyme will drink only one cup of watered wine with me. As a matter of social instruction in fine dining and revelry," Delgado grinned widely, "this evening I would like to share a toast with her, and with all of you, of something much finer in taste and stronger in spirit."

"I drank viruna once before," Jyg reflected and told of his first meeting with Ser Nahi Naha Nala, the woman who bought his gyrfalcon. "She paid an extra gold coin because we drank viruna together, and she knew how she was going to break my heart when she took my falcon."

"That money sent you to school," Tyme noted after a respectful silence. "I wonder if we would have met and become friends if you had not gone to school?"

Jyg smiled and then looked at the bottle with interest.

"Viruna has helped seal agreements and oaths," Delgado proclaimed, "and been shared to rejoice...and to grieve. Will you join me in a drink?" He looked to Tyme and then the others.

"Yes," she smiled impishly, "I would like to try it."

"Sure," Jyg enthused.

"I would love to have some viruna," Klew grinned agreeably.

Delgado pulled out a box with four small, engraved metal cups and set them on the table. He opened the bottle and carefully filled the cups. They each picked up one. "Traditionally, you are to drink the cup in one swallow," he told Tyme. "But if you prefer, do it in two or three sips, that is also fine." He lifted his little cup. "To new friendships!"

"To new friendships!" they repeated the toast, and drank. All of them banged their empty cups back on the table as Delgado had instructed. The viruna was powerfully strong and burned like fire down their throats.

"Whoa!" Tyme coughed as her eyes watered.

"Whoo!" said Jyg as he squeezed his eyes shut for a moment.

"Smooth!" Klew was impressed by the quality.

"This is the finest viruna made!" Delgado boasted. "From the King of Sikes special distillery!"

"How do you possess liquor from the King's own estate?" Klew asked with interest.

Delgado chuckled. "Neither the people selling the liquor, nor those buying it, want to pay taxes to the Czarzina." He shrugged his shoulders. "Let us just say there is a big incentive for getting liquor shipped around the toll booths."

"Are you saying the King of Sikes works with smugglers?" Klew asked.

"My guess is the King doesn't know," Delgado laughed. "Someone in his family or inner circle probably needs cash. If the King inventoried his private stock of viruna, he might get quite a shock."

Delgado changed the narrative. "I know a bit more about *this* end of the smuggling supply line." He told some humorous bootlegging stories of sneaking liquor past the Karvor bridge guards. Klew responded with funny stories of Heart Legion guards catching and foiling ill-considered smuggling schemes while he was a sergeant.

Delgado realized that when he began smuggling, Klew had been posted at the tollgate. "That means all that time you were there," Delgado laughed with glee, "you never caught me! And I'm still smuggling liquor today!"

Klew also found great irony in the situation. "I hated that job! Bullying people for money at the tollbooth day and night so the Czarzina could build another monument to herself in Ambrit. I got out of the Legion as quick as I could buy my bond!"

"This calls for another round!" Delgado declared enthusiastically, patting Klew on the back. "We have history together!" He turned to Tyme. "For you I would recommend less than a half a shot, just a wee bit. Jyg is on his own."

"I will take another *full* shot, thank you," Jyg instructed.

"Just a wee bit," Tyme agreed.

Delgado poured the viruna and they all lifted their little metal cups. "To life long friendships!" he toasted and they joined in.

Tyme gasped. "Even a wee bit is strong!" Everyone laughed.

They talked and told stories into the evening. Tyme told Delgado about Crown Prince Epohco, and how she believed that he was still alive. He sat soberly listening to the tale, and uncharacteristically, did not ask any further questions.

Finally late after dark, Delgado rose to leave. "I thank you for your hospitality. This has been a most interesting night. I want to extend my invitation to all of you, please know you are always welcome at the Blue Moon. I would be thrilled to have you as my guests. Moondays have the best music, but you are welcome any time. Viruna is on the house."

He turned to Tyme. "If I get any new information on Gribono, I will have a signal set in your alley. That way you do not have to hike up to the Blue Moon daily to check the flagpole. I could also come down to report as well."

"I like hearing your reports up at the Blue Moon," Tyme told him boldly. "Have someone leave a sign in the alley and I will come up to see you."

Delgado smiled broadly as he put on his old cloak. He gave Tyme a formal embrace, hugged Klew and Jyg in a more boisterous style, said goodbye to Bones, and went out the door.

A NEW GANG
MEMBER

"**A** most interesting young man," Klew said after Delgado had left their apartment.

"I like him," Jyg smiled enthusiastically, feeling quite happy from the two shots of viruna.

Tyme could not help but smile herself. "He is easy to like," she admitted. "And quick to lay out his intentions."

"You called him moonboy!" Jyg laughed. Klew chuckled as well.

"That is how he was acting!" Wiir Waar had taught her the term for a starry-eyed man who thinks he is in love but is only in heat. Tyme missed her Ser Cus friend, and the advice she would certainly give about Delgado.

"He is a valuable ally," Klew said. "But he could also be a liability. Let's not forget he is a smuggler and law breaker."

"Do you think he is honorable?" Tyme asked Klew. She valued his counsel.

"Yes," Klew replied. "I believe he is honorable--at first glance." He shrugged. "As much as I like him, I hardly know him. I would trust him, but cautiously."

She turned to Jyg.

"I am with Klew," he said. "We should get to know him before we trust him more." Jyg smiled triumphantly. "And I will volunteer!"

"For what?" Tyme asked.

"To hang out at the Blue Moon," Jyg exclaimed. "Check the action. See what others say about Delgado." He looked at Klew. "It makes sense. You are playing the mercenary. I will keep an eye on the Jawbone Ridge gang."

Klew thought for a moment.

"And what are you going to tell Delgado?" Tyme asked. "You are there to spy on him?"

"I am just being friendly," Jyg shrugged as if 'twas obvious. "I have never been out of Dayrstad. I want an introduction to music and culture." He used Delgado's words for the Blue Moon. "It seems natural that I would want to go there."

"Do you?" Tyme asked.

"Of course!" Jyg laughed in return. "Sounds more fun than your sword training!" He rubbed his arm where she had given him another bruise--one of many.

"I think you are right," Klew agreed seriously. "You would be perfect. Give us the inside view." He playfully punched Jyg's shoulder. "Our own member of the Jawbone Ridge gang."

"Hey! I am already an *honorary* member," Tyme reminded them both. "How many members do we need?"

"You are different," Klew answered. "Delgado won't be moonboy around Jyg. He will see Delgado in a more true light." He turned to Jyg. "Keep your relationship with Tyme secret from everyone else. When she goes to the Blue Moon, act like you don't know each other."

"Don't worry," Tyme told Jyg. "When I go to the Blue Moon, we always sit at a little private table anyway."

"Then I will start tomorrow," Jyg announced. "I'll go up after the heat."

"Tomorrow!" Tyme was surprised. "You just saw him tonight!"

"He said come and visit anytime," Jyg reminded her with a chuckle.

Klew nodded his head in agreement. "No sense in waiting,"

he concurred. "Best go tomorrow and start seeing what you can find out."

The next evening Jyg walked through the front door of the Blue Moon and turned left like Tyme had instructed, along a back wall away from the bar and behind the tables for quick access to the screened area on the far wall behind the lights. He breathed a sigh of relief when he went through the opening and saw Delgado sitting with a few others at the center table.

"I was hoping you would come tonight!" Delgado stood up and gave Jyg a friendly embrace. "I cleared out my schedule, so I am free." He pointed to a private table in a small alcove, the table Tyme had described. "Let's sit where we can easily talk."

They each had a shot of viruna. "This is very good," Delgado told him, "but not as good as the bottle I gave you!" He smiled widely. "You must appreciate every drop from that bottle!"

They got along easily, laughing and telling stories, and had a second shot of viruna as it grew dark. A woman had been singing and now a small band with drums, guitars and a violin was setting up. "I think you will enjoy this," Delgado told Jyg. "The band is from Vlice. They are very lively." He looked shrewdly at Jyg. "Do you know how to dance?"

"Are you asking me to dance?" Jyg innocently mocked.

Delgado laughed loudly and slapped him on the back. "I am asking if you know how! Dancing is fun, cheap, and a great way to meet women, men, fifirs. Whatever you're looking for. Do you know what you're looking for?"

"A slight interest in girls, certainly not overpowering. I have high standards." He thought of Tyme and Wiir Waar. "I can wait."

"I also have high standards," Delgado agreed. "That is why I am so attracted to Tyme. A young woman like her is a rare gem to be honored and exalted!"

Jyg laughed. "She would call you moonboy if she heard that!"

"Go ahead and tell her," Delgado waved him off. "She knows my feelings." He chuckled mournfully and then grew serious.

"Would you mind telling me a bit more about Crown Prince Epohco?" he asked. "She called him Epoh."

"He and Tyme had this strange connection right from the start," Jyg began. He told of Epohco's interest in meditation and dreams. "He knew right off that she was special. I figured they would marry and she would be a famous Barbarian queen."

Delgado asked all about the Epohco's accident, and the health of the new crown prince.

"Dracoro will be a soldier king, so the army likes him," Jyg replied. "Epohco would have been a philosopher king. The librarians and scribes liked him, and the teachers at the school. But he never hung out at the training field or armory with the soldiers and guards."

Delgado waved for a final round of viruna. "Let us have a toast to acknowledge those who are not here with us." They drank their small, metal cups and slapped them on the table.

"And now let us enjoy the music and talk of other things," Delgado said with a smile. But his eyes were not as bright as before.

The next morning Jyg woke up with a terrible headache.

THE LARGE BOOKS

E poh thought about the Hool words as he stared at the
text he had uncovered in the pile of manuscripts.
Sultan. Emperor. The words sent his mind reeling with
implications.

Names used by the Ancient Ones long ago, now used by the
Hool. Both names for male leaders!

Did the Ancient Ones have male leaders like the Hool?
Surely the Ancient Ones were not brutish like the Hool!
Although the Ancient Ones *did* destroy their world--that
seemed like something the Hool might do.

The other sobering implication, if the Hool and the
Ancient Ones had language similarities, the Hool must also be
descended from the Ancient Ones. Just like the Ambri claimed
to be. That meant the Hool were not foreign savages from
across the Endless Waste, but closely related to the Ambri.

Epoh resumed working his way through the layer of
manuscripts, finding more strange details. The Ambri used *ser*
as a term of respect for women. The Ancient Ones used *sir* as a
title of respect for men. The Ambri word *condition* was a place
to rest during the heat. The Ancient Ones had *air condition* to
escape the heat.

The bottom layer of the manuscript pile held boxes of large
books. Epoh used his knife to precisely cut away the top of
one of the stacked paper boxes, and lift it off. Underneath was
another piece of the corrugated paper. Beneath, two books,

side by side, both with a dark paper covering with a smattering of white and blue colors smudged in a circle of dust. He gently lifted one of the books and set it in the reflected sunlight. He carefully opened the thick, hard cover.

The first page had decomposed to white dust. He tried to lightly brush it away but everything fell apart in his hand. He softly blew and the dust flaked away to reveal green colors. A painting of plants? He blew again. Red and yellow blossoms. With each tiny breath the picture emerged.

A waterfall surrounded by dense, thick foliage of green plants with large colorful flowers. The sky a strange color of blue. The painting was unlike any he had ever seen. So detailed and precise 'twas as if he was looking directly at real life.

When the grubbers came out for a break and bite of locust patties, Epoh showed them the picture. They all stared silently at the thick green growth, the flowering plants, the waterfall, and the odd blue-colored sky.

"What is it?" asked Harvig in wonder.

"'Tis a forest in the clouds," Epoh marveled. Tyme had told him of Lost Valley in the high Barrier Mountains where clouds of mist swirled through the air and plants grew on top of each other. He pointed to the waterfall. "The power of that water can pull you right in. If you can't swim, you drown." He had told them of falling into such a river, being swept over waterfalls, then knocked and tumbled through tunnels and caves as the water descended from the mountains into the Maze.

Grinst looked at the waterfall in horror. He had never quite believed Epoh's river story. He could not imagine so much water running together.

"Why is the sky blue?" asked Horton. "That looks strange."

"I am not sure," Epoh replied. The sky they knew was always fire tinged with yellow, orange, and red colors by the sun in the mornings and evenings, and dazzling white all through the day. Never blue!

THE KISS

"Thank you for your hospitality the other evening," Delgado's eye's sparkled. He was sitting with Tyme at their private table in the Blue Moon. "I enjoyed being at your apartment, meeting Klew, and making friends with Jyg. I hope he was not too hung over after he came up to visit me. I warned him of the consequences, but he is his own man and makes his own choices."

"He was quiet the next morning," Tyme acknowledged with a smile. "Not his usual chipper self for a few hours, but then he cheered up." She chuckled. "He was ready to come again tonight, but I told him 'twas my turn. That you had sent a message."

"Whatever it takes to get you up here," Delgado purred.

She rolled her golden-green eyes but then smiled warmly. "I had a great evening the other night as well. 'Twas fun having you meet Klew and Jyg. I enjoyed seeing you outside the Blue Moon."

"Can we meet at your apartment again?" he asked her. "Mayhaps next week?"

"Mayhaps," she said with a smile. "We still have plenty of viruna."

He grinned happily in return.

"So what is the latest news?" She wanted to get business out of the way.

"The black lacquered coach with the palominos," he told

her, "is the personal carriage of Ser Gina Gain Gani, a wealthy merchant. Very ambitious in Karvor politics. Interesting that Gribono tips a stable worker to know when she arrives at the Plumed Bird. My guess is, he then shows up as though by chance, in hopes of meeting or gambling with her," Delgado shrugged. "Don't know much yet beyond that. Mayhaps Klew will have heard of her."

"That is it?"

"That is it," he confirmed. "Business all taken care of."

She looked at him thoughtfully. He certainly was handsome. And fun to be around. But he was the leader of a gang of lawbreakers. If Epoh were here, she would not even consider him. But Epoh was not here.

He noted her pondering. "We can just relax and listen to the music if you like," he told her. "'Tis okay to sit quietly."

She leaned forward and kissed him lightly, lingering for a moment with their lips close, and then drew back. Their first kiss, over and out of the way. Now she could relax.

His face lit up. "My lady, ever you surprise me!"

"And myself as well," Tyme replied, now shocked at her own boldness.

They talked, laughed and listened to the music. Tyme drank watered wine. When her cup was empty, she agreed to half a cup more. When she finished Delgado leaned closer.

"Before...you kissed me. Now," he asked, "may I kiss you before you go?"

Tyme nodded her head.

His kiss was stronger. Longer. Wow.

He smiled broadly and stood up to give her a formal embrace. "I hope to have more to report soon. Please consider coming up to enjoying the music on full Moonday!"

PART III

Nothing can stop the righteous from their goal.

Kabaal Prophecies

She had no fear of death, only of failure.

Hope the Proclaimer

ESCAPE

Once a month a doctor inspected all the prisoners at Ralston Garrison and the Box. One moon a different doctor came to Riin Ruel's cell. She was a thin, older woman with rich ebony skin and short, kinky silver hair. With the guard standing outside the door, the woman began to examine Riin Ruel.

The doctor stood with her back to the guard to hide what she was doing. She motioned for Riin Ruel to keep silent as she lightly tapped a Dagger code of sisterhood on her arm. The two women stared intently into each other's eyes.

Riin Ruel had been waiting over two centuries for such a sign! She had always believed that the Daggers would not forget her. At last they had found a way to get her out. Riin Ruel felt ecstatic. She wanted to hug the woman, but instead she forced herself to appear nonchalant.

"You will escape the Box through the morgue," the doctor whispered softly. Such an escape meant there would not be any chase after her. She would be presumed dead.

Riin Ruel smiled grimly at the irony. Dying to a new life.

The doctor slipped a long, thin reed filled with a dark paste from inside the folds of her coat and set it along the end of Riin Ruel's sleeping mat where the size and color blended perfectly with the other reeds of the mat.

"Three dark Moondays from now, start at this end and eat one marked section of the reed each night. The type of drug and the effect will change. The first two weeks you will just have diarrhea. Then you will become more and more feverish and sick. Drink as much water as you can each day. You must continue eating the reed to the very end. After the last is eaten you will appear as dead. I will be on duty that night only to transfer and watch over your body." The doctor straightened and called for the guard to open the cell door and let her out.

Riin Ruel sat on her mat in thought. She would need to suspend her *Prayers for the Damned* and her battles with the demons on her Yoke. She had finished off the demon in the third hell, and now had only one active demon, the fiend from the fifth hell. She knew his name, although she would never say it aloud, nor even write it. He was greatly weakened, and no longer able to infect men's souls. Yet he was still tenacious and strong in his own lair in the fifth hell. She had him cornered and weakening with every battle. Once again she would leave the demon fearfully waiting for her next move. She would need her full strength for the strain on her body with her upcoming fake death. She put her Yoke away.

The next moon the regular doctor resumed making the rounds. Riin Ruel focused on praying and building up her vital forces for the ordeal ahead. Three months later on the third dark Moonday she put her head down close to the hidden reed in her sleeping mat, and bit off the first small, marked section with the black paste inside.

PART IV

*Greed and treachery have bitter reward
while a generous heart gifts all with joy.*

       Kabaal Prophecies

All these events began to form a tapestry, each coloring a small portion of the weaving, together creating portraits of good and evil.

       Hope the Proclaimer

A CHAMPION
FOR THE FIRE

When King Eyrico of Dayrstad first installed Eddarko, his younger brother, as Duke of the Siren, Eddarko was thrilled to be out of Dayr Castle and in charge of his own mini-kingdom, away from his prissy older brother, the King.

As a boy Prince Eddarko had chaffed under the strict and proper example shown by his older brother, Crown Prince Eyrico. It rankled Eddarko that he could beat his older brother in all the ways that mattered. He was a superior wrestler and fighter in every category of weaponry, a better leader of soldiers, and more shrewd and ruthless in court. He was also a better rider, drinker and womanizer.

But 'twas his older brother who was destined to become king. Secretly Eddarko agreed with the Hool that the strongest king was best chosen on the tourney field.

When Eddarko became Duke, he immediately began to establish his own rules and protocol. When nefarious rumors of Duke Eddarko's bad behavior drifted to Dayr Castle, King Eyrico sent couriers with letters of reprimand. But neither advice nor threats seemed to sway the Duke. Nothing short of his complete removal seemed effective, which King Eyrico never considered. He knew full well that the Duke would die fighting before giving up the Siren. And the Duke knew his brother did not have the stomach for such a fight. Therefore all of the King's threats were empty and hollow. Duke Eddarko ignored all missives from his brother and continued to live and rule as he pleased.

This festering stalemate and lack of respect between the two brothers further pushed them apart. At first Duke Eddarko reveled in this division, stirring things up. But over time he began to miss aspects of court life in Dayr Castle and felt even more jealous of his older brother's power and position.

The Siren was isolated and removed from contact with the rest of Dayrstad, and the old cities. The Ser Cus never came to the Siren, nor many of the minstrels or traveling dance troupes. The Duke felt like he had been pushed aside and life was passing him by.

He began scheming to change his fortune and overthrow his brother. The Duke surrounded himself with disgruntled soldiers of fortune and disgraced mansers and nobles who were all eager to point the blame for their troubles upon others. They reinforced his feeling of victimhood and desire for revenge upon those in Dayr Castle who had more power and prestige.

When the Duke first heard of the Fire, he had no interest in the group. But as their numbers began to swell, Eddarko realized there could be advantages and opportunities in ingratiating himself into the ranks of the disgruntled and outcast groups of Dayrstad society. He saw the Fire as his chance to build a group of followers and unify a growing movement around his own banner.

Duke Eddarko became a voice and rallying point to those who were seeking a new order, a champion for the Fire, demanding the group have the rights of a full Attribute. The Duke encouraged placement of Fire shrines in the refuge of the Womb, over the objections, and the resignation, of the head priest.

The remaining priest was a young woman who had grown

up in the Bait and had no outside education. She lacked the confidence and experience to challenge the Duke over such matters of theology. If the Duke proclaimed Divine Fire to be an Attribute and worthy of a shrine in the refuge, the newly elevated priest was not about to quibble over secondary men's issues in the refuge. She performed all the important rituals herself in the sanctuary with the women.

The Duke was also the first sovereign to meet with Shamano, the shaman from Birjj, and give him full honors and recognition at court. However, the Duke preferred to meet the shaman at the refuge in the Womb, or better yet, down at the old kiva in the Bait, which was being cleaned and repaired. That way he could show his respect by coming to visit, but also have the freedom to leave soon if the shaman began droning on about the Fire. 'Twas all the man wanted to talk about. The few times that Shamano had come to court, he had ruined the evenings. The shaman's presence did not inspire drinking and dancing, or much laughter. Luckily he seldom visited the Siren.

Another shaman named Rogoto was now living in a shelter by the old kiva. The underground stone chamber had been constructed by the old tribes and considered heathen to the Ambri, who covered it over with terraced vineyards when they created the Bait in the fertile valley below the Siren. Now the followers of the Fire embraced the kiva to reclaim their own heritage and beliefs. The one true religion for men.

Rogoto performed daily ceremonies at the kiva. He never came up to court, which left the Duke free to live as he pleased without interference from overtly pious Fire devotees. Soldiers and idealistic young men from the Bait and Valhal visited the kiva to say prayers and make offerings, then headed up to the Siren for food and drink. In this way Duke Eddarko, who always provided lively entertainment, became acquainted with many of the restless and dissatisfied men living in Dayrstad and the Barrier Mountains.

Things were going well until the Duke met Bokono, who claimed the title of rebel leader. The Duke considered himself a superior candidate. He had a highly fortified base, the Siren, and a small army. Bokono's imaginary army was scattered through the mountains with no headquarters, nor safe haven. From the moment they first met, Duke Eddarko began a secret campaign to lure into his own camp as many of Bokono's followers as possible.

Bokono dreamt of becoming the King of Birjj. Duke Eddarko planned on becoming King of Dayrstad, which he considered a much more likely possibility. Eddarko knew he would get few converts from Bokono's followers who lived in the mountains of Birjj. But he wanted to make sure he got back every one of Bokono's followers who lived in Dayrstad. Those were *his* people. Their loyalty belonged to the Duke! He needed them to accomplish his plans.

SHAMANO

Shamano believed that a man's body, more than a woman's, was stained and impure. 'Twas decreed by Divine Council and an obvious fact. Women's bodies were first created by Divine from the ether as angelic beings. Men's bodies were first created through worldly passion.

Boys were far more susceptible to risky behavior and violent emotions. Boys created more problems. They fought, got into trouble more, and were more likely to be arrested. Men perpetrated most crime. Men did most of the killings. Men filled the prisons.

The shaman believed that men needed special purifying, and that only Divine Fire could cleanse and refine a man's body and soul. Only the Fire was strong enough to transform men into more spiritual beings. The Fire was an Attribute of Divine given to help men mold themselves into a new creation.

Just as a woman's body has a special bond with the moon, which affects menstruation and fertility, Shamano believed that men's bodies had a special link and affinity for the sun. Like men, the sun was stained and impure. The afternoon sun killed most everything. Only specialized cactus, yuccas, and palms could live in direct sunlight during the heat. Yet the sun, like men, was needed for life to exist. Without sunlight all plants died. Without sunlight people became sick. Without the sun the world would be dark and cold and all life would cease.

The sun represented the fundamental truth of the Fire.

The sun was a sign in the sky, given by Divine, to show men their need to subjugate their emotions, to burn away their destructive passions, to cleanse both their physical and spiritual bodies. The afternoon sun, the heat, also reminded men of the terrible consequences of a failure to constrain and curb their evil compulsions and obsessions. The destruction brought about by the heat represented the inevitable result of uncontrolled passion in men.

After Shamano met Gribono at Dayr Castle, and accepted the gambler's pledge of devotion, and his offer to be a spy, Shamano journeyed on to Sikes. The shaman first went to the capitol where he oversaw the placement of a large, polished sun disc onto a new Fire altar in the refuge of the Mother Womb. King Gorijo of Sikes had just recently allowed the altar to be established, over the strong objections of the women priests. Shamano had hoped he might meet with the priests, to better explain Fire theology, prayers, and offerings. But the Womb officials refused to speak to him, fearing they might give some legitimacy to his beliefs and position. Instead, they labeled his actions as heretical and accused his followers of being sun worshippers.

Undeterred, and without surprise, Shamano left the city and headed into the mountains, traveling with a few other monks. He had separated from Bokono, who was meeting with other freedom fighters--as they called themselves. The priests, sers, and nobles called them rebels.

Shamano wanted to meet Singer, who had not yet caught the attention and disapproval of the priests. The fact that he was out of sight on the farms, and sponsored by the Manser of Agave, had kept Singer from running afoul of the authorities. The shaman had visited the farms before, leading worship ceremonies. He had no difficulty getting directions from the field bosses to find the area where Singer was located.

The steep valley hillsides were covered with the orange and red spiky-fingered agave cactus. Many sprouted a single, tall, dried stalk topped with the shriveled remains of a large flowering head. None of the plants had blossomed since the last rains more than two centuries ago. Spread across the hillsides, the agavrs toiled with their long machete knives and carried their loads, the thick heart of the agave cactus, down to the wagons to be weighed and hauled to the farm distilleries.

When Shamano first heard Singer's voice he felt a surge of emotion. He had always liked men's drumming in the kivas and listening to the boys' choir in the refuge. Now hearing a grown man singing Divines felt profound and empowering. Singer's voice had a strong, striking beauty, a joyous, vibrant and uplifting tone and spirit. The shaman hiked closer to a small outcropping of rock where he sat listening until all the workers returned to camp to eat and rest during the heat.

In the evening Shamano joined a crowd of men that gathered on a hillside shaped as a natural amphitheater. He did not introduce himself, but sat quietly observing while Singer led a few songs with a group of men singing along as a choir. Then a young tween named Swindovo brought out a drum for songs that were formerly Praises but now with a fast rhythm. Repetitive, catchy and easy to learn. Everyone in the audience sang along.

Later, Draktono was introduced and spoke. He talked of the discrimination between girls and boys, between women and men. 'Twas quickly apparent that he was highly educated in theology and philosophy.

Shamano had never been trained at a University. He was trained in the mountains of Birjj by other shamans. He had never performed the men's rites in a temple refuge. The priests did not recognize his title, as he had no certification. Shamano had come to believe that much of the training and theology given to shamans by the priests was brainwashing, and that he had been lucky not to have it.

Now as he listened to Draktono's speech about girls

and boys being taught together equally, Shamano grew uncomfortable. He believed boys were best kept more apart from girls. Girls either subdued and ridiculed a boy's confidence, or inflamed his passions. Boys were best controlled within a strong and rigid group of like-minded peers. Their own tribe.

Shamano was unsettled by the direction of Draktono's preaching. Draktono was advocating for changes to the Mother's Milk, the refuge, and even the sanctuary itself. He wanted to change the basic theology of the priests. Shamano had no interest in changing the social order of the priests in the Womb.

He only wanted recognition of the Fire, the Holy Spirit of Divine specially given for men. His singular goal was to spread the word about the changes the Fire could bring to men's lives.

THE TRUE BELIEVER

"**S**hamano is a true believer," Draktono said.

"What is that?" Swindovo asked. 'Twas late at night and they were sitting with Singer around a fire pot under a waning but mostly full moon. Shamano had been in the crowd for the evening singing, stayed to listen to Draktono talk about discrimination and social and religious reform, then had spoken with him afterward. Draktono could tell that the shaman from Birjj had not been pleased about what he had heard.

"Shamano's convinced he has special insight. That what he believes is direct from the Fire. To him, questioning is the same as doubting, which is his biggest fear. True believers are so convinced of their righteousness that even when there's solid evidence against their beliefs, they will not let it influence or sway their opinion. In that way they believe they are standing strong in faith."

"Sounds to me," Swindovo suggested, "more like standing strong in thick headedness."

"Shamano believes faith is about embracing Fire theology-- as he sees it--and then putting a blind trust in those teachings," Draktono sighed. "He's had little education and distrusts those like me who have. Critical thinking is not in his skill set. Any attempt to do so only aggravates him."

"What do *you* believe is faith?" Singer spoke for the first time that evening.

"Faith is about putting one's trust in Divine," Draktono replied. "Having faith means letting go of stress. Not wasting time and energy worrying. To have faith is to have a deep feeling and awareness of Divine within." He smiled. "We have faith when we sing."

"Yes," Singer smiled. "We do. Strong faith."

"Sadly," Draktono continued, "Shamano believes having faith is about having a strict adherence to a narrow doctrine. And he wants me—us--to embrace and preach the Fire." Draktono shrugged. "I told him I would be very interested to talk with him more about his views. About his beliefs and interpretation of Fire theology. How he does his practice. A number of things. But I can't embrace or preach his version of the Fire. Even though I agree with him in having Divine Fire as an Attribute. I just would not teach about it in the same way.

He shook his head. "'Tis interesting, Shamano always refers to their beliefs as the Fire. Not Divine Fire. He's quick to say the Fire comes from Divine when asked, but he never labels it such. Always just the Fire."

"What *is* the Fire?" Swindovo asked.

"Depends on who you ask," Draktono smiled ironically. "Shamano says 'tis the Holy Spirit come to cleanse men's souls. Divine Council says Divine Fire is a heresy and not an Attribute of Divine Herself."

"What do you say?" Singer asked a second question for the evening.

"I don't want to discount Shamano's belief. He's sincere in his commitment and has used his faith in admirable ways. And it seems he has a strong practice," Draktono acknowledged. "But I have a problem with some of his teachings. The biggest is that he believes men to be inferior to women. He accepts the doctrine that women were made by Divine in Her image and are, therefore, purer and more closely embody the Womb of Life. Women then gave birth to men. Because of that, men are a step further away from Divine."

"Makes sense to me," Swindovo said, "Men always get into

more trouble!" All the tavern brawls and fights were between men. And 'twas mostly men who were sent to prison or to work on the farms. "Men just seem like they are wilder."

"Many men *are* wilder," Draktono conceded. "But," he was quick to add, "with proper education, men are capable of doing any job a woman can do. Even being a doctor. A male shaman should have the same respect as a woman priest. Men are capable of having the same feelings of love and the same pureness of spirit as women."

"So you don't think men need special grace?" Swindovo asked.

"I think Divine grace is strong enough for both women and men," Draktono answered confidently. "But men, male energy, deserves some recognition for being a part of the Divine plan. Men contribute a spark of life and passion to our world. Should men choose to call that Fire, I have no quibble with the term. Therefore, I agree with making the Fire an Attribute."

"However, Shamano believes the Fire is specifically for men," Draktono shook his head in exasperation. "His concept of the Fire is a reaction to the fact that he believes men, because of their more fallen nature, need something special to redeem them. I don't think men need special prayers. What boys and men need is a fair and equal opportunity for education when they are young, and fair and equal possibilities for work and business as they grow through life."

"What if we change the hymn?" Swindovo asked one evening. They had been practicing a Gloria with a slow melody but a livelier chorus. "Let's do the melody at double time and take out the part we keep stumbling over."

"The song is very old and sacred," Draktono started to argue, "and should not be changed."

The Singer put a hand on each of their shoulders. "Swindovo may have an excellent suggestion," he said with a twinkle in his eye. "I think we should try it."

Having made the change, and all agreeing that the hymn had been greatly livened up and made more impactful in the process, Swindovo felt emboldened to offer possible changes to other Glorias and Hallelujahs. He started by taking small parts of songs and repeating them over and over in catchy rhythmic loops. Many of the songs that Swindovo tweaked and changed quickly became the favorites of the evening crowds who liked to sing along.

UP THE HILL

On the full Moonday festival, three nights after their first kiss, Tyme felt a tingle of excitement as she made her way up the hill toward the Blue Moon to see Delgado and listen to music. She was curious to see how she would feel now that they were officially dating. She was also looking forward to hearing the band from Vlice that Jyg had been raving about. And she wanted to dance.

'Twas just after the heat and the narrow, steep, and brightly painted streets, stairs, and passageways of Karvor were filling with people coming out for the evening celebrations. The white sky had begun to color, and a gentle warm wind was flowing down from the mountains. Shopkeepers were opening their stores, taverns and food carts were setting out chairs, while others staked claim to their positions selling food from baskets. By sunset the alleyways, plazas, and parks would be filled with people strolling and enjoying the moonlight and the cooler night air. There would also be firepots for those who felt a chill and colorful lanterns everywhere.

A line was already forming at the Blue Moon. The doorkeeper waved her through ahead of everyone else. She dodged a few couples, who were racing to get to their favorite tables, and went to the far side of the room through the ornate screen to the headquarters of the Jawbone Ridge gang.

Delgado's face lit up when he spotted her. He immediately got up and gave her a friendly but formal and proper greeting.

"Would you prefer to join in with the group?" Delgado asked discreetly. "Or would you like to go to our private table?" Now that they were dating, he felt those decisions were up to her.

"Let's join the group," Tyme replied. She only glanced at Jyg. She was afraid she might smile. The plan was to pretend they had never met. He was sitting with a trio of musicians.

Delgado introduced everyone. The woman singer had just started a story, so she began again. She was an obvious performer and soon had everyone laughing at her tales of being a traveling musician. Tyme noted that she kept eyeing Jyg, and that he seemed unaware. His red hair and freckled skin were certainly dramatic. Tyme enjoyed relaxing and having the focus be on others.

When the music started, Tyme remembered that in Karvor 'twas the Ambri way for women to ask the man to dance. She had learned how to lead from Wiir Waar and had danced at the banquet at Dayr Castle and another night with Wiir Waar on the streets and plazas by moonlight. But that was moons ago and she was out of practice. Delgado did not mind in the least. He seemed to relish every moment of her learning and was quick to laugh and urge her to try again when she made a mistake.

Tyme had a wonderful evening. She and Delgado stayed at the group table. When she left she gave Delgado a kiss on the cheek in front of everyone, which delighted him greatly, and another kiss on the lips when they hovered together discreetly by the door.

"Please come again. Soon," he implored as she passed through the screen and left the saloon.

JYG

J yg went up to the Blue Moon three or four nights a week where he joined the leader of the Jawbone Ridge gang with his inner circle. Delgado introduced Jyg as a manser falconer and friend, and began acquainting him to a more sophisticated clientele.

One evening Delgado revealed to Jyg that the gang was having difficulty following one of the players from Gribono's all-night card games at the Anvil. "He keeps giving our tail the slip. He ducks into the warrens and we lose him."

"Bones and I can track him," Jyg volunteered. At dawn the next Moonday, he was tucked into the shadows of an alley next to the Anvil on Cracken Street in Old Town. When a tall, dark skinned man with dreadlocks emerged, Jyg pointed out the man to Bones with a grawk.

The man set off rapidly along a tortuous route, down but also around and up stairs and alleyways, one way and then another as he descended through Old Town past Cergi Rim and into the warren. With Bones showing Jyg the route, he could stay further back and out of sight as they trailed the man. Occasionally Jyg saw a familiar street or landmark, but most of the time he was unsure as to where exactly he was. Bones excelled at finding perches that Jyg could easily spot to lead him along, positioning her body to give clues as well. Beak held high meant up the stairs, head held lower signaled to go down.

The man was taking every precaution to insure he was

not being followed, and Jyg could have never done so without Bones. They came through steep back alleys into a canyon with larger homes where the man slipped through the back gate of a walled compound. Jyg knew the fact only because Bones landed before the door and croaked out a satisfied grawk! She loved playing follow the leader.

As Jyg and Bones returned to the apartment, they came across three men in a corner arguing over the contents of a shoulder bag.

"City guards!" A rough voice gave a warning cry from somewhere else. The group scattered down an alley. Moments later two guards ran after them in pursuit.

When Jyg resumed walking, he came to an alley with a group of men huddled playing dice in a corner.

"City guards!" Bones cried out from the nearby branch of a dying sun palm using the same urgent voice she had just heard earlier. The group of men jumped up and ran the other direction.

Jyg burst out laughing. "You like words that make people react," he said with a realization. "You like stirring people up. Playing tricks."

"Sshh! Quiet!" Bones admonished Jyg, and she didn't say anything more that evening.

Delgado began working to find out who owned the property where Jyg and Bones had followed the man. A few days later he reported to Jyg.

"The compound is owned by smugglers. You may have been following Telapo himself. He brings in most of the viruna from Sikes." He patted Jyg on the back and ordered a round of drinks. "You do very good work! Now we must celebrate!"

Delgado enjoyed mentoring Jyg in Tanis culture and song. The Blue Moon was known for its soulful and heartfelt music, sometimes slow, other times lively. Different bands brought different customers and a different vibe. Previously Jyg had heard only tavern music, echoing up out of the commons to his back patio at Dayr Castle. Now he had a prime seat to watch and hear talented and fervent musicians performing dramatic songs with feeling, rhythm, and beat.

Delgado convinced Jyg to learn to dance and arranged for him to take lessons. When Jyg arrived at the studio, he was surprised to find an attractive instructor just a bit older than himself.

Her name was Rona Roma Rola. She was a fluid and athletic, black-haired dancer with great expression and flair. She hoped someday to be the lead dancer at the Feathered Plume casino and show hall. Right now she was struggling to get into her first chorus line and paying her bills by giving dance lessons.

"Just call me Rona," she said after introducing herself. She was immediately intrigued by his red hair and freckles. He was mesmerized by her smooth face and the almond shape of her eyes.

"I am manser Jygero," he replied, "but my friends call me Jyg."

He was surprised by her casual forwardness when she grabbed him in her arms and began her instruction. He had not danced at the banquet with the Ser Cus at Dayr Castle, and he had never embraced a girl in either a formal or romantic way. He felt like a bumbling, stumbling, red-faced idiot. But she was patient with him and said all he needed was a bit of practice.

Jyg practiced with Tyme through the week. At his next lesson, he did much better.

"You could be a good dancer," Rona told him approvingly when they finished, "if you just put in some effort."

"I am surprised 'tis so much fun," Jyg confided. "I never really thought about it before."

"Well, you still have much to learn," she chided him with a smile, "before I am done with you."

"Good. I am glad you are not done with me," he replied, his face growing red as he regretted his choice of words.

But she just smiled and asked, "Where are you from?"

"Dayr Castle." It seemed so far away now. "I am a manser

falconer." Delgado had instructed him to proudly use the title, which was guaranteed to impress nobles and everyone else. From the look on Rona's face, it appeared to be working. "My family also raises chickens and pigeons," Jyg added, wanting to be real and acknowledge his humble roots. "I am in Karvor for awhile on business."

She smiled with delight. "I guessed you might be a Barbarian."

"You did?" he answered in surprise. He had thought himself more worldly and cultured after his time at the Blue Moon.

"I mean that in a good way," she explained with a laugh. "I guess I've always wanted to meet a Barbarian."

The next evening at the Blue Moon, Delgado introduced Jyg to a pigeon breeder who officiated and judged pigeon races. The man talked incessantly about the sport, which held little interest for Jyg. He had enough of pigeons. He made a few attempts to get away, but the man only followed wherever he went, naming everyone he knew who raised birds in Tanis. Finally there was a lull in his chatter.

"Do you know Pran Parn Panr?" Jyg asked on impulse.

The man was taken for a moment. "I've heard of her but never met her. I think she lives in the Alkali Hills," and then added, "if she's even still alive. She has never bred racing birds to my knowledge. I believe she breeds squabs for the grill," he sniffed.

"Is that far from Karvor?" Jyg asked.

"About two hours on horseback along the Tepu road, turn and go up Dry Creek canyon. She lives on the ridge at the top of the canyon."

Later Jyg told Klew and Tyme about it. "She is one of my uncle Pio's business partners," Jyg shook his head in mock concern, "of whom I'm sworn to secrecy, so don't tell anyone." He had a hard time taking his uncle's never-ending and unexplained business stealth seriously. He turned to Klew. "Next time I take Zill for a long ride, rather than following your paint trail, I would like to see if I can find Pran Parn Panr."

"Why the sudden interest in pigeons?" Tyme asked.

"A bunch of the money Pio used from selling my gyrfalcon went to build her new dovecotes. I would like to see why selling Zaru was so important."

The Alkali Hills were swirls and splotches of white-crusted minerals in dusty red soil amid intermittent piles of burnt-looking rock. Jyg rode up the parched side valley along a broken ridgeline of black stone to find a tottering ramshackle house perched against the top of a cliff amongst a warren of crumbling dovecotes. He did not see anything that looked newly built except a heavy, locked gate for wagons and a large fortified front door.

Jyg tied up Zill to the hitching post and knocked on the door. No one answered. He knocked again, louder. After another wait a small shuttered window in the door opened.

"Yes?" a man's voice asked.

"I'd like to talk with Ser Pran Parn Panr."

"She's busy," the voice answered and the shutter began to close.

"Tell her Pio's nephew would like to speak with her."

The shutter opened slightly. "Who's Pio?" the voice asked.

"My uncle," Jyg replied in consternation. "She will know who Pio is."

The man seemed a little uncertain. "Wait here," he said. "I'll go see if I can find her." The small shutter in the door closed again.

Jyg looked around at the house and the buildings. Everything looked run down and decrepit. However, the windows had recently added metal bars. The wagon gate had two large metal bolts and locks.

After a long wait the small shutter on the door opened again. "Are you alone?" the same voice asked.

"Yes, quite alone," Jyg replied.

"Did you bring any birds?" the man asked.

Jyg looked up at Bones perched on the edge of the roof. "I do not have any pigeons," he answered truthfully.

The small shutter closed again. Jyg sighed in consternation. A few more minutes slowly passed until the shutter opened again.

"How do I know you are really Pio's nephew?" an old woman's voice asked with suspicion. "Why would he send you?"

"My name is Jyg. I came on my own. Pio does not know I am here."

"Then why should I let you in?" the old woman asked.

"Common courtesy," Jyg answered, trying not to get mad. "Pio paid for your new dovecote with money from the sale of *my* gyrfalcon." He shook his head in disgust. "Or is there no new dovecote?"

"What was Pio's base breed?" she fired back, ignoring his question.

"Rock pigeons. I caught most of them in the rafters of the Kings Stables." After a long pause, Jyg heard the bolt on the door move. The old woman opened the door to stand at the threshold and look him over. She had dark skin, wild and tousled gray hair and a penetrating gaze.

"So you captured the eyass and raised the gyrfalcon!" she said begrudgingly.

"Yes." He pointed to Bones sitting on a corner eave of her house. "Now I have a talking raven."

The old woman appraised him warily and turned her eyes to Bones to ask, "What does she say?"

The big black raven swooped down to land with a loud whoosh and flourish of her wings on a nearby post. "What does she say?" Bones mimicked the old woman's voice perfectly.

Pran Parn Panr gasped and cackled with glee.

Jyg hid his surprise. Bones had never imitated a high screechy voice before. "Tell her your name," he prompted.

"Bones!" the bird said in a low, gravelly voice.

"Yeeiii!" the old woman exclaimed excitedly. Bones postured before them with her head held high.

"Quork," Jyg made the raven territorial call. Bones spread her wings and flew back up to the eave of the roof. "You can talk to Bones again later," he said to the old woman. "But now I would like to come inside." She was still standing in the doorway, her servant behind her. At last she moved out of the way.

"You can call me Panr," she introduced herself and motioned toward the man behind her. "This is my son, Pranamo."

Jyg was led through a maze of small dovecotes and storerooms with crates for pigeons everywhere. Everything was set up to raise squabs for the grill. Panr stopped at a large, stout, newly built door and pulled out a key from around her neck. She opened the door and entered with Jyg. Her son stayed outside. She shut the door and they went down a rock passageway and around a corner of the cliff to the newly built wooden framework on an overhanging cliff face filled with cubbyholes of roosting pigeons.

"This was where the old dovecote framework burned," Panr told him solemnly. "This is where we kept the special birds. Pio's birds. The money rebuilt the dovecote," she patted the framework, "but the bloodline of those birds was lost. That was centuries of breeding." She had been resupplied with another starter group of birds from Pio, and was still building back her aviary. Half of the cubbyholes and cages were still empty.

"How did a fire start back here?" Jyg asked.

"How indeed," Panr replied mysteriously. "Birds don't start fires."

"You think someone started the fire?" Jyg asked with surprise.

"I never found any charred feathers, birds nor bones," the old woman told him. "No birds ever returned to roost." She leaned closer in a whisper. "Someone took those birds, then set the fire to cover their tracks."

"Birds could have all been burned to ash if the fire got

hot enough," Jyg replied. He looked over a railing to the rocks below. There were still a few charred struts and burnt cinders down in the rocks.

"'Twas Jakiko," the old woman hissed. "Pranamo's so-called friend, who he has not seen since the blaze. I hired him to help," she shook her head sadly. "Biggest mistake I ever made. Jakiko stole the birds and then set the fire to hide it."

PICTURES OF A LOST WORLD

E poh had been thrilled to find in the book the picture of the waterfall and the forest in the clouds. They had all been amazed by the greenery and bright flowering plants. And the sky a strange color of blue. He looked at the picture for hours before trying to turn the page.

But no matter how he tried, he could not turn, lift or scrape away to another page. Everything collapsed into dust.

He tried another book, and another. He could always gently blow away the thin coating of white dust inside, which covered the first picture, to see the waterfall and forest in the clouds, but all the other pages fell apart.

Each of the books also had thin paper covers. Most of them were little more than powder, but a few were more intact with a round circle and two lines, maybe words.

After a moon of fruitless effort, Epoh was getting closer to the bottom of the book mound. Then one day he opened a box of the books where the paper cover was for the first time more distinct. It looked like a large blue and white marble. The two words were legible, one above the marble and the other below. He thought the first word might mean plant, which certainly matched the first painting inside the book. He did not know the meaning of the second word.

When Epoh opened the book, the paper cover fell away into dust. With care he blew away the white dust inside to see the picture of the waterfall. Slowly he peeled away the page. To his surprise and excitement, the page below stayed intact. He could see a title page with the same two words along with some smaller writing underneath.

Epoh assiduously began peeling away the title page to reveal intriguing snippets of the picture underneath. 'Twas a detailed and precise close-up painting of red feathers. As he worked the large head of a gorgeous bird was revealed up close with a thick curved beak and a striking eye. The meticulous close-up portrait showed each of the tiny feathers all around the bird's eye along with the fine lines and texture of its face in a small area with bare skin. Epoh finished the task of revealing the picture just as the grubbers were coming back out of the tail to take their afternoon break. They all studied the painting thoughtfully.

"What kind of bird is that?" Harvig asked in amazement.

"I am not sure," Epoh replied. "I have never seen or heard of anything like it."

"'Tis beautiful," Horton said in awe.

Each day Epoh painstakingly revealed a new picture from the book. Every afternoon the grubbers would gather around to examine and comment upon the paintings. There were an astonishing variety of strange animals. Giant hairless beasts with enormous tusks. Fearsome giant cats. Animals with long, towering necks. Horses with stripes. All sizes of deer with huge beautiful antlers. More colorful birds.

"Have you ever seen pictures of any of these animals or birds in other books?" Horton asked. He knew that Epoh had studied in places called libraries, where entire walls were filled with shelves of books.

"No," Epoh answered. "These are all new to me. There is nothing like this in Ambra."

"Then where do they all live?" Harvig wondered. He could not imagine such creatures surviving in the Endless Waste.

"I don't know," was all Epoh could say.

Day by day Epoh uncovered more pages. The book showed green and fertile lands like they had never imagined. And blue sky! So many pictures with the sky a bold beautiful color of blue.

"This is obviously what the world was like before the Ancient Ones were destroyed," Epoh said. There was no other explanation.

He was interested to see there were vast deserts, dunes, and stunning flowering cactus during the time of the Ancient Ones as well. There were also massive groups of colorful fish and brightly colored plants and bushes living underwater in the Dead Sea, where now only worms and water bugs survived.

PIO PIGEONS

"Panr thinks a man named Jakiko stole her birds and set the fire to cover his tracks," Jyg told Klew and Tyme. 'Twas a hot evening and they were sitting out on the moon deck of their apartment. The darkening sky was muted orange.

"Did she appear reasonable and sane?" Klew asked.

"Sane as anyone could be cooped up alone with that many pigeons," Jyg answered. "Actually, she has wild unkempt hair and seems a bit crazy. Her house is full of hundreds of squabs that her son raises while she works on her experiments behind a big locked door. She is even more paranoid than my Uncle Pio."

"What was your Uncle Pio worried about?" Klew asked.

"Somebody finding out what he was doing with his experiments and stealing his birds. He has always been that way."

"What was he doing?" Tyme wondered.

Jyg sighed. He had been told for so long not to talk about it, or ask questions, it felt strange to say or reveal anything.

"Pio has never actually told me," he began, "but I think I figured it out. People have always used pigeons to send messages. But it only works for short distances. About a two-day ride from the dovecote is all you can send a bird. Release a bird further away and the bird will not return home. It will simply find a new place to roost nearby." Jyg brushed his red hair back. "I think Pio has been breeding birds that can take messages much further," he confided. "I think he is breeding birds that, if released here in Tanis, can fly all the way back to Dayr Castle."

"Across the Barrier Mountains!" Klew marveled. "That means they could fly messages from here to Ambrit!"

"The birds will always fly back to where they were born and raised, to their own dovecote. Even if it takes days of flying to get there."

"So to send a messages here," Tyme inferred, "a cage of birds born in Panr's dovecote has to be transported to Dayr Castle. Then whenever a message needs to be sent, they release one of those birds to fly back home."

"Exactly," Jyg nodded.

"That could be revolutionary," Klew pronounced. "To send a message so quick. It would be a tremendous advantage in warfare. Or politics. Or in business. Whoever had such ability could certainly profit in many ways. Especially if others did not know of their advantage."

"Pio once told me that when the pigeons he was breeding had exactly the right traits, he would announce his results." Jyg recalled the comment well because 'twas the only time his uncle ever gave him a straight answer. "He plans to sell the birds for a modest price so that most everyone can afford to buy them." Jyg grinned at the thought of it. "He is going to call them Pio Pigeons."

"How long has Pio been partners with Panr?" Klew inquired.

"Since before I was born."

"Did Panr tell Pio of her suspicions about the fire?" Klew asked.

"I don't know," Jyg shook his head. "I assume she did. But Pio never tells me anything."

"I think we should take this seriously and tell Delgado to put a lookout for Jakiko, or any new or expanded dovecotes," Klew said. "If Jakiko stole the birds to sell, he most likely brought them here to Karvor."

"Did Panr give any other hints about Jakiko?" Tyme asked.

"Just that he was always snooping around and thought himself a bit too clever."

"There is a good chance some of those birds are still here now," Klew guessed, "And some most likely in Ambrit or Pintone."

"By now they would have birds born in the new dovecotes who are old enough to fly long distances," Jyg said. "Their parents, the original stolen birds, have to be kept caged and only for breeding. They can never be released again, as they would fly straight back to Panr's, to where they were born."

JAKIKO

J akiko had always been curious about things, and it seemed to get him into trouble. His teachers complained that he asked too many questions. His betters all complained when he tried to make comments and suggestions. He bounced from one apprenticeship to another.

Then he was hired to help his friend Pranamo raise squab pigeons up Alkali Valley. The work was mostly repetitive manual labor, straightforward and easy to learn. Jakiko was quick to see that the pigeons in the smaller back dovecotes, where Pranamo's mother worked, were never sold for meat like the rest of the pigeons. Why that was, Pranamo would never say, replying simply they were for Panr's experiments, of which he had no knowledge or interest.

But Jakiko had an interest. 'Twas like a puzzle. He began snooping about whenever he had a chance, scanning the notes and letters on Panr's desk, and even peeking in the drawers if he got a chance while he was cleaning and the crazy old woman was turned away and distracted. Slowly he had pieced together hints and clues. Panr was breeding messenger birds that could fly long distances.

Jakiko hatched a plan to steal Panr's birds and burn her dovecote to conceal the theft in one momentous and brilliant insight. The birds would be worth bags of money to the right buyer. Imagine sending off a message from Karvor and having it arrive in Ambrit the next day!

Jakiko's attempt to sell the birds, along with himself as their breeder and caretaker, quickly led him to the spies of Major Bayn Baya. The major arranged a meeting with a fictitious buyer. Jakiko was hired to set up a dovecote and begin establishing a new generation of pigeons for a test. The unassuming dovecote was in a run down workers neighborhood. The previous owner had died.

Jakiko hired laborers to clean the dovecote and, like Panr had done, set up charts to monitor each bird. Then there was little to do other than keeping the birds fed and healthy and waiting for them to breed and mature. He had anticipated this very fact and had insisted on a generous allowance to cover his expenses during this period.

When the new generation of birds were grown, four of them were taken eastward in a cage. The first bird was released in Pintone. The second and third along the way in the Hollow Hills, and the last bird from Ambrit. All the birds made the journey back to their home dovecote in Karvor in a single day.

Jakiko was given a splendid bonus. Major Bayn Baya had dovecotes set up for a few birds to be transported to begin breeding in Pintone, Ambrit, and Ralston Garrison.

JYG & RONA

During their third dance lesson, Rona asked Jyg all about raising and training Zaru. On the fourth lesson, he asked her about being a dancer.

"I have always wanted to get up and move when I hear music," her dark eyes twinkled. "'Tis deep inside of me. I can not explain it." She grinned wildly as she took the lead and twirled them about.

"I like it when you lead," Jyg laughed. "You feel so strong and sure. I am happy to follow."

"I love leading," she smiled confidently. "But being a Barbarian, you should learn to lead. And some Ambri women like being chaperoned on the dance floor, heaven forbid that we call it being led."

"If we ever went out, you would have to be the lead dancer," Jyg vowed. "That would be much less stressful for me."

"Oh, I am sure there are plenty of women who would just love to lead you around the dance floor," she teased.

"I only want to be led around by you," he joked. His comment brought her up close. Her face was like a beautiful, smooth mask. She kissed him.

"I have been wanting to do that since last week," she confided to him. "When you told me about having to sell Zaru." She was still standing close.

"Can I see you again?" he asked. "Somewhere else?"

"You *are* a Barbarian," she teased. "Asking me out."

"How about tomorrow?" he pressed on boldly. "After the heat?"

She laughed at his eagerness, and said, "Okay."

"But not at the Blue Moon," Jyg told her. "Just down the street is a plaza overlook with a stone bench. I have a raven I would like you to meet."

The next evening Jyg was sitting at the stone bench with Bones when Rona approached. He stood up to introduce them.

"This is Bones," he motioned to the intimidating, two-foot tall black bird with a heavy sharp beak standing resolutely on the bench. "Bones this is Rona."

"She is beautiful," Rona squealed with delight.

Jyg looked at the bird expectantly. "What is your name?" he asked.

"Bones!" the raven replied in her deepest, base voice then regally spread her wings.

"She is so big and powerful!" Rona exclaimed.

"Well, don't just stand there, let Rona sit down," Jyg told the bird. When the raven did not move, he made a quork noise. Bones took off with a loud whoosh and flew up to perch on a ledge close by.

"Sorry," Jyg apologized. "She is being weird." As if to prove him right, the big raven swooped back down onto the ground before them.

"Manser Jygero!" Bones whined, using her most annoying and pitiful voice. "Manser Jygero!"

Jyg shook his head. "Why are you using that voice?" He laughed to make light of it. "Bones knows I hate that voice." He said quork again and Bones flew with a whoosh back to her perch. Rona chuckled at the bird's antics.

Jyg told Rona about finding the two raven chicks and the injured condition of the smaller one, which gave rise to the name Bones. He related how he had made a plaster cast to splint her neck and raised both chicks. How he had lost Despot. And of Bones learning to speak.

"That is amazing!" Rona gushed, in awe of his doctoring

abilities and touched by his connection and devotion to birds.

"I would like to keep seeing you," Jyg told her, his heart thumping in his chest.

"I would like to keep seeing you as well," she responded enthusiastically.

"Then I need to tell you about the real reason I am in Karvor," he began solemnly. "About my friends, and what we are trying to find out."

NOT ONE OF US

The rebel leader, Bokono, was from Birjj. He had no recollection of the Mother's Milk, where he was born in Rhing and nursed behind the Womb temple. On his 25th moon, he was sent to the farms in the mountains to live and work.

He had fond memories of the dorm where he grew up, having fun getting into innocent trouble with his friends, shirking work details, and playing tricks out in the fields on the older laborers. But when he continued his antics into his tweens, he was labeled as a troublemaker by the sers and sent to detention. The direction of his life changed.

Bokono embraced the role of agitator. If the sers thought to intimidate him, he would prove to them that he was not afraid of their punishments and would continue to live, act, and say damn well as he pleased. He had always been a good wrestler and street fighter. Now he began learning the sword. By his second century when he became a full adult, he had already been briefly jailed for a few disorderly conduct offenses including once coming to work drunk.

He was sent to the isolated men's prison at Tolk valley where he met other angry and dissatisfied men. He raged against the sers and their laws for imprisoning so many young men like him for harmless pranks and partying. When he got out, he began to organize meetings and gatherings to create a network of help for those in jail, and soon he became a messenger between the various men's groups.

The men in the mountains had long talked of overthrowing the sers and their Ambri ways, and transforming Birjj into a Barbarian Kingdom. Lately the talk had become more serious, no longer just a dream, but something that could happen soon. Men were asking themselves what they might be willing to do, how far they might go, if real fighting were to break out.

More Fire shrines began to appear in the hills. At first Bokono did not share the devotees' faith in the Fire. He was only interested in harnessing their discontent into a military force. But when he met Shamano, he began to grow in faith and asked to become a devotee.

Although Bokono embraced the Fire, he did not embrace all aspects of Shamano's teachings. Bokono believed rebellion was inevitable, and he remained leader of the freedom fighters in the mountains of Birjj and Sikes. He also had many friends in Dayrstad, who supported his cause, and claimed that they would rally around his banner to help Birjj break free of Ambri culture and governance—and place Bokono as the new king.

Despite his allies, Bokono knew that without the backing of the Fire, he did not have enough soldiers to see his plans through. Bokono needed the Fire, stirred up for revolt and firmly on his side.

Unfortunately, Shamano did not share Bokono's passion for a change of power and government. The shaman believed that the desire and struggle for political power was the problem, not the solution. Shamano believed 'twas the inner struggle, for a man's heart and soul, which was the true battlefield. The rest was all ego and illusion.

The shaman harbored no misconceptions about Bokono's motives. He knew the self-proclaimed freedom fighter saw himself as a political savior to men. But Shamano also knew that Bokono could be instrumental in spreading the Fire to soldiers throughout Birjj, Sikes, and Dayrstad. For that reason, the shaman tolerated Bokono's rebel intentions. The important thing was to grow the Fire with more converts.

Shamano believed that goal justified his alignment with a man so hungry for power. He daily prayed that the Fire would purify Bokono's spirit of such ambitions.

After Shamano visited Singer, he met up with Bokono in the mountains of Sikes. The rebel leader sat in silence as Shamano told him of what he had seen and heard at the agave farms. Bokono did not need to meet Singer to know he did not like him. Singing Divines was no way to start a revolution.

"I admit at first I was caught up in the singing," Shamano said regretfully. "But in retrospect, I believe the singing to be a fanciful yet dangerous distraction." The shaman shook his head. "The far more serious and important task is igniting a burning Fire in the heart of each devotee."

"Singing is no way to gather followers with any mettle," Bokono agreed. He could not imagine such a group would have any spine for the task ahead.

"There is also a teacher," the shaman informed him. "His name is Draktono. He talks of the discrimination of men and of using words and language to reform Ambri society and religion."

"Words?" the rebel leader asked with a dumbfounded expression.

"He claims that changing the way we talk can change the way we act."

"The way we talk?" Bokono was incredulous. He had long ago given up on talk, of emasculated men begging for crumbs at the banquet table of the women oppressors. Bokono wanted a radical change. And he wanted it now.

"Draktono has no passion for making Fire devotees," the Shaman continued. "He only wants to discuss theological implications. He does not want to actively teach the Fire."

"If he will not preach the Fire" Bokono stated coldly, "he is not one of us."

Over the next few months, they got updates of the growing popularity and influence of Singer and his followers. Bokono became increasingly concerned. While Shamano viewed Singer's movement as frivolous, Bokono saw the group as a real and growing threat. Every follower of Singer was one less potential soldier for the Fire. Bokono knew 'twas up to him to stop Singer's growing influence.

Bokono needed someone who could get close to Singer. An agavr and fellow worker who could catch him at an unguarded moment, in an isolated valley or even at the latrine, and slit his throat. Hopefully, if Singer was killed, that would reduce the following and influence of Draktono. If it did not, then the self-described theologian would have to be dealt with as well. His teachings were nothing but fanciful talk and dreams.

There was only one man that Bokono could trust with such a delicate task. First, he would start him working at the farm. Then he would be told who to strike, when Bokono was far away, giving him an alibi of innocence.

WHO CAN ONE TRUST?

D uke Eddarko kept a close watch on everything that happened at the Siren. He had spies everywhere, including the Bait and Valhal, and of course, Dayr Castle. He was curious to begin receiving reports concerning one of his couriers. Lartso was often partying and spending more money than he should have, in view of his small stipend from the Duke.

Lartso was somehow making extra coin on the side. It did not appear he had made the money gambling, for he was known to be poor at cards and did not favor the dice. The money had come from somewhere else. And the money appeared to be ongoing.

The Duke considered his options. He could confront Lartso and give him a chance to reveal his schemes and redeem his behavior. Or the Duke could let him go on with his little sideshow, unaware that he had been found out, and use Lartso for a more dangerous mission. If Lartso did not come back from the mission, then the Duke would not lose anyone he valued or could trust.

Lartso was pleasantly surprised when the Duke invited him to a court banquet and seated him on the right as an honored guest.

"I have not seen you much these last moons," the Duke told him. They talked about the shipment of liquor Lartso had taken previously to an outpost of Vargo Garrison in the mountains of Vanttan. The Duke had made a tidy profit.

Lartso hoped the Duke might want him to go again. 'Twas about time that he reported back to Captain Targono. Plus, his partying funds had shrunk considerably, and he was eager to receive another payment from the Captain for spying. But when Lartso tried to suggest another liquor smuggling trip, the Duke said he had a more important errand in mind.

"To Zerenlo," Duke Eddarko toasted his deceased business partner and Lartso's former boss, who had killed two men in a knife fight for which Lartso had taken the blame, and the prison sentence. Lartso had been sent to the Hammer Legion and was then recruited to spy on the Duke for Captain Targono. Zerenlo had later been executed in Sikes on other charges.

"And to you," the Duke tipped his cup at Lartso, "whom Zerenlo trusted above all others when a bit of nasty work needed taken care of." But Lartso was no real fighter. Zerenlo had chosen him as someone he could intimidate into keeping his mouth shut and taking the fall should the authorities discover the two bodies, which they did. "That was some bold knife work," Duke Eddarko praised Lartso with respect.

"Twas what 'twas," Lartso shrugged his shoulders modestly. His heart thumped in his chest. He was unsure if the Duke was being sincere or trying to trick him. Captain Targono had somehow figured out that it had been Zerenlo who actually killed the two men. Did the Duke know the truth of it as well?

"I need a man with your kind of knife skills," the Duke continued. Lartso nodded his head grimly, playing along. Mayhaps the Duke did not know what had really happened after all. "I need someone who is not afraid to take action. Someone like you, who is not afraid of a little blood."

Lartso did not like what he was hearing at all. He wondered if he should just confess, but he was afraid of the Duke's anger and rage. The Duke was not asking, he was ordering. Lartso did not want the Duke's knife at his own throat. He felt he had no choice but to follow along.

"By rights of battle, I will be the true King of Dayrstad," Duke Eddarko said with a cold fury. "I will lead an uprising and challenge my brother on the tourney field." He closed his fist and thumped his chest over his heart. "That is my destiny. That is my right."

Lartso thumped his fist to his heart in a show of fealty. He thanked the Fire that the Duke had not asked him to kill King Eyrico!

"There can be only one rebel leader," the Duke continued sternly. "*I* will be that leader."

"Bokono," Lartso blurted out in horror.

"You must slit his throat," the Duke said matter-of-factly. "I will give you a gift to take to him. A bottle of the finest viruna. You will drink together and when he is drunk, you will kill him."

Lartso's mouth tasted like metal. Bokono was an experienced fighter who knew the sword. A terrifying and formidable opponent, even if intoxicated. Lartso did not know if he had the courage and brutality to carry out such an act.

THE BLUE AND WHITE MARBLE

As Epoh performed his slow, delicate task of cleaning and picking away tiny paper scraps to reveal the last pages of the book of the Ancient Ones, he thought of the picture of the blue and white marble on the paper cover. The more he thought about it, the more he wanted to see it better. The cover was important. Why would it be a painting of a marble?

Epoh spent weeks constantly running out to realign the dune mirror as the blinding sun moved across the sky so he could see to slowly open boxes and hopefully find a book cover that was in better condition. He used his knife to gently cut the thin membrane across the top and ends of each new box. He used two knives and gently hinge-lifted the flaps of thick, corrugated paper into the air before the pieces broke apart into his hands. Underneath was a single piece of the thick, corrugated paper. He cautiously lifted it using just his knives. The cover picture of the blue and white marble underneath was ruined smudges of color. With care he lifted each of the books out of the box. None of the covers were intact. He stacked them aside and went out to realign the dune mirror yet again.

When Epoh opened the first box on the bottom row, he

found a book cover nearly intact. Clearer and sharper than ever before.

Epoh held his breath as he bent down to examine the cover more closely. Part of the marble had a tan, brown and green textured surface. The blue part was made of various shades that softly blended together with no definition, with sections of turquoise along the edge against the tan and green. The white was wispy as if on top of the other colors, more thickly appearing over the blue, but also obscuring parts of the brown and green.

He looked at the painting for hours, repeatedly going outside each time the black glass mirror on the dune had to be realigned for the sun, then coming back in and letting his eyes readjust to the dimmer light before reexamining the picture. When the grubbers came by in the afternoon, he excitedly showed them his latest find.

"What is it?" Horton asked after he had backed away a few steps. Epoh had repeatedly warned each of them about breathing on it and disturbing it in any way.

"At first I thought 'twas a marble," Epoh said.

"What is a marble?" Harvig questioned. He had never heard of such a thing growing up in the desert.

"'Tis round and made of clay or hard glass. You use them in a game. The fancy ones have swirls of color." He shook his head. "But that does not make sense on this book cover. The cover should represent what is in the book."

"The book is pictures of what the world looked like when the Ancient Ones lived," Harvig stated.

"I wonder if that is it?" Epoh guessed to himself.

"What?" Harvig ask.

"The world," Epoh answered.

"What do you mean?" ask Horton.

"The world as seen from way up high," Epoh said with growing excitement. "Like up real high in a cargo bird."

"The world is round?" Harvig asked uncertainly. "Like a shield?"

"'Tis round like a ball. Like the moon, and the sun, and the stars," Epoh stated. The great Ambri scientist, Pian Pina Pani, had proven it in her monumental work, *Mathematics of Celestial Spheres*.

"So we live on the top?" Horton speculated.

"'There is no top. It spins and rotates," Epoh replied. "That is what makes day and night. We could be anywhere on it."

Epoh looked closely again at the different textures and patterns of the picture. 'Twas like a giant map. "All these bumps and ripples must be mountains," he pointed. "And this must be the coastline." Some regions had a stunning turquoise color. The sea was a beautiful blue.

"Look how much water there was," Epoh pondered. "I wonder if some of that water dried up and left the Endless Waste." He shook his head. "Or mayhaps the Dead Sea is so large it would make the lands of Ambra look small."

"What is all this wispy white?" Horton pointed.

"That must be clouds," Epoh marveled. "Not of dust, but moisture and rain!"

JAKIKO'S DOVECOTE

Tyme now climbed up the hill to the Blue Moon more often and sometimes popped in at different times of the day. She had much more free time than when she lived and worked at the stables at Dayr Castle. She shared the job of buying food and cooking, which neither she nor Jyg had done before. Luckily Klew revealed himself to be a great chef and teacher. She had her sword practice, spiritual practice, exercising the horses, and following trails. But that still left her with free periods in her day and open evenings.

She visited the Mother Womb down the hill when there was singing and chanting, and often sat quietly in meditative prayer. She regularly volunteered to help with the soup kitchen and was put to work scrubbing pots and pans once the cooks realized her lack of culinary abilities.

Now 'twas nearly the heat, and Tyme was returning from Old Town where she had gone to buy candles. She decided to stop in the Blue Moon. A woman was singing a sad song and playing a flute. Tyme went behind the screen on the far wall. Vorcono and a few other members of the Jawbone Ridge gang were sitting at a table. He waved at a door.

"Delgado just went in there to sit quietly," Vorcono told her. He was not sure what he thought of the gang leader's new habit. But he was in awe of Tyme and not about to dispute her over anything.

Tyme knocked lightly and went through the door. They

THE WAY OF THE WORLD

were in a storeroom. In a back corner Delgado had cleared a small area and made a little altar with a bell and prayer beads. He was seated on a prayer rug and cushion. When he turned and opened his eyes his face lit up.

"Can I join you?" Tyme asked.

"Yes, of course," Delgado gestured to a spot on the floor beside him. "I would love it."

They sat quietly for about ten minutes and then Delgado rang his bell lightly. When the sound faded, they both got up. "Would you stay for a light lunch and a nap?" he asked.

They joined the others who were eating a cold meal in the group condition. They sat to the side and talked quietly as they ate.

"Usually I practice a bit longer," Delgado told her. "I like to imagine you are sitting with me and it calms me down." He shook his head in bewilderment. "So today, you *are* sitting with me, and I was more scattered than ever. Too excited. I could not keep my mind from racing."

"Consistency is not easy," she offered. "'Tis hard not to be judgmental over a good or bad meditation experience. But, you must learn to release all expectations. Start from where you are and continue on from there."

"But how do you quiet your mind?"

"First, become aware that the loud talking brain is not the only you. There is another, separate part of you," Tyme said. "Have you ever had your brain tell you to do one thing but you did another?"

"Yes," Delgado grinned. "Sometimes rightly, and sometimes wrongly."

"That other part of your being that chose differently is the part of you that is aware of deeper yearnings and beliefs," Tyme shared. "It does not just listen to the loud talking brain. It listens to the heart. It listens to nature. It listens to Divine."

Tyme smiled. "Tao Tau said the brain was a wonderful tool for us to use, but 'tis not our master. Mayhaps it would be better to stop trying to calm the mind for now. Instead practice not listening. Don't pay attention. If your mind brings up something, let the thought go. Gently bring yourself back to a quiet place. Without judgment. Focus on taking slow, deep breaths. Relax and feel your body rest and rejuvenate with each inhalation and exhalation. That will help your mind to settle."

"So the listener is the real me, and not the talker?" Delgado asked.

"They are both you. But the listener is closer to your heart and spirit."

The others had long ago finished eating and begun their naps. Now Tyme and Delgado quieted and joined them. When the heat was over, they returned to their normal table to hear some music. They heard only one song when a gang member arrived.

"We found a suspicious dovecote in Old Town," he informed Delgado. "The owner used to sell squabs to street vendors. He died. Someone unknown bought the dovecote and hired workers to clean it. 'Tis being used again, but no one is selling birds."

Tyme was quick to return to their apartment and share the news with Jyg and Klew. They set off that evening to check out the dovecote, which was located in a poor, sunny side neighborhood clinging to a steep narrow draw. The structure was made of adobe, a round, tapering twenty five-foot tower ringed with geometric patterns of small inlaid tiles and stones. The conical top cap overhung and protected the shuttered entry vents under the eves, which could be opened or closed in the morning and evening to allow the birds to fly in and out, and kept closed at all other times to keep lizards, rats, and other predators from gaining entrance.

"I can start climbing it from the roof next door on the west side," Jyg reported. ""I'll need a boost to reach up and climb the trim work," he grinned. "It should hold me. If I can get the shutter open, I think I can fit through one of the top vents."

"And you will be able to tell if those are Panr's birds?" Klew asked to make certain.

"One candle will be plenty enough for me to see if the pigeons are from Pio's breed line," Jyg promised. "Panr's birds will have to be caged and isolated from the flock that was born here, to keep them from flying back to their old home," Jyg said assuredly. "The layout of how the birds are penned will tell me everything I need to know."

They went back to their apartment and waited until a few hours after sunset. The moon was three-quarters across the sky before they returned to the dovecote. Tyme kept watch while Jyg and Klew climbed onto the neighboring roof. At the base of the dovecote, Klew braced himself against the wall so Jyg could climb onto his shoulders to reach the bottom row of trim stones. The first one came out when Jyg yanked on it. He gently placed the stone back into its hole. But the stone beside it felt solid, as did another for his other hand. He heaved himself up and pasted his toes onto the blank wall so he could throw one hand higher to a larger trim stone, then quickly pulled while he shifted his lower hand to palm and push, balancing carefully to bring a foot up to test and then stand up on the row of stones. Because of the slight tilting angle of the structure, Jyg was able to keep nearly all his weight on his feet, his hands balanced lightly against the wall.

Klew slipped back into the shadows as Jyg moved smoothly and gracefully up to the next row of trim stones. From there 'twas an easy step up to a row of tiles. The next row of stones for his hands were out of reach so he balanced gently with his palms on the blank wall as he stepped his feet up two more rows of stones. Now he was able to reach an upper row of stones. He smeared his feet into slight depressions as he smoothly walked his feet up the blank area, reached for higher trim stones, pulled himself up, and stood on top of the upper row of tiles. Again he balanced with his palms and fingers open and against the smooth adobe as he cautiously stepped his feet up the last two rows of patterned stones. As he stood up, the stone under his right foot popped out.

Jyg bobbled and stepped back onto the top of the tiles to

catch his balance as the rock landed with a loud crack on a nearby rooftop. He put his foot up onto another stone and tried again. This time it held. He moved up again onto the top row of trim stones and was able to firmly grab the wooden struts under the top cap. He stood up and leaned back with one knee against the wall as he examined the shutter in the darkness under the eve. He tried to push it open. It only moved slightly before hitting a stopper.

Most dovecotes in Karvor had blocks behind the shutter to keep big lizards and ringtails from pushing their way inside. Jyg slid a knife blade along the edge to jiggle and lift the safety block out of the way. After just a few tries, the shutter opened.

The pigeons awoke as he lowered the rope ladder from his backpack into the hollow chamber. He climbed awkwardly through the vent, closed the shutter again, and descended the swinging ladder. The birds rustled and cooed with concern, but none took to wing in the darkness.

At the bottom Jyg struck his flint to get a flame and light a candle. Half of the dovecote was enclosed behind walls of netting divided into four chambers of various sizes, each with its own door and small sign. The inside of the dovecote was arranged the same as Pio's and Panr's. Jyg opened the door to the largest enclosure. He examined the birds closely and could tell immediately that these were Pio's pigeons. He did a quick inventory of the number of birds in each of the chambers. He also counted the number of birds that were habituated to the dovecote and could fly free when the shutters were opened.

Jyg extinguished the candle and let his eyes adjust to the darkness, then climbed up the rope ladder, back out through the vent, and carefully down-climbed the outside of the dovecote back to the ground. The eastern sky over the Tanis Hills was slowly growing with the reddish break of day as Jyg, Klew, and Tyme met back on the patio of their apartment.

"There are five pens inside," Jyg told them. "The biggest holds the original birds from Panr, which are now just breeders. The others are labeled and hold pigeons from Ambrit,

Pintone and Ralston Garrison."

"And they are all bred from Pio's pigeons?" Klew asked.

"Definitely," Jyg replied. "There are no pigeons from here in Tanis, or anywhere else, that look like rock pigeons from Dayrstad. And Pio's birds have more purple around their neck than normal rock pigeons," Jyg explained, "which all these had."

"So, now what do we do?" Tyme wondered.

"If Panr will help, we can switch some of the birds," Jyg said with relish. "Then we can intercept and read the messages."

A BOTTLE OF VIRUNA

L artso checked his saddlebag before mounting his horse. He wanted to make sure the special bottle of viruna was packed well. The liquor was of the highest quality, made in the King of Sikes' personal distillery and pilfered by the King's nephew before being smuggled through the back mountains to the Siren. Now 'twas wrapped in a quilted and embroidered pouch to be presented as a peace offering to Bokono, the rebel leader, from Duke Eddarko.

Except the gift was only to facilitate a knife slit across the throat, which Lartso was to deliver after Bokono had finished the bottle. Duke Eddarko had ordered Lartso to kill his competition for the title of rebel leader.

Lartso was filled with anxiety as he rode the steep and hidden Scout trail up and out of the Siren Canyon and through the mountains of Dayrstad. He consoled himself with the promise to get good and drunk whenever and wherever possible along his route. On the third day he stopped to spend the night partying at Dayr Castle, and then returned to the Ambri Scout trail to take the quickest way to Birjj, where he spent another night of drunken revelry and womanizing. Then 'twas on to Karvor and the wildest nights of all. Finally, he took the long, lonely road to Sikes, with only a few small taverns in a week of travel. The rest of the nights, he slept on the ground and spent the heat in roadside conditions.

He arrived tired and worn in Sikes on the day before full

Moonday, when Bokono was to be arriving. Lartso stabled his horse and checked into a cheap inn. At a nearby tavern, he ate a big meal and drank a bottle of wine on a bright, moonlit patio, but could not relax for the nagging feeling in his stomach. He wondered if this would be his last night alive. He spent the night drinking and visiting the cavort for sexual release before staggering to his room and passing out on his bed.

The next day passed slowly. He promised himself that he would not drink but then broke down and had a mug of ale with his lunch. He was restless and agitated through the heat. Afterward he went straight to the refuge inside the Womb temple. Sure enough Bokono soon showed up with two others to leave an offering and say a prayer. Lartso kept his head and face concealed with scarves and did not approach. The Duke had made it very clear that he should wait until Bokono was alone.

Lartso followed the rebel leader out onto the street and hung back until Bokono had parted from his companions before he approached. Luckily Bokono recognized him when he dropped his scarf and did not question his credentials as a representative of the Duke.

"I have a message and a gift from Duke Eddarko," Lartso told him. "But we must speak alone. The message is for your ears only."

Bokono had come back to Sikes to deal with Singer and the problem of his gaining followers and converts that Bokono believed were being stolen away from the potential ranks of the Fire. Bokono was to meet that evening with an assassin he had placed among Singer's followers and give the order for the execution of the dangerous cult figurehead. But that order could easily wait.

"My room is nearby," the rebel leader told him. "No one will bother us there."

Lartso covered his face and discreetly followed behind. They went down an alley to a battered door, which opened into a small private room behind a saddle shop, whose owner supported the rebels and let leaders of the Fire stay in the room without charge.

The two men sat at a small table. Lartso brought out the embroidered pouch and handed it to Bokono, who grinned knowingly as he opened it up. "The Duke always has fine liquor," he said approvingly. "What does the Duke want in return for this gift?"

Lartso took the bottle, broke the seal, and removed the ornately carved wooden stopper. "He asks that you have a drink and accept his offer to come to the Siren for a special meeting of the Fire to be held in your honor."

"My honor?" Bokono asked in surprise. He had felt the Duke was resentful of his leadership.

"The Duke regrets that his actions and lack of faith might have driven a wedge between the two of you. He now sees that for the good of the Fire, 'tis important that you remain rebel leader. He is willing to proclaim it so if you come to the Siren now, where he can publicly state his fealty to your leadership."

Bokono was momentarily silent. He was taken back by the clumsy ruse. He did not believe for a moment that the Duke would lay down his arms in support of Bokono's claim to rebel leadership. Surely it must be a trap. Most likely the Duke hoped to lure him to the Siren to be killed.

"I am glad to hear that the Duke supports my dominion. His backing means everything to me." Bokono toasted his supposed new bannerman, then poured them each another shot of the viruna. He was not fool enough to fall into Duke Eddarko's trap, but he would gladly drink his liquor.

"Sadly, however, now is not the right time for me to come to the Siren," Bokono apologized. "Mayhaps in a few moons. When Shamano might accompany me." What he meant was when the shaman could protect him. Even the Duke would not be so foolish to attack Bokono when the leader of the Fire was there to witness his actions.

Surprisingly, Lartso did not make any objections to this answer or to Bokono being escorted to the Siren by Shamano.

"Yes," Lartso replied. "Let us drink to reconciliation. We must all do our part to consider what is best for the Fire." He shakily downed another drink and nervously licked his lips while trying to get into a better position to strike. As they talked he repeatedly failed to summon the nerve to attack.

Bokono began feeling suspicious. He shifted in his seat, subtly twisting his sash to better reach the dagger beneath the folds of his robe at his hip.

Lartso realized that he had somehow tipped Bokono with his jitters. What little hope he had of carrying out the Duke's plan now vanished. He was too terrified to attempt anything. He kept imagining Bokono twisting and breaking free from his grasp and plunging the dagger back into his own heart.

After a long silence Lartso had no choice but to stand up to make his exit. "I will inform the Duke of your intent to visit the Siren as soon as possible," he said.

"Please thank him for his support," Bokono smiled pleasantly, "and for the viruna. Tell him I look forward to the ceremony at the Siren."

Lartso shakily departed out the door.

Bokono put the stopper back in the bottle as he prepared to leave. He was going to meet up with his own spy and assassin and give the order to have Singer killed.

SWITCH THE BIRDS

J yg returned to Panr's house the day after he found her birds in an Old Town dovecote . Even though her son, Pranamo, now knew Jyg, he was unwilling to let Jyg inside until he checked with his mother. After a long wait the old woman herself opened the door.

"Bring your raven?" Panr asked.

Bones flew in dramatically to land with a whoosh of her wings before her. "Bring your raven?" the big black bird perfectly mimicked the old woman's voice.

Panr cackled with glee.

"What does she say?" Bones mimicked the old woman's voice from their first visit.

"Yeeiii!" Panr exclaimed with marvel, "She's a clever one!" Bones paraded back and forth in front of them.

Jyg gave a hand signal, and Bones flew up to the eve of the roof. He turned to Panr. "I have news."

"We will talk on a back patio where Bones can join us," the old woman said matter-of-factly. "Pranamo will bring us tea." The old woman led Jyg through the dovecotes and storerooms to a small, shaded cliff ledge overlooking a steep gully of crumbling black stone.

"Kaw!" Jyg cried out a raven greeting. A few moments later Bones flew over and swooped in for a landing.

"Bring your raven?" Bones asked with a tilt of her black head and a glint in her eye. She hopped up close to Panr and nibbled at her fingers with her long, thick bill the same as she did with Jyg.

"She likes you," Jyg smiled. Hopefully that would make it easier for Panr to agree to his plan.

"She is a magnificent bird!" Panr replied, wiggling her fingers playfully and groping Bones' bill in return. After a few moments she grew serious and turned to Jyg. "What is your news?"

"I found some of your birds."

"How many?" the old woman gasped.

"Nearly a third of them," Jyg estimated. "The others are in Pintone and Ambrit. A few are at Ralston Garrison."

"Ralston Garrison!" Panr hissed in dismay. "That means 'tis someone from the military that has them!" Her hope of getting the pigeons back plummeted.

Jyg was relieved to see that Panr grasped the complexities of the situation. He had been worrying that she would want to take immediate action to get the birds back no matter the consequences. He waited until Pranamo served tea and left before saying more.

"I have a plan," Jyg told Panr. "We might be able to get some of your birds back, but not right away." He licked his lips. "Jakiko is caretaker for the birds in Karvor."

"Jakiko!" the old woman shrieked. "He can't properly care for those birds!" she cried accusingly. "He knows *nothing* of pigeons!" She began to wail and tear at her hair. Bones jumped off the patio and glided away to a nearby rock ledge.

Jyg surprised himself by giving Panr a hug to calm her down. The pigeon lady wiped her eyes and gritted her teeth. Bones flew back to stand solemnly in a corner.

"There is a way we can find out who now owns your birds," Jyg said. "If we know that, we might be able to get some of them back." He explained Klew's theory. "Whoever owns the pigeons is not sharing birds with Vargo Garrison."

"'Tis just the Heart Legion using the messages," Panr replied.

"We think 'tis someone outside normal military channels." He told her briefly about his own quest, of Noot's murder, and the search for his killer leading to plots of treason against King Eyrico and the Czarzina herself. "There is one way we can find out," Jyg said hopefully. "But I will need more of your birds to do it."

Panr looked at Jyg approvingly. "You are a sharp lad," she said with a sly smile. "Let me guess. You want to break into their dovecote and switch some of the birds."

"So when they release a bird for Pintone, Ambrit, or Ralston Garrison," Jyg continued, "it will actually be one of *your* birds. It will fly straight here, where you will have all the pigeons bred for those places. You remove the message, read it, and hook it onto the correct pigeon to fly on to its rightful destination, no one the wiser."

"And you will switch and keep all the pigeons separated and labeled in their pens.

"Exactly," Jyg said. "But we can not mark the birds in any way they might see."

"That won't be any problem," Panr smiled confidently. "I know my birds."

Jyg returned to Karvor with a stack of full pigeon crates strapped to the back of his horse. Late that night he returned to Jakiko's dovecote with Klew, Tyme, and a few extra members of the Jawbone Ridge gang, who were posted in the alleyways for lookout. This time Jyg would take longer and be more exposed as he pulled up each cage overhand while Klew held out the bottom of the rope away from the dovecote so the cage did not scrape any of the trim stones or tiles. Jyg hung each cage just inside the shuttered opening. When he had them all up, he slipped inside the dovecote to stand on his rope ladder, lower all the cages in the darkness, and then slowly climb down the swinging ladder to the ground.

He struck his small tinderbox to light a candle, grabbed an empty cage marked Ambrit, opened the door marked Ambrit, and carefully gathered all the birds. From another cage marked

P-Ambrit, he released the same number of Panr's birds back into the pen. He did the same switch with the birds marked for Pintone and Ralston Garrison, and he put Panr's birds in their place. When he finished he hoisted all the pens back up next to the shutter and climbed out. An orange band of color was starting to glow in the eastern sky. He lowered the cages one by one back down while Klew held the rope out to keep the cages from scraping and marking the outside of the dovecote.

As Jyg began to climb down, one of the sentries gave a soft owl hoot in warning. Jyg stood motionless, balanced on a row of tiles half-way down the side of the dovecote. Someone walked down the alleyway underneath, but they did not look up. When the walker turned the corner, Jyg finished his down climb to the ground where Klew and Tyme had strapped the crates of pigeons onto his horse. There was just light enough to ride. He had the birds back to Panr's not long after sunrise.

The old bird woman was ecstatic to examine and scrutinize a selection of Pio's pigeons newly bred from three different dovecotes. She had feared Jakiko would not give the birds adequate care and was relieved to find that the new generation of pigeons all appeared healthy and well.

THE WHOLE EVENING
SEEMED SUSPECT

Bokono, the rebel leader, had just met with Lartso, the envoy from Duke Eddarko, who had come with a gift of the finest viruna liquor and a promise of fealty to Bokono's leadership, if he would come to the Siren for a special meeting and endorsement by the Duke.

The problem was the whole evening seemed suspect. Not only the promises of the Duke, but also the behavior of the messenger, Lartso, who was visibly nervous and skittish as a colt.

But Bokono had no time to sort that out now. He was to meet up with his own spy and assassin working in the agave farms. Tonight he would give the order for Singer to be killed. For the sake of the Fire, Singer had to be silenced. For the sake of Birjj becoming a new Barbarian Kingdom, Singer, and his daydream followers who would battle with words, had to be eliminated before they spread their ideas.

Bokono put on a cloak and headed out the door. He did not walk far down the street when he felt a wave of dizziness. By the time he arrived at the tavern for his rendezvous, he was staggering in confusion. He heard a loud ringing in his ears and the light from the lanterns blinded him. He felt himself stumble and fall, striking his head on something hard, the world spinning and swirling. The small portion of his brain that still worked, that watched his final moments play out, realized that the viruna, the gift from Duke Eddarko, must have been poisoned.

Lartso barely made it back to his own inn before he felt the first wave of dizziness. He staggered to his room.

"Have a drink or two of the viruna yourself," the Duke had told him. "It will help calm your nerves for what you're going to do."

Poison!

That had been the Duke's plan from the beginning. To poison them both.

The Duke had known all along that Lartso was not a cold-blooded killer. That he would not slit Bokono's throat. The Duke knew he had never killed those other men in Sikes.

That was why the Duke chose him. Like his old boss, he had picked Lartso because he was easy to use, and then throw away when no longer needed.

THE TRAITOR

Rocozo, the big, injured gang leader, slowly shuffled down a lone dark alley in Old Town after an evening of drinking at the Anvil. 'Twas his first night back in public after his humiliating beating by the tween girl at the Blue Moon. A few months had passed. He was using his arm again but still needed crutches for his leg. The rogue brute had become leaner and trimmer as a result of his busted jaw and missing teeth. He was only now able to chew regular food on one side.

He was surprised when the traitor from the Jawbone Ridge gang hissed his name in the darkness. Like the first time, the voice came out from the window of a tacked-up and abandoned storefront, the opening crisscrossed with bars and boards to keep people out. Yet there were a few gaps between where someone could look out while remaining hidden and safe.

"I can help you get even," the voice promised, deliberately raspy to hide the owner's identify.

"Like you helped me get into this problem in the first place?" Rocozo jeered back.

"How could I have known she would be there that night?" the voice protested. "I said Vorcono would not be there. He wasn't. The girl ruined my plans as well."

"Then what are you going to do about it?" Rocozo growled irritably.

"She has been seeing Delgado at the Blue Moon," the voice informed him. "She walks home alone."

Rocozo clenched his fists but said nothing. He hated having to rely on the traitor to get his revenge.

"Her name is Tyme. I could tell you where she lives," the voice enticed him. "And what night she will be out late."

"Sounds like I would be the one doing all the work," Rocozo spat.

"You are the one who seeks revenge," the voice pointed out. "I am just trying to be of assistance."

"What do you want in return?"

"Same as before," the voice grated. "You take east Dowd Street. I take the west."

"Why should I give you any of Dowd Street?" Rocozo taunted in anger.

"Because without me you can't get the other half at all," the voice reminded him. Rocozo had never even considered the possibility until the traitor had suggested how it might happen. Rocozo already had control of the lower Chalk Hills. Getting an entry point into Old Town was a bold new step.

"Where does she live?" he demanded, clenching his fists as he listened to the reply. When the voice sought to hurry him to action, he snarled and banged his crutch against the boarded window. "I need a few more moons to heal!"

The voice did not answer.

Rocozo leaned back onto his crutch and continued down the alley, grinding his remaining teeth in anger.

PART V

Every woman suffers. Every life has pain.

Kabaal Prophecies

In our illness we learn humility, in our healing gratitude.

Hope the Proclaimer

A TERRIBLE THIRST

Riin Ruel awoke with a terrible thirst. The mystic warrior of the Daggers was so weak she could not lift her head and could hardly moan more than a whisper. But 'twas enough to get the attention of the nurse watching over her. The old nun carefully spooned mouthfuls of a strange, salty broth into her mouth.

She was alive, barely. She did not know where she was. She tried to speak but the nun shushed her and gave her more broth. She began to remember what had happened. A sister Dagger had come into the Box at Ralston Garrison disguised as a doctor and given her a long, thin reed filled with a dark paste to hide in her sleeping mat. She had eaten one marked section of the reed each night. She had diarrhea for two weeks before becoming much more feverish and sick. The last week had been delirium. The final days had seemed never ending, but she had made it through. Died, nearly, and was now coming back to life.

When she woke the second time, she was given the same salty drink in a cup and was able to sit up briefly in the bed.

"You are in a nunnery north of Ambrit," the nun told her. "You have been here before. Do you remember the name?"

"Falcana," Riin Ruel answered. She had visited the abbey as a young girl. The nunnery included a number of hermitages along the shore of the Dead Sea. She guessed she was in one of those secluded hideaways. "How long was I sleeping?" she asked the nun.

"Four days," the woman replied. Much of that time she had been lying in a casket in the back of a wagon travelling from Ralston Garrison. "You will be here for three or four moons at least," the nun told her, "until you start to get your strength back."

"Three or four moons?" Riin Ruel asked with concern. She hoped to be on the road much sooner than that.

"Three or four moons until you are strong enough to sit on a horse," the old nun nodded her head. "But it will take much longer to get into fighting shape."

PART VI

When a ruler loses her path and way with Divine,
plots of treason sprout from the rocky soil.

> *Kabaal Prophecies*

A constant craving and desire for power consumes those seeking
dominion and control.

> *Hope the Proclaimer*

BAD WIND

The grubbers had just finished going through a mound of jewelry at the back of the dragon's stomach. Nearby was the collection of long, round, metal cylinders, standing packed and precisely arranged in a metal frame. The top of each cylinder had a rounded and elongated metal protrusion.

"Like nipples," Grinst commented as he brought the light closer to the rows of top caps. Each one was the size of a loaf of bread, with a single small hole in the side. He stuck his metal probe tool in the hole of one and gave it a few prods. As he did the cap rotated slightly.

"'Tis loose," Grinst declared. He used his metal tool to lever and continue turning.

"'Tis coming apart," Horton noted as the cap slowly moved up and away from the cylinder.

Grinst repositioned himself to keep turning when the cap stuck a few times. After more turns it came loose, and Grinst lifted it off with his hands. He set it aside to look at what was revealed.

Strange, bulbous metal tubing with a junction and opening to one side and what looked like a round handle at the top. Grinst put his hand on the handle. There were bumps in the handle that fit between his fingers as he held on. 'Twas wonderfully made. Grinst could not help but try to turn it. He went the same direction that the cap had come off the cylinder.

Nothing happened. He tried the other direction. Nothing. He motioned for Horton to try.

Horton put his big black hand on the handle. He tried to turn it both directions, but it would not move, even with two hands. He placed his metal probe tool through holes in the handle for extra leverage. After a couple of attempts with the lever, he felt the handle move the same direction the cap had come off. He turned the handle a complete circle and then it stuck. Horton could not move it any further.

"I think I hear a hissing noise," Horton said. He put his ear up to the opening in the tube. "I can hear something." His eyes grew wide, the whites bright against his black face in the low light.

"Let me listen," Harvig exclaimed. He handed Horton the deep-bowled skillet with their tiny fire and put his ear closer. A wide smile crossed his face. "I can hear it too." Grinst tried to listen but could not hear anything.

They left it and took off another one of the cylinder caps. Using his tool for a lever, Grinst was able to turn the inside handle one revolution before it stuck. He put his ear to the hole in the tube and shrugged his shoulders. "Mayhaps a little hiss."

They attempted another cylinder. The cap came straight off. Horton was able to turn the handle with his lever tool until they heard a loud, high pitched hiss from the opening. Horton put his hand over the round hole and could feel air coming out.

"'Tis like wind inside," he said in amazement.

"Plenty of wind outside already," Grinst snorted with little interest. "Who needs more?"

Horton wrinkled his nose at a strange and repulsive smell and said, "Bad wind." He tried to turn the handle back but it moved just a little before sticking. The hiss lessened but was still audible.

They left the cylinders of bad wind standing in neat rows and made their way back out of the dragon's stomach, done for the day.

DIRECTIONS TO
THE KIVA

K lew had been posing as a soldier for hire, a True Warrior who had a mild interest in the Fire, which was his personal feelings as well. His custom was to say his prayers near the statue of Tatano, whom he considered his role model in life. He occasionally went to the refuge of the Canyon Womb, where many of the minor offisers of the Heart Legion attended, a step up from the large, plain Womb in the garrison compound itself. But the refuge was often bustling and distracting with arguments between the temple staff and Fire devotees over their use of forbidden red candles.

Klew preferred the tranquil atmosphere of the beautiful Mother Womb of Karvor. The refuge was beautifully built in its own right, not as an afterthought to be squeezed into a narrow outer ring of the temple.

Tanfaro, the shaman, nominally obeyed the priest's orders to discourage any worship of the Fire. He had the custodians make frequent rounds to remove all red candles, wax, and sun disk medallions from the altars. However, Tanfaro instructed the custodians not to argue with worshippers, but let them do what they wished. Then after the devotees left, their offerings could be quietly and respectfully cleaned away.

Klew enjoyed sitting on a back bench of the Tatano shrine,

against the wall. During busy times he observed who came to the shrine, but at quieter times he closed his eyes and did the meditative prayer that Tyme had taught him. A simple, repetitive devotional to his breath. *Divine is All* with each inhalation. *All is Divine* as he exhaled.

When he opened his eyes, he was surprised to see Tanfaro standing and looking at him. The shaman smiled and introduced himself.

"I have seen you here a few times," Tanfaro said with an easy smile. He was in his early fourth century, tall, dark and handsome. He had been schooled in Pintone, the capitol of Tanis, and given his first posting at the refuge in the Womb in Tepu on the dry Iridi River. Just recently he had been transferred to the Mother Womb in Karvor. They chatted for a while before moving together toward the doors.

The shaman asked Klew about his practice. "So many men here are swept up in the Fire," Tanfaro confided. "'Tis reassuring to see a True Warrior with a similar enthusiasm for traditional teachings."

That evening Klew told Tyme and Jyg about his findings. "Tanfaro is trying to mediate between the Fire and the priests of the Mother Womb. He is not able to get them to actually talk to each other yet, but he has managed to calm tensions and conflicts within the refuge itself."

"Delgado told us that he plays cards with Gribono once a week," Tyme reminded them.

"Yes," Klew nodded. "The gambler seems to be spying on him as well. All the more reason for me to learn about him."

"True," Tyme nodded.

"One other thing," Klew added. "I have heard rumors of a shaman performing ceremonies in a kiva about a half day up the old trail to Birjj." He knew that Tao Tau had been curious about the older rites the shamans might perform, and that Tyme shared that interest.

"I would like to meet a mountain shaman," Tyme agreed, "and learn about his practice."

Jyg did not say anything. He was staring off into space. "What are you thinking?" Tyme asked.

"Oh, nothing," Jyg shrugged his shoulders.

"You were thinking about something," Tyme prodded gently.

"'Twas about Bones and Rona." Jyg admitted with hesitation. He had told them of his friendship with the dancer. "When I introduced them, Bones was real stand-offish. 'Twas weird. Not that Rona could tell. She thought Bones was great. But Bones would not pay any attention to Rona at all. I could tell Bones was giving her the cold shoulder."

"Ho, ho!" Klew chuckled. "Is Bones jealous?"

"Why would she be jealous?" Jyg asked doubtfully.

"Because she can tell you have a girlfriend," Klew explained.

"Do you?" Tyme asked with interest.

"I have seen her a few times since I finished my dance lessons," Jyg turned redder than normal and grinned sheepishly. "We meet up at the Blue Moon." Rona had been continuing his dance instruction for free. They also enjoyed talking and listening to music. Jyg was impressed by her determination and focus to be a dancer. Rona was intrigued by Jyg's whole story. He seemed so sure of himself.

"Where is Bones?" Klew asked.

As if on cue, the big raven came flying in through the window, tucking and folding her four-foot wings to fit through the frame, then snapping them open again to swerve and land with a dramatic whoosh on the table before them.

"What does she say?" Bones mimicked Panr's voice perfectly as she proudly lifted up a foot to display a small message tube attached to her leg. 'Twas the evening after Jyg had returned to Panr the pigeons that Jakiko had stolen.

"Bones visited Panr!" Jyg said with astonishment. He untied the tube, opened the end, and pulled out a small piece of rolled up paper. "We can send messages with Bones," he read. "If no message, I will tie string to show Bones was here."

"If Bones flies to Panr's," Klew noted with approval, "that will save us from having to ride out to see if any messages have arrived from the pigeons."

"In that case," Tyme said happily, "I think I will saddle up tomorrow and ride the old trail to Birjj to see if I can find the kiva and the shaman you were talking about."

Long before the Ambri built the current city of Karvor, even before Old Town was founded, earlier inhabitants built kivas throughout the Tanis Mountains. Ambri herstorians dismissed most of the kivas as simply conditions and communal living areas for primitive tribes. Kivas were filled in by the Ambri, supposedly for safety, or stripped of their stonework and left as holes in the ground.

Older traditions in the mountains claimed many of the kivas were built for special ceremonies performed by men. Whatever the true herstory, Tyme was curious to see a kiva ceremony and meet an ancestral shaman.

As she rode up through the limestone canyons and cliffs along the old trail to Birjj, Tyme was surprised that the few people she met reminded her more of Dayrstad peasants than citizens of Karvor or Tanis. Unlike Dayrstad, however, they were not used to seeing a nimble daya horse on the steep and exposed path.

The hamlet of Perich was a ramshackle collection of stone huts built in a shaded valley near a small stream. There was a mill, a blacksmith, and a tavern and inn, without a hitching post or watering trough for horses. Tyme led Cadie to a spot where she could drink from the creek and left her with the reins draped over her neck.

Inside the tavern Tyme ordered a buttered tea and asked the waiter for directions to the nearby kiva. He seemed startled by the question and gave her directions in a stilted voice. She finished her tea without seeing anyone else and left town as the waiter had told her. The directions made sense at first as she followed along a northeast ridge, but then she got lost dropping into a canyon.

When she returned to Perich, she stopped at the tavern for another buttered tea. The waiter was unhelpful and confusing when she asked him to repeat the directions. Finally she politely dismissed him to enjoy her tea.

With the heat approaching, Tyme rode Cadie back down the old trail to Karvor. She would look for the kiva another day.

Tyme had no awareness of how her brief visit would unsettle the men of the village. When she left Perich, the tavern waiter went to a nearby stone house and banged on the door. Inside was a large man who was sharpening a pile of swords with a grindstone wheel. The waiter reported what had happened.

"And you gave her directions to the kiva?" the big man asked in outraged astonishment.

"I was so taken by surprise at her asking!" the horrified waiter tried to explain his mistake. "I started telling her the truth before I could think what else to say!"

"Did she go there?" the man demanded to know.

"She couldn't find it," the waiter tried to calm him down. "I told her the wrong few turns at the last valley. I said nothing about the hidden handholds. She went back to Karvor on a daya horse."

"A daya," Otovo scowled. "She must be a noble from the Womb. Sent to spy on us. If you see her again," the man hissed, "I want to know about it right away. Do not wait until she leaves town." Otovo lightly touched the blade of the sword in his hands to test its sharpness. "Let me know when she is still here, drinking tea."

I RELEASE YOU

When Grodoro watched his boss, the rebel leader Bokono, stumble, fall and die of poisoning on the floor of a tavern in Sikes, he panicked. Bokono had hired him to infiltrate Singer's group at the agave farms. Most likely to assassinate someone. Was that why Bokono was now killed? To stop the attack? Was someone now going to kill him as well?

Grodoro had been growing continually anxious and nervous about his assignment. He did not like it. He had spent moons listening to the Singer's group sing and talk. There was power in the music and truth to the words. Grodoro saw little hope in the world and did not want to be any part of destroying the good that was happening at the farms.

Walking back from town, Grodoro realized he had to confess everything. Early the next morning, he met with Singer and the apprentices in Manser Shelodo's office, and he revealed Bokono's plan to kill one of them.

"Most likely Singer," Grodoro guessed, "But could have been Draktono. I am not sure."

"And now this Bokono, this Fire rebel leader, is dead?" Manser Shelodo said with horror yet relief.

"Poisoned the very night he was to have told me who and when to strike here," Grodoro affirmed.

"Would you have done it?" Singer asked with a calm curiousity.

"I did not want to," the man began to whimper. "I did not know what to do. I was afraid of Bokono."

"You came to us now and told us," Draktono said, "and for that you have our gratitude."

"And what do you plan to do now?" Manser Shelodo asked.

"If I could," Grodoro answered, "I would stay working and being here with you. My old life no longer has appeal."

Manser Shelodo shook his head sadly. "I am not sure any of you should stay here. You have caught the attention of ruthless fanatics."

He knew the King of Sikes would not be happy to hear of zealot infighting at his best agave fields. The King would certainly investigate and most certainly view the group as a cult. 'Twas one thing to allow the Fire a polished metal disc on the altar of the refuge of the Womb, 'Twas another to allow them to overrun his farms and endanger his supply of viruna. The King would want the proselytizing stopped.

"I believe our experiment here has come to an end," Manser Shelodo said with growing certainty. "Despite the increase in production during the day, the King will not want the attention that your evening get-togethers are creating at his agave fields."

"No more singing?" protested Swindovo.

"Or teaching?" Draktono asked in shock.

"Not here," declared Manser Shelodo.

They all gasped.

"Because of this situation," the manser continued, "I release you all from your positions. I will not force you to stay here if you cannot sing and discuss theology. You will each get a farewell bonus for the productivity you increased."

"What do you suggest we do?" Draktono asked.

"Keep doing what you have been doing," Manser Shelodo advised. "But do it someplace else. Not in Sikes. There are some old kivas near Karvor. You could try there. I think you could build a following. There is power in what you sing and teach."

A LITTLE STINK

The morning after the grubbers found the metal cylinders of bad wind, they returned early to the dragon's stomach for more scavenging. Epoh stayed outside. The sun was not yet high enough in the sky to provide adequate light for his black mirrors to work.

As the grubbers entered the dragon's stomach, they could smell the bad wind from the cylinders. When Harvig complained of the odor, Grinst chided him.

"A little stink going to keep you from dragon treasure?" he asked with disdain.

"No, I suppose not," Harvig answered. He grabbed the fire skillet and started a small fire of splintered wood and burnable debris. As he led Grinst and Horton around the first corner into the darkness, he held out the fire skillet before him, then turned it to cast light back toward the others so they could see.

Suddenly there was a tremendous BOOM and bright, terrifying hot flames all around. The fire skillet slammed into his face, and Harvig felt his body being violently lifted and thrown backwards into the air by a terrible force as everything went dark, and he knew no more.

GENERAL CATA CARA

Czarzina Hana Hama Hala had more important things to do than listen to some Barbarian peasant defend his Fire heresies. She dismissed the prisoner with a bothersome wave of her hand before he had a chance to speak.

"His actions speak loud enough," the Czarzina proclaimed. "He placed a heathen idol in the men's refuge of the Exalted Cathedral of the Divine Womb. He defiled the Mother temple! For that he must be punished the full extent of the law."

General Cata Cara of the Heart Legion stopped reading the indictment and nodded her head in agreement. "You are right to be firm with these heretics." She scanned the report as the guards took the man out. "He follows a shaman who is said to be raising an army in the mountains of Birjj."

"The mountains of Birjj are of little concern to me, and this man even less," the Czarzina continued, already bored with the subject.

"Very well, my Czarzina. That is all for today," the general bowed and left the room, her footsteps resonating in the vaulted chamber. Despite the Czarzina's disinterest, General Cata Cara would continue to have the heretics watched. The general sensed something that made her uneasy.

General Cata Cara did not come from a military family, but a powerful merchant family from Ambrit that nearly disowned her when she ran off to the Military Academy upon becoming a tween on her 150th moon.

She excelled rapidly to become the youngest captain in Ambri Legion herstory. However, she was well into middle age before finally attaining the rank of general in the Heart Legion. She long believed her career was delayed by outside political influence, along with favoritism and corruption in the military. Her anger had grown over the centuries and did not slack upon her eventual promotion in rank. But the General hid her anger well. She channeled her anger into plans of revenge.

The recent change in the Czarzina did little to appease General Cata Cara's unhappiness. The current holder of the title was worse than her predecessor. The herstory of the Czarzinas was filled with corruption. General Cata Cara believed the whole system needed to be cleaned out and rebuilt on a new foundation that was based on a return to stricter principles and morals. She believed she was the person to bring about that change and order.

The general plotted a coup of minimal bloodshed in which she felt victory was assured. She planned to take over the Heart Legion garrison in Pintone, the capitol of Tanis, along with all the eastern tollbooths along the royal highways. She would arrest and hold the Queen of Tanis hostage, and either bribe or coerce the mayor of Karvor to stay out of the fight with her city guard.

General Cata Cara did not believe the Senasers would allow the Czarzina to use the Hammer Legion to fight the Heart Legion. The Hammer was needed to keep safe the silver mines of Vanttan. Once she controlled Pintone, Karvor, and Tepu, nearly all trade in the eastern mountains could be taxed, not just on the toll roads, but in the markets and businesses as well. When the Senasers saw her restoring the ideals and values of a truly Divine Empire, she believed they would flock to her banner.

She planned to force a vote of no confidence in Czarzina Hana Hama Hala and forge an agreement with the Senasers to proclaim herself not just Czarzina, but Empress--Empress of the rebirth of the Ambri Empire, with a new government and stronger military.

THE MAYOR OF KARVOR

Ser Yaar Yaay Yaan was the Mayor of Karvor. She was a beautiful, curvaceous woman with lustrous black hair and beauty-marked dark bronze skin. She came from an influential family of potters and artists. Her knowledge and background in the arts, along with her vivacious and infectious energy, made her an effective and well-loved mayor by the people of her community.

She loved her position as representative, advocate, and host for the city of Karvor, which she believed to be the finest in all of Ambra. As a representative of the city, the Mayor met a wide variety of people and was accustomed to unusual solicitations. However, one evening she had an especially strange and unsettling encounter.

She was at a military ball. A waiter informed her that she had a private message and escorted her to a quiet, unoccupied meeting room.

"I represent someone who cannot be revealed at this time," the waiter told her with a bow. "My employer is unhappy with the corruption of the present Czarzina. If, at some time in the future, the Czarzina should find herself in political difficulty, and there was no help forthcoming from you, a new Czarzina would support you to become Queen of Tanis."

"And why should I not call out treason and reveal you," the Mayor replied, wondering if the encounter was mayhaps a joke in bad taste. "What would happen then?"

"I would escape through the back," the woman pointed to a door. "It will be found that I was not a real waiter," she shrugged without concern. "The staff will be punished for not noticing me. The guards court-marshaled for the security breach." She boldly stepped forward. "Remember this promise. A new Czarzina will welcome and support a new, wiser and stronger Queen of Tanis." The woman abruptly turned and disappeared through the door.

The Mayor of Karvor stood shocked for a moment then went back to the banquet with unsettled thoughts. Someone was plotting to overthrow the Czarzina and offering to support *her* to become Queen of Tanis! The Mayor had never dreamt of such a thing, even though the present Queen was old and inept, and her only surviving daughter timid and weak, and without a female heir.

The next evening Bones flew into the apartment courtyard with a message tube attached to her leg.

"What does she say? What does she say?" Bones imitated Panr's high, scratchy voice perfectly as she paraded before them on the patio, then hopped onto a table so Jyg could easily remove and open the tube.

"1A," he read from the small, unrolled piece of paper. "That means Panr got one message pigeon bound for Ambrit. The message the bird carried says, 14 V first contact--no alarm." Jyg thought for a moment. "Fourteen at the beginning is probably the message number," he said. "By numbering each message it ensures the recipient will know that if a number is skipped, a previous message has been lost and needs to be resent."

"V first contact--no alarm," Klew mused. "V could be a name or symbol for someone who was approached. No alarm could mean they did not report the contact to any authorities." Klew wrote down the date and message. "We must keep a record of every detail if we hope to decipher their meanings."

EXPLOSION

E poh was doing chores at their work camp under the wing of the cargo bird when the ground shook, and he heard a loud explosion. A cloud of smoke, dust' and debris came pouring out of the door. Epoh tied a scarf over his face and ran up the dune to the entrance. He could hardly see to make his way down the hallway to the warehouse inside the bird.

He did not get far before he came across Horton, who was moaning and lying barely visible on the floor.

"Are you all right?" Epoh yelled repeatedly, but Horton seemed unable to hear. He helped Horton get onto his hands and knees and then haltingly and painfully stand up. With Epoh's assistance, Horton was able to shuffle up the dim hallway and get outside. Epoh left him sitting in a wordless daze in the sand and went back inside.

He found Grinst lying just a little further along in the smoke, right before the corner to the passage running the length of the dragon. Grinst was groaning and talking gibberish about Harvig and the flames of hell.

"Where is Harvig?" Epoh yelled repeatedly, but Grinst was unable to answer. Epoh took a few more steps, but the dust and the darkness was so thick he could not see anything. He went back to help Grinst rise and wobble up the hallway to reach the door and join Horton on the sand.

Epoh adjusted his face scarf and went back into the smoke

filled cargo bird. When he came to where he had found Grinst, he could see no further. He got onto his hands and knees and blindly used his hands to touch and scour the ground in search of Harvig. He coughed from the bad vapors. His eyes stung fiercely. Even though he could not see anything, he tried to squint his eyes open occasionally on the chance that he might catch a glimpse of Harvig's body.

The air was filled with a terrible miasma of choking fumes. A flickering red glow of fires emanated through the smoke. Epoh was on his knees, sweeping his hands across the floor, trying to feel for Harvig in the soot, dust, and debris. He took a breath of something acrid that burnt his lungs and throat and sent him into a painful, wracking coughing fit. He had to get out of the cargo bird! Without taking another breath, he frantically retreated, stumbling madly as fast as he could back up the hallway and through the door for fresh air.

Grinst was lying nearly passed out in the sand. Horton was sitting up but staring dumbly around. Epoh had more coughing fits and gasped for huge breaths of air as he unwrapped the scarf from Horton's neck with quivering hands. Horton sat in a daze without helping. Epoh doubled up the scarf around his face and head. He took deep breaths of good air.

Back through the door into the cargo bird he raced. He allowed himself a few careful breaths as he strode down the hallway to the warehouse, turned right, then dropped to his hands and knees before getting to the corner. He closed his eyes, took a final breath, and held it while he frantically scooted forward, swinging his hands from side to side through the smoke and debris searching for Harvig. He turned left around the corner and shot forward toward the glowing fires but still could not feel Harvig anywhere.

He should be closer to where I found Grinst, Epoh thought with distress as he skittered around and went back toward the corner. He felt only rubbish and litter. He did not have much more air in his lungs. Rather than turning at the corner, he felt through the rubbish up against the front wall.

Epoh touched a leg. *Harvig!* He yanked at the body and found a hand, but when he pulled on it, bloody skin peeled off, too slick to grasp. Epoh frantically searched to find the other foot. He could not hold his breath any longer. He took a short small breath of acrid smoke and yet another before resuming coughing. His eyes burned as he got hold of both of Harvig's feet and dragged his body out of the warehouse and up the hallway to the door outside.

Epoh collapsed coughing and gasping for breath on the sand dune. Harvig lay motionless beside him on his back. His hands were puffed and bloody with burns. All the hair on his head was burnt and singed down to stubble. His face was red and puffy with no eyebrows or eyelashes.

Grinst was now sitting up and looking around. His eyebrows and the front of his hair were singed. Horton was talking gibberish to himself. He had blood coming out from one of his ears.

KA-BOOM!

The ground rocked from a much more powerful explosion. The back of the cargo bird detonated, ripping a hole in the top and sending a giant black cloud erupting into the air. A scattershot of flaming and smoldering debris was thrown up with the cloud and began raining hot, burning refuse back down around the area.

"We have to get out of here!" Epoh cried in alarm. He took off his face scarves and began wrapping them around Harvig's blistered and bleeding hands. "Horton!" he ordered. "You have to carry Harvig over your shoulder. He can not hold on." Epoh did not even know if Harvig was alive, but there was no time to check now.

The giant cloud of dark smoke broiling and towering high above them woke Grinst from his stupor of confusion.

"We have to leave now!" Grinst joined in to help Horton stand up. "Every Hool and grubber in the Sea of Dunes and beyond will see that cloud. They will all come scurrying like rats to investigate. We'll lose our treasure and mayhaps our lives if they find us here."

A MISUNDERSTANDING

On her next ride to exercise Cadie, Tyme went back up the old trail toward Birjj in hopes of finding the kiva. She stopped again at the tavern in Perich. The waiter brought her tea, then nervously excused himself and scurried around a corner to the stone house where he banged on a door.

No one answered.

He banged again, harder.

Still nothing. Reluctantly he returned to the tavern and managed to avoid talking with Tyme, who again noticed his odd behavior but just assumed 'twas customary. After she left town, the waiter went back and banged on the door again.

Otovo opened the door with a scowl.

"I came earlier but you were not here," the waiter apologized even though 'twas not his fault. "She was at the tavern, but left toward the kiva on a daya."

"She picked the wrong day to come snooping" Otovo vowed. "I'll get a couple of the burners and we'll make sure she does not find anything." They needed to protect the kiva! Divine Council had ruled them heretics. Divine Council had destroyed kivas in the past.

Tyme rode further down the northeast ridge before

dropping into a side canyon. She used her new trail finding skills to pick up a faint track that took her winding along a steep and dramatic canyon rim. She confidently encouraged Cadie to walk at the edge for better views. Riding the daya was not as thrilling as riding Spike in the high mountains, yet Cadie was still exhilarating and a joy to ride.

Leaving the trail further for a better view, Tyme rode out onto a small overlook. As she gazed down the canyon rim, she noticed what looked like a few faint marks or steps carved into a cliff face up ahead. As she resumed riding along the trail, she looked for the marks again but was not able to see anything. The trail ended at an area of smooth, sculpted rock along the edge of the cliff.

Tyme tied Cadie in an alcove of shade and then walked along the rim of the rock to look down and see if she could spot the steps she had seen from a distance. Nothing. She leaned further out over the edge to peer down but could not see anything below. Only a few narrow rock ledges. She climbed down to the first ledge, held on to the cliff with one hand, leaned out, and still could not see anything below. But she did notice that the stone handhold was rubbed completely smooth.

She climbed down more smooth handholds to the next ledge. Now when she leaned out, she could see a double line of foot and hand sized steps carved into the side of the cliff below.

"Hello," Tyme called out. "Anyone here?" Her voice echoed lightly.

Facing into the wall, Tyme descended the ladder-like steps that spiraled down the cliff to a narrow strip of rock, which led to an open cave with a flat floor. At the back of the cave was a small spring and cup. Tyme said a prayer of thanks before drinking. At the far end of the cave was a pillar of stone. Tyme could see that 'twas polished from the touch of many hands. She instinctively reached out and touched it herself.

Behind the pillar was a low, narrow doorway.

"Hello," Tyme called out again. She entered the passage into a dimly lit room, perfectly round with a low arch ceiling with stone walls and benches. Ten fire shrines were set at equal intervals along the outside wall. The largest shrine held a sun medallion of polished tin. Tyme studied it thoughtfully. She had seen smaller medallions left in the refuge of the Womb at Dayr Castle, which had been abruptly cleaned away by the shaman. Sun worship the priests had called it.

Tyme did not sense any evilness. She thought it would be interesting to talk with a mountain shaman about the Fire, and what they believed.

Otovo and two burners watched with disbelief from a distance. The Womb spy had gone straight to the rock ledge above the kiva before they could catch up to her. Then she had somehow found the hidden steps down to the kiva itself. She was going inside and they were too late to stop her!

Otovo considered waiting for her at the top of the rock ladder and pushing her to her death. But such an act might also defile the kiva. She needed to be dealt with away from the kiva where suspicion would not fall on them. While Tyme explored the kiva, Otovo and the burners returned to Perich to set up their ambush.

When Tyme came back up to the village, she stopped at the tavern for tea, hoping she might find where the shaman lived. She was surprised to find five customers at two tables close to the door. She walked between them and took a table at the back.

As she waited for her tea, Tyme innocently asked the men in the room, "Does anyone know where the shaman for the kiva might be?"

"What do you know about the kiva?" one of the men scowled in anger. A large and fierce brute nearby swiveled in his chair to face her.

"Not much," Tyme replied. "That is why I would talk with

the shaman."

"You went in the kiva," the big man said accusingly.

"I did," Tyme noted. "Respectfully."

"You admit you went into the kiva?" Otovo replied with astonishment. The men all grumbled. Tyme tried to explain that she meant no disrespect but he rose from his chair to stand before her. "You are a Womb spy," he spit accusingly.

"I am not a Womb spy," Tyme replied calmly. "You mistake my intentions."

"Then you are with the Czarzina," Otovo spat. He pulled his sword a few dramatic inches from its scabbard. "Either way, you are coming with us."

"To see the shaman?" Tyme asked.

The man started to laugh but then caught himself. "Yes, to see the shaman," he repeated unconvincingly.

Tyme easily read the lie. "No," she shook her head. "I am not going anywhere with you." Her voice took a much stronger tone. "Just let me pass, and no one will get hurt."

"You are coming with us," Otovo snarled and began to draw his blade. He brought his feet together.

Tyme pulled out her knife and dove to the ground beneath his scabbard. As she somersaulted she sliced the tendons behind one of his ankles, dropping him instantly. She popped back up to her feet to stand with her back to the door, facing the rest of the group.

"Kill her!" Otovo screamed as he helplessly tried to get up. "Kill her!"

"I do not want to hurt anyone else," Tyme held the knife ready to throw. "Just let me leave peacefully."

She eyed the closest brute but he did not attack. He realized he was no match for her speed. She already had a second knife out in her other hand.

"Back up and give me some room," she ordered. They all shuffled back.

"I respectfully went into the kiva to meet the shaman," Tyme told them solemnly. "To learn about his practice and beliefs. He was not there. I said my prayers and left. I am sorry for the misunderstanding. I am not your enemy."

She opened the door carefully to make sure no one was waiting outside, then slipped out, hurriedly mounted Cadie and rode out of Perich.

THE SER CUS
IN KARVOR

A few days before bright Moonday of the White Dust, the Ser Cus came to Karvor to perform at Skyline Stadium. When Jyg heard of their arrival, he excitedly returned to the apartment to tell Tyme, who was ecstatic to see Wiir Waar, her one and only girlfriend. The thrill of surprising and seeing their friends was tempered by the story of Noot's death, and how they had come to be in Karvor.

During the heat Tyme told the whole clan about becoming a member of the Jawbone Ridge gang, and Jyg told everyone about Bones, Panr, and the dovecotes. When the others all laid back for a nap, Tyme and Wiir Waar left the main condition with Jyg and the Z's, Zintowo and Zandero, and went to a smaller room where they could talk through the remainder of the heat. They were too excited to nap.

"I know Delgado," Zintowo confided.

"You do?" Wiir Waar looked at her cousin with surprise, "Why did you not say so?"

"I did not want Mams or Norvogo to find out," Zintowo replied as if it should be obvious. "Delgado is where I get my viruna. I sometimes party at the Blue Moon."

"So *that* is where you go when you give me the slip," Zandero exclaimed. "I thought as much." He could not help but smirk. "Probably visiting Sultry Nights as well." The thriving escort service and brothel was on the second floor above the saloon and music hall.

"You wish," Zintowo jibbed his younger cousin in return.

"I have met a few escorts from Sultry Nights," Wiir Waar told them. "At our shows. Mostly men, but sometimes women."

"How do you know they are escorts?" Zandero asked.

"Sometimes they will be at one show with one ser, and then with a different ser for another show," Wiir explained. "They are young and handsome and very attentive to the ser."

"How do you watch the crowd when you are spinning swords and throwing knives?" Zintowo asked in amazement. For him the crowd was a blur, *out there*, separate and removed from the stage and his focus on his performance.

"I always keep an eye on the audience," Wiir Waar replied. "Sometimes the sers talk to me after the show and bring their escorts to my dressing area," she explained. "The escorts are easy to spot because of the way they dress and hang on the sers."

"How do they dress?" Zandero asked.

"Showy. Provocatively. But not as much as Ser Cus performers!" They all laughed at the irony.

When the heat passed, the whole Ser Cus gathered outside on a patio courtyard and Jyg called Bones, who flew in with a dramatic whoosh. "Manser Jygero!" the big bird greeted him with a deep booming voice that amazed everyone.

"What is your name?" Jyg prompted.

"Bones!" the raven croaked in a low voice, then asked, "What does she say?" in Panr's high voice, followed by a frantic, warning shout of "City guards! City guards!"

"What a goof!" Jyg laughed. "She has never been in front of so many people. I think she is showing off."

"We have all done that!" Mams laughed approvingly. She had worried that Jyg had lost his familiar when he sold his gyrfalcon. Now she saw *this* was the bird. "Bones will be a blessing to you and keep you from harm," Mams proclaimed with authority.

Since the Ser Cus performers were not working on any new routines, they had to train only during the day. That meant they had evenings off. Jyg and the Z's headed for the Blue Moon.

Delgado was a big fan of the Ser Cus and delighted to find out that Jyg was good friends with Zintowo, who Delgado had met only a few times. The Z's were equally impressed that Jyg would know Delgado and be a regular at the Blue Moon.

Although Jyg was close to Zintowo's age, because of his sheltered upbringing at Dayr Castle, he always hung out more with Zandero. Zintowo had seemed so adult and worldly. But now Jyg felt more comfortable and like a peer with Zintowo and a protective older brother with Zandero.

Tyme and Wiir Waar went to a quiet saloon nearby with a moon deck overlooking the colorful city hillsides and the Jintiga River Valley. Tyme told her more about Delgado, their evenings together at the Blue Moon for his reports, and his occasional visits to their apartment.

"He and Jyg have become good friends," she said. "Even Klew seems to like him."

"And you?"

"I like him," Tyme smiled. "He is a very loveable scoundrel."

"Do you love him?"

"Not in the way I love Epoh," Tyme shook her head sadly. "I have told him about Epoh but he does not care. He said he would take whatever scraps of love I can give him."

"He said that? Those exact words?"

"Those words and more. He can be very poetic."

"The bard of the Jawbone Ridge gang!" Wiir Waar exclaimed in surprise. "He sounds more interesting than ever. A man like that is hard to find!"

"Oh great!" Tyme replied. "Now you will be taking his side."

"I am always on your side," Wiir Waar grew serious. "Even if I council contrary to your opinion, which I am presently *not* doing." She smiled sincerely. "I'm with *you*. Always, whatever you choose."

They talked into the night. Tyme realized how much she had missed her friend and how important 'twas to have someone to talk with and share thoughts and feelings. They laughed and they cried together, both thrilled that they would have a month before the Ser Cus would be leaving town again.

DRAGON SMOKE

T he dragon had a large smoldering hole in her back. A churning and towering, bulbous cloud of blackened smoke rose from the deadly beast.

Horton was stumbling off across the dune with Harvig over his shoulder while Epoh and Grinst were at their work camp under the wing grabbing their packs, gear, and water.

Boom! Boom! Two more explosions. Not as loud but still unnerving. They hurriedly collected supplies and caught up to Horton, who was wobbling but going in the right direction toward the seep.

"We need to check on Harvig," Epoh said solemnly when they were beyond sight of the dragon and felt safe enough to stop.

Horton set his brother down on the hard-packed sand. Epoh bent down to examine him. His face was blistered and puffy, but the skin was not peeling like 'twas on his hands. He had no hair, just smelly, singed wisps.

"He is breathing!" Epoh said with relief. "He is alive."

"We need to get him back to the seep before the heat," Grinst advised as they helped lift Harvig up and onto Horton's shoulder. The journey seemed to take forever. By the time they arrived, Horton was behaving more like his normal self.

Grinst had stopped a few places along the way to dig up roots from a few different types of cactus to make a poultice for Harvig's burns. He arrived at the seep while Epoh and Horton washed and tended to Harvig's wounds.

"The inside of Harvig's hands are not burned so bad," Epoh reported favorably. "Just the back side."

"He was holding the skillet up in front of his face to shine over his shoulder for Grinst and me to see," Horton remembered. "That must have helped protect his face when the fire came at him."

"Otherwise, his face would look like the back of his hands," Grinst agreed. "Yet even then the flames came around and burnt his hair and face."

Thankfully, Harvig was unscathed everywhere else. His blackened and burnt clothes had protected him well. Grinst dabbed the burn wounds with the milky sap of the fire cactus root, and then Epoh wrapped up Harvig's hands and head with scarves. When they finished, they discussed their situation.

"We need to leave soon," Grinst said. "Within a few days would be best. Horton and I can begin packing up and ferrying loads out this evening. Epoh should stay to tend Harvig."

"Which way will you go?" Epoh asked.

"We head for the Broiled Mountains," Grinst replied. "Going straight to Jchow Oasis would get us killed."

"What if Harvig can not move?" Horton questioned.

"He has to move if he wants to live," Grinst shook his head. "We can not carry him that far."

Neither Epoh nor Horton spoke.

"The longer we stay, the more likely we get caught by others," Grinst reminded them. "In a week there could be cutthroats everywhere." He looked pointedly at Epoh. "Unless you plan to fight and protect us all." He knew the boy was queasy about violence despite knowing how to use a sword.

Epoh shook his head. "You are right. We need to leave soon. Let us pray that Harvig awakens and is able to walk by then."

COMING OF AGE

Tyme joined Wiir Waar the next two mornings as she did her workouts and routines. She practiced throwing the knives she had brought from Dayr Castle. She still struggled with inconsistency, having a string of near perfect throws, and then suddenly one or even two flops, with the handle hitting the target instead of the blade. Wiir Waar had never seen anything like it.

"Once you get to a certain level, the issue should no longer be sticking the knife. The knife should stick on every throw." Wiir shook her head. "Truly, I watch you make each throw, and I can not see anything that you are doing wrong."

"At least you do not have to worry about me taking your job in the Ser Cus," Tyme said with resignation. Knife throwing continued to remain a weak link in her warrior training.

"Actually, you could help me tomorrow," Wiir Waar said with sudden realization. "I am performing at a tween party." Becoming a tween at one's 150th moon was the important first step toward full adulthood at two centuries of age. "'Tis a big event. She is related to the Mayor of Karvor so her family is very influential. You could take Lana's place and be my assistant—she wanted that evening off to see friends. It will be just the two of us. The performance is early, then we are supposed to stay, eat, and join the singing and dancing." She grew serious. "As long as you do not mind standing against the target when I throw the knives. Some people are not comfortable with that."

"I guess we'll find out," Tyme joked nervously. "Should I close my eyes?"

"That is usually less stressful," Wiir Waar advised. She dug through an ornate trunk to find a sequined show dress for Tyme. "This is the reason the Ser Cus has a wardrobe collection!" She went to a different trunk and pulled out the green dress Tyme had worn at the banquet at Dayr Castle. But it was too small.

"You have really grown," Wiir Waar said as she grabbed a larger size of the same dress. "You look more like an adult than a tween. Wear this for the dinner and dance after the performance."

The next day was bright Moonday. Tyme snuck in early to pray and sing with Jyg and Klew in the refuge, the outer ring of the temple. Then she joined the Ser Cus women as they filed into the sanctuary. The sound of their singing filled her heart with happiness and joy. Unlike the temple at Dayr Castle, which was never even half full, the Mother Womb in Karvor was filled with women. The atmosphere was powerful and uplifting.

After they finished their prayers, Tyme and Wiir Waar joined the crowds milling about on the shaded streets nearby. Large groups of women lounged at sidewalk tables and patios. Wiir Waar led Tyme to the second floor balcony of a teahouse where they sat in a quiet corner overlooking a small plaza.

"Let me warn you," Wiir advised, "Tween parties can be fun, but they can also be," she searched for the right word, "... exasperating. Families that can afford me for entertainment have lots of money. Families with lots of money often spoil their daughters, who then likewise have spoiled friends, who sometimes are tiresome and annoying. You just have to ignore them if they say something stupid or mean."

"Epoh used to tell me about drunken mansers and nobles at court," Tyme replied, "fawning and saying dumb things trying to impress King Eyrico."

"Exactly," Wiir Waar nodded. "Except they will not be trying to impress us. For them, we are just performers. Almost servants," she said pointedly. "And you are a Barbarian. They will know by your accent if they ask you a question. Just do not be surprised if you get a few shocked looks or comments."

Tyme left Wiir Waar to take Cadie out for a short ride before the heat and then met her after a quick nap. As the heat was ending, they carried their bags the short distance to the home of the tween, which was on a shaded ridge overlooking the giant dome of the Mother Womb.

The house was bigger than Jyg's mansion. Tyme and Jyg had often sat guessing what the owners of such houses might have put in all the various rooms, but they never imagined it to be so filled with furniture and artwork, or having such a large troop of servants scurrying about in preparation for the arrival of the guests. They were escorted down a back hallway to a dressing room off the stage of a beautiful theater with stadium seating on silk cushions for fifty people. A small group of drummers and dancers prepared nearby.

They changed into their outfits. Wiir Waar wore a small, embroidered red jacket over a silver bra, black leather pants, and red knee boots with heels. Her shiny black hair was woven into an ornate braid with amulets and gems. Tyme wore a racy party dress and matching headscarf. She was supposed to look like a pampered and spoiled tween. They double-checked the wooden target and support, which had been placed on the stage for the knife throwing, then discreetly nibbled from the bowls of fruit and nuts set out for the guests as they waited for the audience to arrive.

A group of servants came first, bringing more food and beverages on trays. Then the new tween entered with her entourage of girl friends crowding in behind. A loud chattering excitement filled the theater. It seemed to take forever for everyone to stop talking and find their place and take a seat.

The drummers began playing and a group of scantily clad dancers took the stage. The female dancers got some applause but the audience of tween girls responded most favorably to the shimmying young men. Tyme was a bit shocked by the constant sexual gyrations and innuendo.

And then they were on stage. At first, all Tyme had to do was gesture and stand in awe of Wiir Waar's sword juggling, exclaiming with excitement and accolades, and cueing the audience when to applaud and show appreciation for each part of the performance. Tyme beamed with admiration and respect as she watched her friend flawlessly go through her routine.

When it came time for the knife throwing, Tyme stood up against the target with her legs spread slightly apart and her arms out. She closed her eyes.

Tyme felt and heard the first knife stick into the door by her left knee. The second knife came a moment later by the right knee. Tyme opened her eyes to watch Wiir Waar, whose face made no change in expression, whose eyes were riveted to a spot near her left armpit, as she threw the knife precisely *there*. And then under her right armpit. Tyme closed her eyes. Thunk. The loudest yet. By her left ear. Then thunk again. The last. By her right ear.

Tyme opened her eyes again and felt her heart beating rapidly in her chest as she bowed before the cheering audience and encouraged them all to cheer again for Wiir Waar. Afterward some of the girls and women came down to the stage to stand against the target inside the silhouette of knives still stuck in the wood. Most giggled or cringed. One came up to Tyme afterward in astonishment.

"How could you stand there like that?" she asked in awe. "How long have you done this?"

"That was my first performance as a target," Tyme laughed nervously and bowed.

The tween's eyes bulged. "You must trust her," she turned with awe to Wiir Waar, who encouraged them to try a throw and gave instructions as each took a turn. Tyme sympathized with their disappointment when the knives all hit badly and fell to the floor.

After the tweens left, they changed out of their show clothes for the party. The green dress Tyme had thought revealing at Dayr Castle now appeared modest by Karvor standards. Wiir Waar slipped into a tight-fitting, short, red and black dress. They both wore fine inlaid sandals with straps that wound up their shapely calves and thin scarves draped over their heads and bare shoulders.

Now the boys and men, who had been waiting elsewhere during the women-only performance in the theater, were admitted into the gathering. More food and drink was served. The banquet hall was packed. They were ushered to a table near the front. The four other women at the table all praised Wiir Waar's performance and abilities, and then after a few polite questions, resumed their own conversations. A tween sitting at a more important table near them kept complaining to her friend about having to leave before the dance because her great grandmother, whom she hardly knew and did not even like, had just died. Wiir Waar and Tyme tried their best to ignore her. Thankfully the food was delicious, as they were both hungry after the performance.

Wiir Waar insisted that they do the first few dances together. They were now much closer to the same height. "This will drive the boys crazy," she giggled as they danced together slowly. "Besides, I want you to myself for a few minutes." She looked at her friend with amusement. "I saw you open your eyes for the two throws under your arms."

"I had to close them again at the end," Tyme felt queasy at the memory.

Wiir gave her a hug. "You did great! And you are way more fun to be with than Lana Pana." She looked around the dance floor and the audience. "Do not forget, this is not a Barbarian dance. You are in charge. You choose your partner."

Tyme looked apprehensively at all the unfamiliar faces. "At least give me a few hints if you know anyone nice. Or who is a good dancer." She had been practicing leading with Delgado and was eager to test her skills.

Wiir Waar nodded her head toward a mixed group of mostly men and tweens near the band. "Those are open partners. They will dance with anyone who asks. So if you are nervous, ask them first, since they will always say yes. Most of them are good dancers." She pointed out a few she recognized as having danced with at past parties in Karvor. "Everyone else in the room is free to say yes or no if you ask them to dance. Generally those up close to the dance floor are happy to dance." She nodded toward a group of tween boys watching from a back corner. "Most of them are either too shy, not interested, or not good dancers and would probably step on your feet and make a fool of themselves. That group might be good for other things," Wiir Waar smiled wickedly, "but not dancing."

When the song finished, Tyme chose a tween from the open partners while Wiir Waar picked out a dashing young man who had been closely watching her with his friends at their table.

They danced through the evening with a variety of young men. The last dance they did together and compared notes.

"They were just okay, I guess," Tyme replied when asked about her prospects. "You are right about me being a Barbarian. 'Tis like a big deal to them. A few thought I was exotic... or mayhaps more like a curiosity. Others thought I would be submissive and easy to order around. The rest all expected me to be wild and uneducated."

Wiir Waar shook her head in sympathy. "Sounds like dreary pickings. Next dance, you need to roam around the room more." Wiir Waar had held court at a variety of tables throughout the evening.

"I just wanted a dancing partner," Tyme explained, "I was not looking for a boyfriend." She had been surprised to think of Delgado more than a few times during the evening, and then, with a pang of guilt, Epoh. She was ashamed to acknowledge how Epoh was beginning to slip from the forefront of her awareness. He felt impossibly far away. Would she ever see him again?

A CRACK IN
THE CODE

T he next evening Bones flew in to the patio as Wiir Waar was visiting the apartment. "What does she say? What does she say?" the big raven cried out in Panr's scratchy, high voice as Bones paraded proudly back and forth before them.

"Bones has a message," Jyg said with excitement as the bird flew up to the table and hopped over so he could remove the little tube from her leg.

Jyg opened the end and took out the paper, which had a 2 written on the top indicating 'twas the second message sent by Panr. "1A," he read. "That means Panr got another message pigeon bound for Ambrit. The message the bird carried says 15 W left for P gmom die."

"W, or someone," Klew said, "has gone to P, most likely Pintone, because her grandmother died.

"A whiny noble sitting at the head table at the party last night had to leave for Pintone before the dance," Tyme recalled, "because her great grandmother had just died. Her family was going to travel by moonlight."

"She is a Little Empress," Wiir Waar used the slang term for a young girl who has been spoiled and pampered so much that she becomes a demanding tyrant. "Her family falsely equated their total lack of disciple with being gentle and loving parents. Giving in to the demands of a child can create little monsters who have no empathy or feeling toward others."

"I wonder who she is?" Jyg questioned.

"I am getting to that," Wiir Waar continued triumphantly. "She was so annoying I asked around to make sure I never do a performance at her house. Her family is mostly wealthy merchants. But her aunt," Wiir Waar paused dramatically, "is Major Bayn Baya."

"She is the liaison between the Heart Legion and the Queen of Tanis," Klew told them, "and also between the Heart Legion and the Mayor of Karvor. She is rumored to have a network of spies."

"Looks like someone is spying on her," Tyme said without sympathy.

"'Tis the way of the world," Klew shook his head at the political intrigue. "The shuffling for power. It will be easy to find out if Major Bayn Baya has gone to Pintone for her grandmother's funeral," he said. "If she did, that makes a good case to assume, until we see differently, that the letter W could stand for Major Bayn Baya."

WHAT TO CARRY?

The day after the dragon exploded, Harvig woke up to pain and delirium. His face and hands felt like they were wrapped with bandages of fire. He did not understand what was happening.

"You were *in* a fire," Epoh repeatedly tried to explain. "Your hands and face were burned. Grinst made ointment and I put on the bandages to protect the wounds so they will heal." Epoh had to stand guard all morning to keep Harvig from flailing and tearing off the scarves. By noon he began to settle down, no longer thrashing in agony, but moaning and exhausted in a pitiful and resigned torment.

Grinst and Horton had left the day before to ferry a load of treasure eastward toward the Broiled Mountains. They did not return until late that evening. Harvig was sleeping fitfully at last.

"Has he woke up at all?" Horton whispered with concern as he looked down on his brother.

"Yes, but he was very confused," Epoh answered. "At first he kept trying to rip off the bandages. I changed them earlier this evening and put new ointment on the burns. It hurt him greatly, but afterward he seemed to feel some relief and was able to fall asleep."

"Us standing here fretting won't help him any," Grinst told Horton gruffly. "Epoh is doctoring him well. Best you and I go take out another load."

When they returned the following night, Harvig was sitting up and able to speak. His face was still bandaged, but his eyes were uncovered and squinting open between blistered eyelids.

"I can be ready to leave tomorrow," he assured Grinst as he held up his thickly bandaged hands. "You just have to load me up. I can still carry a load on my back."

"If you tried to carry any treasure, you would collapse and have to be carried yourself," Epoh shook his head. "If you are strong enough to walk out of here, I don't think you should be carrying anything. Your life is more important than treasure."

"He has to carry water," Grinst said resolutely. "He has to be able to carry his food."

"We can carry treasure?" Epoh asked. "But we can not carry Harvig?"

"Not to Jchow Oasis," Grinst repeated.

"We will not need to carry him all the way," Epoh reckoned.

"We need to leave soon," Grinst reminded everyone. "Or risk being found out and losing everything. We have left a path of footprints between here and the dragon. Other grubbers will be coming this way soon."

"He needs more time to heal," Epoh shook his head and gestured to Harvig, who was nodding off to sleep. "He just sat up for the first time this evening. That alone has worn him out."

"Grinst and I can take out another load and return tomorrow night," Horton said. "We can leave the following morning. Harvig will not need to carry anything. His load will be waiting for him further down the trail. If he can not walk, I can carry him."

THE PLUMED BIRD

"What does she say?" Bones spoke in Panr's high scratchy voice as she paraded on top of the table with a small message tube hooked to her leg. "Bring your raven?" the big black bird mimicked Panr's voice again as Jyg untied the tube, opened it, and pulled out the little piece of rolled up paper with the number 3 written on top.

"1RG," he read, "One pigeon going to Ralston Garrison. The message is *16 meet U bMoon 4day PB patio.*"

"Number 16 means we haven't missed a message since the last one," Klew said. "Meet someone represented by the letter U on the Fourth day of bright Moonday week. That is two weeks away. PB could mean Plumed Bird. I have heard they have a top patio with stunning views. That might be where she means."

They had talked of the Plumed Bird a moon ago when Jyg had found the boy who Gribono paid to signal whenever a black lacquered coach with gold wheels and palomino horses was at the casino. After inquiries by Delgado, they learned the carriage belonged to Ser Gina Gain Gani, a wealthy merchant. But they had not been able to follow up on the lead. As a tween, Tyme felt too out of place to go to the Plumed Bird by herself. Besides, she did not have the appropriate clothes.

But now she did. "I could go with Wiir Waar," Tyme said. "She would be a perfect accomplice. Plus, she has the right wardrobe!"

"Go a few nights early," Klew advised, "to check the place out and find which tables offer the most discreet view of what's happening."

The Plumed Bird was the most luxurious casino in Karvor. The four-story building towered over High Street, set slightly apart from the surrounding buildings in a steep cliff and terrace-filled draw with afternoon shade and open views between the mountains to the east for moonrise. From a few days before bright Moonday, to a few days after Full Moonday, and again for the new crescent moon, the many tiered outside patios were filled with patrons drinking and socializing in the night air.

Tyme and Wiir Waar approached the casino front gate after the colors of sunset faded from the sky and the ethereal light and warm night air of the white dust moon filled the streets. The guard politely waved them through. They were dressed fashionably simple to blend in and not draw attention to themselves, with light gauze wraps and finely woven neck and headscarves.

The front patio was filling with women and couples bathed in moonlight and the soft glow of lanterns amid beautiful artwork and pottery. They made their way slowly through the saloon then climbed the outside stairs to the second floor patio, casino, and dance hall, which was even more fabulously decorated, with shimmering crystal lights inside, and contrasting red and black walls. The third-floor held a variety of more expensive gambling rooms and intimate theaters. They were allowed into the front room of the exclusive fourth floor casino, but after it became obvious they were not taking a seat to gamble, they were politely asked to move on.

Now they were in a corner alcove of the rooftop patio bathed in warm and glimmering moonlight and the soft glow of ornate paper lanterns. They surveyed the groups of women and couples at the surrounding tables, talking, drinking, eating, and listening to music. Unaccompanied men were not allowed on the fourth floor patio, and all the men there were handsome and well dressed. A fact not missed by Wiir Waar.

"I wager a number of them are escorts or moonboys," she said, pointing to a table where the attractive men were all much younger than the older sers they accompanied.

Tyme pulled her headscarf a bit lower as she lightly sipped her drink, trying to make it last. All the beverages were expensive at the Plumed Bird.

"I have been here only once before," Wiir Waar said. "A wee bit out of my price range." She shrugged one shoulder with a smile. "Truth be told, I like Red Peppers better for gambling and the Blue Moon better for music. More relaxed, more laughter. The clientele here is too busy being snobbish and putting on airs to have any real fun."

"I never imagined anything like this place," Tyme marveled. "But you are right, the Blue Moon is more fun."

Two nights later Tyme and Wiir Waar returned to the top patio early, just as the heat was ending, to insure they got the seats in their chosen small alcove. The sun was a bright crimson disk dropping into a giant band of haze on the western horizon. Tyme marveled at the sunsets in Karvor, where one could look out unobstructed across nearly all of Ambra itself, with no mountains to block the western horizon as in Dayrstad.

"They say after the rains the sky is sometimes so clear you can see the Dead Sea in the distance," Wiir Waar said.

"I would love to see rain," Tyme said wistfully. The present drought had begun before she was born. She was, however, one of the few people to ever see and feel clouds of moisture and mist in the high mountains, and the strange plants that grew there. She turned to stare at the unusual white moon, more than three-quarters full, hanging high above the eastern sky, which was still yellow and orange from the setting sun.

They ordered watered wine and watched as the attendants set out and lit all the patio lanterns and even a few firepots. A group of tables were being arranged to accommodate a larger party. Not long after sunset, a group of military offisers began taking their seats. Tyme and Wiir Waar studied the women's faces and ranks to better report back to Klew. As the last colors of the sun faded and the white and dusty moonlight grew stronger, a general arrived with two aides.

"I think that is General Cata Cara," Tyme guessed, remembering the descriptions Klew had given them of various prominent military offisers.

"I do not see any captains yet," Wiir Waar noted. Klew had told them that captains would be very important in any successful coup attempt.

The group had not been on the patio long before a very sexy and voluptuous woman appeared with a small group of friends. The woman, who dressed in the fashion of a wealthy merchant with opulent jewelry and rings, expressed surprise at meeting the General, who she appeared to know just slightly. The General invited the woman and her group to join her for a drink.

The two chatted awhile and the General bought another round of drinks. A half hour later when the woman rose and left the patio, the General appeared to order one of her retinue to follow after the woman.

"I think I will follow behind as well to see what happens," Tyme said, adjusting her scarf to cover more of her face.

"I will stay with the General," Wiir Waar replied. "If she leaves I will follow. We can meet later at your apartment."

Tyme discreetly left the patio. She followed the woman and the spy trailing her down the stairs to a second floor gambling room where the woman took a seat at a corner table with two other women and a man. Tyme could not see the faces of the last two. They played a few games of cards and then got up to leave. As they walked out of the room, Tyme's heart jumped in her chest when she saw the man was Gribono. Noot's killer! He did not see her or even look her way.

"'Twas definitely General Cata Cara," Tyme reported to Klew and Jyg. She and Wiir Waar were at their apartment patio sitting in the bright warm moonlight. "Her retinue took up a couple of tables."

"Any of them captains?" Klew asked. Tyme and Wiir Waar shook their heads.

"The General was not there long when she saw a wealthy ser and invited her to the table," Tyme continued.

"A very voluptuous and heavily jeweled woman with light skin and brown hair," Wiir Waar added.

"'Twas Ser Gina Gain Gani," Tyme revealed. "She met up with Gribono and spent the night gambling. They have chemistry and enjoy flirting with each other. I figured out who she was when she left in her black lacquered coach with golden wheels and palomino horses."

"So Gribono pays the stable boy to leave a signal whenever her coach is at the casino," Jyg noted.

"Did they leave together?" Klew asked.

"He was just a few minutes behind. He walked back to his apartment."

"So both Gribono and General Cata Cara have an interest in her," Klew mused.

"Meanwhile, I stayed to keep an eye on the General," Wiir Waar interjected. "She had one other visitor. A major." She described what the woman looked like.

"Major Bayn Baya," Klew confirmed. "The liaison between the Heart Legion and the government of Tanis. Did the General do the same charade of being pleasantly surprised to see the Major and invite her to sit for a drink?"

"No," Wiir Waar shook her head. "The Major came straight to the table like she was expected. However General Cata Cara acted very differently with her. More official. She was much more lighthearted with Gina Gain Gani, ordering drinks and chatting. She did not drink at all with the Major."

"It appears that she spies on them both," Tyme recalled the pigeon messages they had intercepted.

"Which means they are an important part of whatever plans she is hatching," Klew reasoned. "Whether for her or against her, we do not know yet."

"Why would she spy on them if they were loyal to her and a part of her plans?" Jyg asked.

"Mayhaps she does not fully trust them," Klew answered. He stood up to stretch. 'Twas still warm and now almost morning and the nearly full moon was finally turning orange as it set into the haze of the far western horizon.

"The question remains," Klew said as he bid them good night. "Where Gribono fits in? Is he also one of General Cata Cara's spies? Or Major Bayn Baya's? Or does he spy for someone else?"

FLEE!

Grinst and Horton were ferrying loads of treasure east of the seep. Epoh was taking care of Harvig, whose pain had lessened and energy was slowly returning. Epoh had just cleaned Harvig's wounds and applied a new layer of fire cactus ointment. When he finished tying on the bandages, he went to the door of their cave to stretch and have a look around.

Grinst had advised them to move a short way from the seep to a new, small cave with a view of the area, just in case Hool caught up to them. Now Epoh was shocked to look down into the ravine and see four large figures with drawn swords sneaking up to the entrance of their former camp. Epoh darted back into his cave to alert Harvig.

"We need to leave now!" he whispered, "Four Hool with swords are at camp." Epoh threw a few remaining things into his already packed bags. Grinst had insisted that they be prepared to leave at a moment's notice.

"I can carry some bags," Harvig insisted. "Food and water. And at least one small bag of treasure."

Epoh did not want to take time to argue. He loaded a bag for Harvig and helped to put it on his back.

"I can carry more," Harvig urged.

"It will feel much heavier in an hour. Once we leave here, we can not abandon anything on the trail if the bag gets too heavy. That would be leaving a marker for others to follow. We must do like Grinst said."

Throughout their scavenging in the dragon, Grinst had hidden their hoard of valuables in a multitude of caves and crevices throughout the eroded ridges and valleys above their base camp. With each new load of treasure, he had scurried from cache to cache, redistributing everything in a dizzying sequence of arranging and rearranging.

Grinst had kept everything organized for just the type of emergency they were now facing, the need to quickly grab the most important valuables and leave. Grinst had also hidden and buried all the lesser treasures in a variety of locations. Some of the loot was designed to be easily found, to catch any inquisitive Hool or grubber's attention. Other caches were increasingly harder to find, to lure those Hool into continued success in discovering treasure all around the seep.

"That way they won't follow us," Grinst had explained. "Keep them at the seep and occupied while we get away."

Epoh helped Harvig to slip out of their cave undetected. Their escape route was a steep narrow gully back up to the dunes. Harvig was soon breathing heavily. Epoh knew he could not maintain a fast pace for long. They came to one final place where they might be seen from below. No one was about. Now was their chance. They began to scurry across the spot, when they heard a shout.

Epoh looked down to see that one of the Hool had come out of a cave and was now looking straight at him. The man with a sword immediately charged up the hill.

"Run!" Harvig shrieked, then stumbled and fell to his knees as he turned to flee.

GINA GAIN GANI

Ser Gina Gain Gani loved colors. She had apprenticed at the Potters Guild Department of Colorant in Karvor to learn the precise science of mixing clay to create different and exact hues and tones. Early on she had blended and gave name to her own special blue clay mixture, turmala, which became popular with artisans throughout the city. As a result of this and other fine work, she had risen through the ranks of the Guild to become an expert on the creation, judgment, and critique of colors.

She soon realized her influence and approval could be quite dramatic in generating a demand for certain colors. And by limiting the availability of those colors, a higher monetary value could be obtained. Rare colors were expensive colors. Because of her control over the purity standards, she was also a member of the Guild Council. She oversaw the Guild warehouses and also the wagons that transported clay from the independent pickup stations in the Painted Hills to Karvor. In all of her dealing, she sought ways to skim a portion of the profits into her own special purse. Her gambling money.

Gribono first met Ser Gina Gain Gani as a mark. Occasionally he needed to make fast money to maintain his comfortable lifestyle. He had heard she was rich and liked to play the cards. He bought new clothes for the occasion of meeting her, planning to take her for everything he could.

But half way through a surprisingly enjoyable evening, he

decided to lighten up and not push her so hard. He would still reward himself handsomely, but he would keep it friendlier. She was a very clever and witty woman, which alone would not have swayed Gribono's purpose. But he began to realize her potential in helping him meet other sers from the highest levels of Karvor society. And he detected a cunning and resolve in the woman, which intrigued him. He found himself charmed.

As Gribono made his rounds one evening after the heat, he swung by the Plumed Bird for a sign of Ser Gina Gain Gani. The stable boy had moved the potted plant signaling the arrival of the black lacquered carriage with golden wheels and palomino horses. She was at the casino. He repositioned the pot and slipped a coin beneath it, then strode back to his apartment and changed his clothes, much more excited about the evening.

He found her on the second floor, at an open table where she knew an unescorted man like himself would be allowed inside to play. Gribono was not permitted to visit the third and fourth floors or the top patio by himself. She took him up to the third floor.

Ser Gina Gain Gani told Gribono about her chance meeting with General Cata Cara earlier that evening on the patio. Gribono listened intently. He did not believe that the General would invite a woman such as Ser Gina Gain Gani to her table to chat on a whim. The General was measuring up the noblewoman for something.

Neither of them noticed Tyme, wearing headscarves and watching them through the evening.

SKYLINE STADIUM

On the evening before full Moonday of the White Dust, the Ser Cus gave the first of three moonlight shows at the Skyline Stadium in Karvor. The magnificent tiered theater was built by the Ambri of the finest stonework, the perimeter graced with exquisitely carved statues of the Founding Mothers of the Ambri Empire. The stadium in Ambrit was larger, but many believed the stadium in Karvor more beautiful, built on a giant prow of rock facing the fading sunset colors of the western horizon. The twinkling white light of the rising moon behind the audience illuminated the stage with a magical, glowing light. Rows of stage lanterns gave an additional trim of golden incandescence in the warm night air that brings the white dust.

Tyme peered out from behind a curtain at the crowd. The population of Karvor, like everywhere else throughout Ambra, was smaller than it had been during the days of the Empire. Still, half the stadium was full

"Does it make you nervous?" Tyme asked.

"More like excited," Wiir Waar answered. She wore a revealing two-piece outfit of colorful scarves and thin veils, with decorative silver gauntlets around her forearms, and silver sandals with straps criss-crossing up her calves. Her thick black hair was braided with yarn, amulets, and gems. "How about you?"

"I am totally excited," Tyme grinned back. "And nervous as

well."

"You can do like Zintowo," Wiir Waar joked. "Don't look at the people watching. Just blur the audience out of your consciousness. Focus only on the stage."

"No," Tyme shook her head. "I want to be aware of the audience, even if 'tis scary at first." She was not doing much more on stage than she had at Dayr Castle, just helping out with some of the props and equipment, but now 'twas in front of fifteen hundred people.

A bell rang and they left their dressing area for the stage. Tyme was also wearing a small costume with wispy scarves. Lana Pana had done her make-up again and put a dramatic glitter in her shiny black hair. She joined Jyg beside the gear for the low rope line. He was wearing a headscarf with a billowy shirt and tight acrobat vest and looked very nervous. They both wore enough face paint that no one in the audience would recognize them. They watched through a seam in the curtain as Wona Weer, the Ser of Ceremonies, took the stage and waved her black riding crop to quiet the audience. She wore her ornately jeweled corset, tight riding pants, and lace-up the back high-heeled boots.

"Most noble sers," she cried out, her voice loud and clear. "Tis great to be back in Karvor." The crowd cheered. "At the most beautiful stadium in the whole Ambri Empire." The crowd cheered wildly. "I present to you, the Ser Cus!"

Norvogo drummed, and most of the troupe came out, bowed, and began jumping and tumbling acrobatics in every direction. When the drum beat changed, the group dispersed as Tyme and Jyg set up the low rope three feet off the ground for Lana and Tana Pana's comedy routine of each trying to balance on the rope, only to bump off the other. When the twosome finished, Tyme and Jyg hurriedly took down the equipment so that little Weethee and Wuleeno could somersault and cartwheel repeatedly across the stage, followed by Zintowo and Zandero doing multiple flips, handstands, and feats of strength and power.

Tyme's favorite part of the evening was watching Wiir Waar do her sword juggling and knife throwing. Tyme marveled at her friend's abilities and skills. And her commanding stage presence. Wiir Waar knew how to dazzle and thrill the audience.

Her mother, Waar Weer, performed the riveting finale as the Ropewalker, on a line strung high in the dazzling white moonlight across the width of the stadium. The crowd was hushed watching the tiny figure make occasional bobbles and looking like she might fall, which Tyme now knew was all part of the act.

Later that night after the show, Tyme, Wiir Waar, Jyg and the Z's all went to the Blue Moon. Delgado had seen the performance with some of his gang and insisted on buying them all a round of drinks.

"Watered wine," Wiir Waar interjected. "And only one glass each. We can not stay long. We have shows the next two nights." Delgado chatted for a few minutes and then got called away on urgent business matters. Tyme and Wiir Waar sat together and talked.

"I admire your work and accomplishments," Tyme told her friend. "You have very defined goals and a sense of purpose. Have you ever questioned your life or your path?"

"Not really," Wiir Waar answered. "The Ser Cus is the only life I have ever known. Or ever wanted. There are hardships of course. But whose life is without hardship and some pain?"

Tyme nodded thoughtfully. "Tao Tau says trials and tribulations can build character and strength, or they can make a person fearful, angry and resentful. The difference is in how we choose to respond to adversity."

"Choose to respond," Wiir Waar repeated. "I believe that as well. Because I feel I definitely make conscious choices about my actions and the kind of person I want to be. How I want to embrace and live each day."

"Embrace each day," Tyme nodded. "You certainly do. I also want to embrace and live each day. But now everything is uncertain. And after all this spying is finished, I am not sure where I want to live, or what I want to do."

"When we last had this talk, you said your home was in the stables at Dayr Castle," Wiir Waar recalled.

"Everything's changing," Tyme shook her head sadly. She described the last trip she had taken into the mountains with Tao Tau, who had revealed that she had collected all the herbs she required.

"She does not really need me anymore," Tyme explained ruefully. "She plans to travel to Ambrit and publish a book on how to make her healing salve. You are not going to believe it, but the most important ingredient is actually from mushrooms she grows in her cellar!"

"Mushrooms?" Wiir Waar exclaimed with delight. She knew how the Manser of Medicine had tried to steal the old woman's secrets. "Does Fagedo know about this?"

"Tao Tau plans to surprise him and give him one of her books. He will find out then," Tyme laughed. She would love to be there and see his face and reaction. He was such a pompous fool.

Wiir Waar chuckled and then grew serious. "That would be sad if you didn't go with Tao Tau anymore into the mountains." She knew how much the trips meant to Tyme, as well as the herb woman's advice and friendship.

"I always knew it might not last," Tyme admitted. "Most adults are too big to ride an ibex into the high mountains. The only reason Spike can still take me is because he is so stubborn and proud. But if I keep growing, I'll be too big." She grew teary eyed.

Wiir Waar gave her a hug. "Remember, I said you would be welcome living with the Ser Cus. Although not as the knife thrower," she could not help but gibe her friend.

"No," Tyme chortled. "Not as the knife thrower! But I can not run away with you yet. Not until we find out who Gribono reports to, and who he is conspiring with in Dayrstad. And also find out who is sending the messages using Panr's stolen birds.

We could be in Karvor for decades."

"'Tis such a fluke connection to Jyg's uncle's pigeons," Wiir Waar remarked. "Jyg was certainly clever in switching the pigeons and intercepting the messages to read before sending them on with the correct bird." She had a newfound respect and appreciation for Jyg. He had grown and matured greatly. And he was also getting rather handsome.

"Jyg's been wondering what he wants to do as well," Tyme said as they watched him flirt with Rona. "Being in Karvor so long has made both of us question the direction of our lives. I don't think he will go back to Dayr Castle." She shook her head sadly. "If Jyg's not there, and Epoh's not there, do I want to still live there? I used to think I *had* to be there in case Epoh returned. But that is not necessary now. If I stay in Karvor and Epoh comes back, I would find out right away through one of Pio's pigeons."

"I don't think Jyg will go back either," Wiir Waar shook her head. He was laughing with delight at something Rona had whispered in his ear.

"If Jyg stays here," Tyme mused, "I have thought about staying as well. I don't really know."

"Would you keep seeing Delgado?"

"More than you would guess," Tyme answered wryly. "He wants to hire me to be his bodyguard."

USELESS TO RUN

Epoh helped Harvig back up off his knees. He knew 'twas useless to run from the Hool with the sword, but he did so anyway, following a shaky Harvig toward a low ridge of dunes where they had hoped to make their escape.

Epoh looked back to see the large man was gaining on them. Epoh stopped trotting and felt a sad and detached calmness as he turned to slip off his load and accept his coming fate. He adjusted his cape to keep hidden the large knife of the Ancient Ones tucked underneath.

Just then he heard loud shouting. Another Hool came out of a different cave and was yelling ecstatically. The man racing toward them slowed.

"He found some of Grinst's treasure," Harvig said.

The man chasing them stopped and turned.

Another Hool came out of a different cave to yell excitedly.

"He has found treasure, too," Epoh said with a new hope. The man chasing them noted Harvig and the bandages on his face and hands. He could tell by the way Harvig was tottering that he was not carrying a heavy load. Epoh knew the man was thinking he could easily catch up to them later. Now, he wanted to join his friends who were screaming about piles of treasure. He spun and ran down to their camp to make sure he got his fair share.

Epoh and Harvig scurried behind the ridgeline of small dunes.

"We need to set a pace that you can maintain," Epoh warned Harvig. "Even if 'tis slower than we would like."

"Yes," Harvig agreed between breaths. He was gasping from the work of carrying his meager load up the hill, and his heart was pounding from the shock and fear of being attacked. "We have to trust Grinst's plan."

"If the other grubbers are continually finding stashes of treasure," Epoh repeated the idea hopefully, "they will not take time to come after us."

They had to remind themselves of this slender hope as they labored along through midday, continually looking over their shoulders nervously for any signs of pursuit. They were traveling east as Grinst had instructed them should an emergency arise, walking between two large dunes on earth so hard-packed they did not leave footprints nor any sign of their crossing.

"I don't think they are coming after us today," Harvig said as he staggered to turn once again to look behind them. The sky was a blinding white. 'Tis getting close to the heat."

"Yes," Epoh agreed. "I think we might be safe for today. We need to find shade and dig out a condition." Harvig, head and hands all bandaged, had walked much longer than Epoh had thought he could.

"How do we find Horton and Grinst?" Harvig asked uneasily as he looked eastward.

"I am not sure," Epoh replied truthfully. "Let's just hope they find us."

PARTY AT THE MAYOR'S

The Mayor of Karvor, Ser Yaar Yaay Yaan, lived in a mansion on Travertine Heights. Her patios and rooftop terraces afforded spectacular views of the city and the sunset colors. The marble halls of her home were filled with artwork, colorful pottery, and statues of famous sers. Her large banquet rooms were frequently filled with important nobles, dignitaries, and military officers, which included the most powerful women from all across Ambra.

Every quarter century the Mayor hosted a military gala celebrating the alliance between the Czarzina and the Queen of Tanis. Vital to that partnership was the cooperation between the Heart Legion garrison at the toll station, and city guard of Karvor and the Mayor. The military gala was a chance to publicly confirm the strength of that relationship in a festive atmosphere. The Czarzina did not attend personally, however. She rarely left Ambrit. A group of diplomats and officers would represent her. Nor would the Queen of Tanis be in attendance, as she was rumored to be ill. She would be represented by the Mayor of Karvor.

Because the gala was on dark Moonday, an auspicious time for both rebirth and renewing of commitments, the Mayor did not plan on using the outside patios. She wanted the celebration and entertainment inside. When the Ser Cus had come to town, the Mayor was thrilled to hire them to perform in addition to a music and dance troupe.

"Ser Yaar Yaay Yaan," Klew mused. "The sound of her name implies a very influential family."

"Do you know anything about her for certain?" Tyme asked. She was wary of inferring too much from a woman's name. Or a man's name. She found it ironic that Klew preferred to drop *ono* from his name, which signified that he grew up in a Mother's Milk, yet was quick to attach meanings to other people's names.

"I know she is generally well-liked," Klew replied. "She was not yet mayor when I was stationed here with the Legion."

"She is hosting a military party," Tyme reported. "With all the Heart Legion offisers." Tyme paused with a grin. "She invited the Ser Cus to perform."

"Which means us as well," Jyg pointed at himself and Tyme.

"And invited us to stay for the banquet and dancing afterward," Tyme continued.

"Which means we will have lots of eyes and ears to spy on the guests," Jyg agreed. He looked at Wiir Waar for support and then told Tyme, "We were thinking about smuggling in Delgado."

Wiir Waar had told Jyg about Tyme's poor luck at finding fun or interesting dancing partners at banquets where they performed. He had joked to Wiir Waar that it would be fun to sneak Delgado in as a Ser Cus member and stagehand at the next performance so he could dance with Tyme and be a part of one of the opulent celebrations.

"That was before you knew the performance would be at the home of the Mayor," Tyme said. "What if someone recognizes him?" she worried. "We do not want to draw any attention to ourselves if we are supposed to be spying."

"We can disguise him," Wiir Waar laughed. "We have a makeup kit with a fake nose and cheek pouches. No one will know him. He can help spy."

On the afternoon of the performance the Ser Cus wagon, with Narvago at the reins, pulled up to the back servants gate of the Mayor's residence and was waved through by the guards and directed past the back of the kitchen to the stage door of the banquet hall. After the wagon was unloaded, Delgado took the reins and moved the wagon to the Mayor's stables out of the way. Rather than going straight back to the banquet hall, Delgado ambled through the corrals and buildings, chatting with the workers and checking things out.

When he did join the others, he was quickly sent back out to the kitchen. Since he was not needed for the set-up or the show, the plan was to constantly send him on errands to learn the layout of the mansion. He ambled his way into the kitchen to brew a cup of herbs, claiming to make a poultice for a swollen ankle. As he was waiting, he overheard a cook instruct a new waiter the directions through the servant corridors to reach the Mayor's study.

While Delgado snooped, Tyme and Jyg did the same around the banquet hall, ostensibly to view the stage from different angles to make sure the crowd could see well from all directions. In fact they were learning the layout of all the entrances and servants passages, as well as listening for anything of interest by the workers, who were busily bringing in trays of food and drink.

The banquet hall was much larger than any Tyme or Jyg had ever seen. Statues of famous women artists, a number from Karvor itself, were carved into alcoves and colonnades, along with whimsical sprites, fairies, and angels. The floor tiles were exquisitely detailed pathways through mosaics of trees bursting with colorful fruit and birds.

Once the stage was set, the doors were opened, and the musicians began to play as two women dancers performed.

The banquet hall filled rapidly from the treaty room where the accords had been formalized. A group of military offisers arrived with the Mayor to take seats at the head of the hall in front of the stage. The Mayor made a toast to the alliance and the party began.

Tyme, Jyg and Delgado sat in the shadow of a curtain where they could see the Mayor with General Cata Cara, Major Bayn Baya and Captain Kin Kell sitting in front.

The drums began to roll and the Ser of Ceremonies in her sequined jacket and boots opened up the performance with the troupe tumbling and hand-standing across the stage. Zintowo and Zandero did a number of strength and power moves, which the audience appreciated, but more cheers were given to Wiir Waar's sword juggling. And even more to her knife throwing, which Tyme watched from backstage as Lana Pana resumed her normal place in front of the target with her eyes open. Delgado watched in awe by Tyme's side. She had told him of standing at the target, of opening her eyes for a few moments, and then closing them again. He could not imagine doing such a thing. While Tyme and Jyg helped change props and anchor the low rope line, Delgado ran a few more fake errands.

The Ropewalker finished the show on a line strung from the balcony across the stage. The audience enjoyed it, but Tyme thought it hardly dramatic compared to outside high above the stadium. The Ropewalker seemed to feel the same as she took just a brief bow before the whole troupe came out for the final applause.

As they started loading their gear back into the wagon, Delgado pointed to a third floor balcony with a door partially open. "That might be the Mayor's study. Or near it." He turned to Jyg. "If you climbed up to that balcony now, while the door is open, you could slip in the room and unlock one of the side windows. Then if you came back later, you could get inside without making a sound."

"Who said anything about coming back later?" Jyg asked.

"Just in case," Delgado reasoned. "If we find anything suspicious, we might want to come back. Then we would have a way to get in." He shrugged his shoulders. "It might be difficult to find another way. Then you would wish you had taken advantage of this opportunity in front of you."

Jyg studied the stone trim work for the quickest way up the wall. A couple sections looked tricky. "It might take a minute to climb up and back down," he shook his head. There were too many servants coming and going past. "Someone would see me for sure."

"We can catapult Weethee up there in a matter of seconds," Zintowo said. "She can slip in and open a shutter latch then jump back off. Darvio can catch her." After telling the others, Delgado stood guard in the alley while Jyg watched the back door to the banquet hall.

When they both gave an all clear sign, Zintowo, Zandero and Weethee crossed a small courtyard below the balcony and set up the plank and fulcrum for the catapult. Weethee stood on the plank studying the third floor railing high above her head. "From the top," she said, judging the distance.

The Z's set up the stepladder and climbed to the highest step. "One, two, three," Zintowo whispered. Together they jumped onto the elevated end of the plank.

Weethee sprung high into the air, perfectly executing a smooth soaring leap to land gracefully with her feet balanced on top of the stone railing. She dropped quietly into a corner of the balcony. Once she was sure no one was in the room, she slipped in through the door.

At the same time Zintowo and Zandero loaded the stepladder, plank and fulcrum back into the wagon. Darvio stood nearby waiting for the signal. A few moments later, Weethee returned to the balcony, leaving the door open exactly as she found it. When Jyg and Delgado gave the all-clear signal, Darvio rushed in under the balcony while Weethee stood up on the railing. She smoothly stepped off, pulled herself into a tuck, and fell toward Darvio's arms. The Mountain reached up high with his massive hands to catch her and swoop her low with his arms in a big swinging arc of momentum before looping her back up into the air. He released her as she came out of her tuck to land lightly on her feet. They both scampered over to the wagon.

"'Tis a library," she told them. "I unhooked the shutter on the third window to the right."

"Perfect," Jyg said. The outside of the third window offered hidden access from an ornate section of trim stone with a recessed and darkened corner.

They finished packing their gear into the wagon and quickly cleaned up and changed their clothes for the banquet. They were given a perfect table for spying, off to the side yet still with a good view of the front audience and the dance floor. The food and the wine, which everyone from the Ser Cus watered heavily, were delicious.

When the dancing started, Tyme was quick to ask Delgado out onto the floor. Originally the idea was to bring Delgado to dance with Tyme throughout the evening for fun. Now the plan was to do just an occasional dance together to check in, but spend most of the time mingling and dancing with others to see what might be found out.

Tyme found Delgado's disguise slightly unsettling. With the glued-on hump across the bridge and the end of his nose, and the soft wax stuffed along the bottom gums of his jaw to widen his face, he appeared someone else, squinting to hide the twinkle in his eyes. Still sort of handsome, but not dashing. And well dressed, wearing a beautifully embroidered white long sleeve shirt, tight leather pants, and black knee high boots.

When the music ended, they headed toward a group of men that was beginning to form. The ready and available men dancers.

"Oooh!" Tyme joked and pointed discreetly, "I want to choose him before Wiir Waar does."

"I think you are already too late," Delgado laughed as Wiir

Waar suddenly appeared at the man's side and asked him to dance. Tyme chose an older, distinguished looking soldier who escorted her with delight to the dance floor. She looked over her shoulder as a young woman offiser asked Delgado to dance. And a distinguished older noble woman asked Jyg.

"I am a Barbarian," Tyme told her dance partners. She and Jyg were keeping their background stories as true as possible. Tyme claimed she was working to train a horse act into the Ser Cus show. Jyg wanted to be the falconer, and Delgado was a temporary fixer and errand boy with local connections. They answered questions about themselves vaguely and encouraged their partners to talk instead. Everyone obliged.

"People like to talk about themselves," Tyme noted later that evening when the three of them were back checking in at their table.

"Hear anything of interest?" Jyg asked.

"Captain Kin Kell is General Cata Cara's hand and highly favored," Tyme affirmed what they had already guessed. "How about you?"

"I danced with Ser Gina Gain Gani," Jyg said. She was the woman Gribono gambled with and spied on. "She seemed eager for the party to end so she could go play cards."

"I wonder if she is planning to meet up with Gribono?" Tyme wondered.

"I got a few not so subtle come-ons for a rendezvous later," Delgado interjected with a mischievous chuckle. "I was afraid one woman was going to kiss me on the dance floor and knock my nose off."

Tyme shook her head in wonder. His charisma apparently still oozed through his disguise.

"I did overhear," Delgado continued with his fake jowly smile, "two soldiers infer that Major Bayn Baya will be coming back to the Mayor's house for a private meeting tomorrow night."

"The woman with all the spies," Tyme mused. "Mayhaps we should spy on her."

"How clever and convenient," Delgado congratulated himself, "that someone already thought to secure a safe and secret way back into the house for just that purpose."

"Well, if I am coming back," Jyg said, "I would like to have more of a look around, before I return in the dark with no moon. Let's take a walk out on the grounds for some fresh air."

The patio off the banquet hall held a smattering of people sitting and talking in small groups. Colorful lanterns illuminated the nearby paths and walkways. A dry creek bed of flowstones, waterfalls, and small pools wound through the property but had not seen any water since the last rains more than two centuries ago. The moonless sky was filled with stars. The white dust was fading from the sky. A number of windows in the mansion shone with light, helping to give the manor shape and form in the darkness. Jyg and Delgado climbed a set of stairs along the creek bed to a sitting area on the terrace of a cliff. They were nearly level with the third floor of the house.

"That must be the Mayor's study," Delgado pointed to the top front corner of the building with a private balcony and patio.

"Definitely harder to climb up the front," Jyg noted. "And more likely to be seen. Your way up through the back window is much better," he happily conceded. He studied the layout and stonework, along with the walls and cliffs surrounding the house, for alternative options and escape routes. He pointed to a recessed patio with two sun palms. One was leaning close to the outside wall. "That is how I will climb back over the wall when I am finished."

MAJOR BAYN BAYA

Major Bayn Baya was a tall, thin, strong woman with light skin, a chiseled nose and jaw, and blonde hair cut short in a military style. She kept a home in Pintone, where she grew up in the clan of a wealthy family, and also in Karvor, where she spent much of her time.

Her residence in Karvor was built on a hillside with patios aligned for moonrises and early morning sun, along with terraces to view the sunsets over the far western horizon each evening. 'Twas a small home by the standards of her family but it suited the Major fine. She was invited to enough banquets and parties that she had no desire for a large residence to host them herself. She rarely entertained, and if she did she preferred the intimacy of only a few people.

The Major did not crave the trappings of a luxurious and pampered lifestyle. She appreciated fine things to a degree, but manic and never ending consumption bored her. The continual striving to have the latest fashions and jewelry, bigger carriages, and larger mansions, left her unfulfilled.

What the Major desired was power.

Which made her alliance with General Cata Cara inevitable. Her network of spies had long ago reported the General's unhappiness with the continual corruption of the Czarzinas. The Major agreed that the current Czarzina was a vain fool, wasting enormous amounts of money and time building monuments to shore up and glorify her own ego. She was nothing but a needy and pouting bitch pretending to be a great ruler.

The Major also had no illusions about the General. Cota Cara was a fanatic of a different sort, believing the power of the Legion should be used to police and enforce a stricter morality. She wanted to build up an army of laborers, and for that she needed a return to more stringent religious laws that commanded all menstruating women without nursing infants to visit the Cavort each moon to increase the birthrate for the good of all.

Truth be told, the Major had long believed just the opposite. She did not care if women gambled and drank, or kept young men for themselves for pleasure, regardless of their ability to sire children. Weak and frivolous people were easier to control. The Major had exploited those weaknesses and risen in power without needing a large army to achieve her goals.

But now, to rise further, the Major needed to align herself with much larger forces. And there was no one more ambitious than General Cata Cara, who sought to become the Empress who would bring about the return of the Ambri Empire. To align herself with such power, Major Bayn Baya would pretend to embrace a strict fundamentalism.

THE BROILED
MOUNTAINS

E poh dug out a condition in the sand for him and Harvig to lie in for the heat. They were on the side of a large dune that was always shaded, so even the sand on the surface was not very hot. The sand two feet down was wonderfully cool to the touch. Harvig ate quickly. Epoh still had to feed him because of the bandages on his hands. He fell asleep before he finished his meal.

Epoh did his practice by softly singing Praises to himself with his eyes open, then stayed awake to watch for any Hool approaching from the west, or Grinst and Horton from the east. He did not think any of them would be out this time of day, but he was not willing to bet his life on it. He continued humming devotions to try and calm himself.

When the heat ended, he woke Harvig and they packed up to resume hiking. They scanned ahead for any sign of Grinst and Horton, returning to the seep, and looked nervously behind for any Hool. Streaked red and orange bands of color were forming across the white sky. The colors grew richer and vibrant as the sun set. They continued on, worrying more now as night fell. Where were the others? The moon was half full. Bright Moonday.

"There are Hool behind us," Harvig announced with terror

as he turned for a better look.

Epoh spun around as quickly as his heavy load would allow. Two figures. Unexpectedly close. They had kept themselves hidden by a small ridgeline of sand. Epoh unhooked his T cane from the basket and placed it behind to balance his load as he slipped the tumpline from his head and set the basket to the ground.

"No sense in running," he said as shook his head sadly. He helped Harvig with his load. The figures were rapidly approaching in the moonlight. The bigger one waved with excitement.

"That's Horton!" Harvig cried with relief. "And Grinst!"

"Indeed," Epoh grinned widely as they watched them approach. They soon were hugging one another.

"We came back on the hard top of the dune and did not see you," Horton explained. "When we dropped off the dune near the seep, we could hear a group a Hool celebrating."

"I snuck in close," Grinst continued. "I could tell you were gone. They are some rough customers. Best we put more distance between us." He put Harvig's load into his own near empty basket.

"You did good to carry this much," Grinst told Harvig with fondness. "I will carry it to our first cache to give you a break."

"And I can split Epoh's load until then," Horton offered. "We will move faster that way."

They turned southeast, looking away from the half-full moon over their shoulders, which gave their vision extra clarity and brightness in the glowing light. Without any load, Harvig was able to maintain a faster pace. They walked briskly and silently until the moon went down in the middle of the night, and then collapsed on the ground to sleep.

Grinst roused them four hours later at first light. They were no longer worried about the Hool following behind. Now they were excited to be on their way out of the Sea of Dunes. They marched into the dawn light and growing colors of the sunrise. Soon after the sun came up, they had to put on their visors, and then capes. Next fringe shields for their eyes and full sun cloaks. At midday they came to the first treasure cache.

"We have another stash further along," Horton reported, "with more water as well."

"I scouted ahead and found another seep," Grinst said. "From there we can make it to Stink Springs and the Broiled Mountains."

They put everything from the cache into their large yucca fiber baskets woven and reinforced with hidden wire netting from the dragon. Then helped each other lift their loads onto their backs and strap their tumplines across their foreheads. Even when wearing a sun cloak, 'twas quick and easy to flip the strap over the head and instantly shed the bag if the need arose to fight. Harvig could not use a tumpline yet because of the burns on his forehead and face, so his yucca basket was modified with two shoulder straps.

Now the early afternoon sun was over their shoulders and they could take off their fringe blinders. Epoh felt like a beast of burden. He was now carrying his own full load of treasure, along with part of Harvig's. They each also had numerous gems sewn into their clothes. Even if they lost their baskets, they would not be penniless.

That night the moon was brighter and stayed up longer. Harvig impressed them all with his ability to hike long into the night. The following day they came to the second treasure and water stash. They each took on even more of a load.

"The weight will lessen as we travel," Grinst advised them. "The water will go down each day, and Harvig will be able to carry more as he gets stronger."

When they left Stink Springs, the Broiled Mountains were hidden in a haze of dust off the southeastern edge of the Sea of Dunes. 'Twas impossible to see the mountains as one approached, and impossible for anyone in the mountains to ever look out and see the Sea of Dunes below. The mountains were perpetually shrouded in parched, dirty air that smelled of baked rock.

"Once we are in the Broiled Mountains, we will claim to be iron miners with loads of ore," Grinst instructed them. "That is worth enough for a poor miner to dig up and carry out, but too heavy and cheap for anyone else to rob us."

Now that they had left the Sea of Dunes, Epoh found himself conjuring countless scenarios of his return of Dayr Castle. He tried not to dwell on such speculations. He still had a long way to go to get out of the Endless Waste.

When they rested Harvig was full of questions about Jchow Oasis. He could not imagine groups of buildings like the nunnery all clustered together, with people as thick as ants. Harvig and Horton joked and speculated about buying large houses next to each other, how many servants they would have, and how they might spend their leisure time.

Grinst never said anything of his plans. "Not there yet, are we?" was all he would answer. Epoh hoped to be at the oasis only briefly, just long enough to put together a small camel caravan to take him west to Valhal and the Siren.

The grubbers made it over the first pass of the Broiled Mountains and down into the valley where there was a seep. It took four days to fill all of their water skins and catch enough lizards and locusts to build up their food supplies.

When they left the landscape became more dramatic with swaths of every imaginable color splashed across the eroded and exposed hillsides of rock, clay and silt: bright yellows, reds, greens and even blue dirt and stones. The colors were wonderfully saturated and vibrant in the early morning and late evening light.

By mid-morning the colors were washed out and the sky was a bright, dirty-yellowish white. As Epoh carried his heavy load up a loose, dusty hillside, he stared at each step of his dirty, thickly calloused feet in his yucca sandals. His exposed calves were thin and sinewy, bronzed nearly to black.

He had changed so much over the last decades. How would he fit back into court life? And what would his relationship be with Tyme in light of her far more important destiny? What would she do when he told her of the prophecy, and of the Blade, Riin Ruel, who had searched for her at Dayr Castle and also at Ezkia Nunnery? He wondered what had happened to the Blade? Why she never came back? Had she found some other girl? The thought had never occurred to him before. Had the Blade mistaken another for fulfilling the prophecy? Epoh was convinced that Tyme was the Bright One.

Grinst called a halt when they came across a cleft in the rock with a light breeze flowing down a shaded canyon. When they rested for the heat, Epoh did his practice and then napped. Horton and Harvig joined him in chanting prayers. Horton often did a short meditation, while Harvig sat longer with Epoh. Grinst kept busy with repairs and slept.

The last pass was a high, barren ridgeline streaked with hard-packed black sand and yellow dirt. They crossed it in the evening, just before dark when the air was crisp and cold and felt to Epoh like he was in the Barrier Mountains. He was consumed with thoughts of home.

Early the next morning as they resumed hiking down the ridgeline, Grinst looked with interest at the ground down the left hillside.

"Someone has been going down into the Valley of Death," he said with surprise, pointing eastward into a dramatic but dirty pre-sunrise orange sky. He used his T cane to help take off his load and walked that direction, looking at the ground. The other grubbers did the same and followed him down a hill to a rock outcropping overlooking the immense barren valley below.

The old grubber studied the ground. "Someone has been going down into the Valley of Death," he repeated with a grave voice.

Epoh, Horton, and Harvig all scanned the hillside around them. "What do you see?" asked Horton, giving voice to what all three were wondering.

"What do I see?" Grinst thundered. "A group just recently passed." He paused thoughtfully. "Mayhaps seven of them."

"How long ago?" Horton asked in amazement. He could not see any sign of a disturbance.

"A few moons," Grinst answered. "But there is an older trail as well."

"You see other tracks?" Harvig asked, looking closer.

"Been too long," Grinst shook his head. "Only disturbances!"

"Where do you see a disturbance?" Epoh asked with amazement.

Grinst pointed with a sweep of his hand down into the Valley of Death. "No good water down there," He said with certainty. "So must be water on the other side. Because they never came back." Grinst shrugged. "Else they are all dead."

Epoh studied the area. For just a moment the light changed, and he thought he could see a faint path of disturbance. An ethereal line running down the hillside. Then 'twas gone.

They hiked back, hoisted their heavy loads, and began their southwesterly descent out of the Broiled Mountains. That evening Grinst led them off the ridge into a maze of side canyons filled with small caves.

"Tis time to divide our treasure," Grinst told them. "Best to do it before Jchow. We don't want to carry these loads into that den of snakes."

They all grew serious.

"We are one day from a seep," Grinst explained, "and a week from the oasis. A perfect spot to tally accounts." He arranged all their bags of treasure before them.

"Our agreement as grubbers was to divide the treasure by seniority," Grinst reminded them. "For each share to Harvig and Epoh, Horton gets three, and I," Grinst tapped his chest merrily, "get five."

Because of the way he had organized and packed up the treasure when they left their camp at the seep, Grinst was now able to sort everything with amazing speed. His pile was too large for him to carry. Horton's as well. Epoh and Harvig each had smaller mounds.

"Best to bury most of it in these canyons," Grinst told them, "and do not put everything in one spot."

Epoh looked over his pile. He did not want to attract thieves either. All he needed was enough to hire a caravan to take him to Valhal, and a modest bag of gold and gems for home. He put more than half of his treasure into Harvig's pile.

"'Tis yours," Epoh told him happily. "Bury it here for later like Grinst said."

A RETURN TO
TRADITION

The Mayor of Karvor felt honored to be entrusted with the highly prestigious and important position of promoting and overseeing the most colorful and vivacious city in all of Ambra. She worked tirelessly on behalf of not only the Potters Guild and the casino, saloon, and tavern owners, but also the small shopkeepers, street vendors, day laborers, and everyday citizens. As Mayor she represented the city in countless meetings, ceremonies, and banquets.

She was in her dressing room drying off from her bath in preparation for another evening meeting, eyeing herself favorably in the mirror. Ser Yaar Yaay Yaan was a sensuous and buxom woman who had born five children by her husband without need for a trip to the cavort to become pregnant.

With the birth of each child, the cavort grew more and more interested in her husband. Fecund males with aristocratic breeding were in high demand for the fertility rites. Some women were jealous if their husbands were labeled birth desirable by the cavort, and resented any time they spent at the rites. But Ser Yaar Yaay Yaan found it gave her a stronger standing and power. She enjoyed flirting with others knowing she was secure at home with a handsome husband, a prized stud who had provided her with three healthy girls. It added to her allure and flamboyant mystique. And to her authority and mark of Divine favor. As an escort her husband was utterly devoted and well behaved with the most proper of manners and eyes only for her. He was unfailingly polite in deference to her slightest wish. Unobtrusive yet always nearby when needed. He was a perfect helpmate and a potent symbol of her power.

Tonight, however, she had told him he was free to go out and do whatever he wished. She was meeting with Major Bayn Baya and some other offisers in her home, and he would only be in the way. She put on a modest, official-looking embroidered blouse and colorful jacket that still managed to emphasize her curves along with tight pants and beaded boots.

When Major Bayn Baya arrived, the Mayor was surprised to see she was accompanied by just a single secretary. Realizing the informal nature of the visit, the Mayor suggested they have drinks on a west patio viewing the dusty, cinnamon streaked sunset. The new crescent moon appeared briefly in the western sky and dropped over the horizon as they chit chatted over the recently signed accords with the Czarzina.

"Mayhaps we could have a private word in your study," the Major spoke frankly as it grew dark and the servants lit the lamps. The Mayor led them inside and up the stairs to her office.

Earlier that same night Jyg had returned to the Mayor's estate with Darvio and the Z's. When the sky grew dark they gathered in an alley outside the walled compound. Darvio leaned forward against the wall with his huge arms and legs stretched out. Zandero climbed up his back to stand with his feet on the big man's left shoulder and his hands against the wall. Zintowo climbed up to stand on Darvio's right shoulder and brace together with Zandero so that Jyg could smoothly climb up their bodies and stand balancing on the Z's shoulders.

He carefully stretched his arms up but was not able to reach the top of the wall.

"I need to stand on your heads," he whispered to the Z's.

"Whatever," Zandero answered nonchalantly.

Jyg carefully balanced with his arms spread wide against the wall, gingerly stepping on top of their heads, then carefully stretching his arms up to finally reach the top of the wall. He pulled himself up enough to see that the coast was clear, then flopped over the top to hang off the other side by his hands and drop with a twist and a roll into a back corral of the stables. A couple of horses neighed and stomped in surprise. Jyg huddled motionless in the twilight to see if anyone would investigate. When no one came, he cautiously circled the horses along the route Delgado had described through the back of the stable to the alley, the banquet hall, and the small courtyard beneath the back of the Mayor's study.

The far corner where Jyg began to climb was already so dark he could hardly see. But the trim stones were so pronounced and easy to feel and climb, he did not need his eyes to tell him where the holds were. In a short time he moved up to the third floor balcony window where Weethee had earlier unlocked the latch. Jyg hunched quietly listening at the window as a servant entered and lit a lamp. When the servant left and Jyg was sure that no one was in the room, he used a small shim to pry open the un-latched window and silently slipped inside the Mayor's study.

Just to his right against the adjoining wall was a small closet with a key in the lock. Jyg opened it. Shelves with jars of wine and alcohol, and just enough space to squeeze inside. He left the door cracked open to have a clear view of most of the room across the top edge of the frame. A few minutes later Jyg heard someone approaching and entering the study. Two voices chit chatted as drinks were poured and they took their seats.

"May I speak frankly?" Major Bayn Baya asked.

"Of course," replied Ser Yaar Yaay Yaan, the Mayor of

Karvor.

"Tonight I speak for a group of Ambri patriots who believe Czarzina Hana Hama Hala is a disgrace to her title," the Major said bluntly. "I speak for a group of patriots who believe the time has come for a complete change in government. A return to morality and Divine favor."

"And what does this group seek from me?" the Mayor of Karvor inquired.

"We seek your support when the time comes. Our group holds you in very high regard. You are a wise and powerful woman blessed by Divine with a fruitful womb. You are like the Founding Mothers and rulers of old. You are our choice to be the new Queen of Tanis."

The Mayor listened thoughtfully. She had never hoped or dreamed of anything beyond her current position in life until the spy dressed as a waiter had promised her the same title. Truth be told, she had not stopped thinking about it since. Queen of Tanis! How often had she bristled under the foolishness and mismanagement of the current Queen. How often had she wished for a wiser ruler for her country?

The thought that she herself could be that ruler set her mind reeling. Although she had never lived in the capitol, she knew nearly everyone of importance from their visits to Karvor during high summer, when everyone with money fled up into the mountains to escape the lowland heat. She had never desired to spend time in Pintone, but the capitol appeared much more appealing if she was living in the Queen's Palace! Plus, she could refurbish the summer palace in Karvor and make it fashionable again for the Queen to leave the capitol.

"We seek a return to older ways," Major Bayn Baya continued. "A return to tradition and the Womb temple. We seek a vibrant cavort and Mother's Milk for workers to build a stronger and healthier society. You embody that goal."

"And how do I help in this endeavor?" the Mayor asked innocently, even though she had already guessed the answer.

"Your city and country were essentially forced to sign this treaty agreement with Ambrit. The terms all heavily favored the Czarzina. A time will come when the Czarzina will be vulnerable. At that moment you will denounce the treaty for what 'tis--a robbery and extortion—and refuse to come to her aid. All you need to do is keep your city guard out of the fight. We will do the rest."

Major Bayn Baya did not tell the Mayor that the plan was not simply to replace the Czarzina. The plan was to proclaim General Cata Cara as Empress of a new Ambri Empire.

The Mayor of Karvor stood and escorted Major Bayn Baya from her study. She left the door open and called for her servant to turn off the lamps and shut the room for the night. A few moments later the servant appeared. As she was extinguishing the lamps, she noticed the key still in the lock of the study liquor cabinet.

The Mayor must have gotten out a special bottle to share with the Major during their meeting and not put the key away. The servant walked over to the door, turned the lock, and put the key back in the drawer in the Mayor's desk where it belonged. She blew out the remaining lights, left the room, and closed the study door.

Jyg had watched through the small opening in the top of the liquor cabinet door as the servant approached. He heard the lock in the door shut. A few moments later the lights in the room went out and the door of the study closed. Jyg gently pushed against the door. 'Twas definitely locked. He put more force against the door and it did not budge. He let out a slow and anxious breath. He was imprisoned in the Mayor's liquor cabinet!

JCHOW OASIS

When the grubbers left the maze of canyons where they buried most of their treasure, they each carried just one heavy bag of gold jewelry and gems that they could carry in one hand.

The last two nights of their journey, they had looked down from the Burnt Mountains and seen the lights and firepots of Jchow Oasis. Now that their arrival was near, they were filled with nervousness and excitement. They were also physically exhausted. The brutal hike from the Sea of Dunes with their heavy loads, poor diet, and questionable water had taken a toll. When they finally arrived at the oasis, they camped outside of the city walls by themselves and away from the other groups of squatters, and entered the gates of the city early the next morning with the inflow of poor laborers.

Jchow Oasis was made of sculpted mud walls, graceful archways, and high domed ceilings dried hard as rock, uniformly whitewashed and tidy in the town center, and rustic and crumbling along the edges. Narrow lattice covering the alleys, lanes, and courtyards provided shelter from the direct sun. The bulk of the city was a warren of underground rooms and dwellings, four and five stories deep, networked together in a subterranean maze with residences and businesses all accessed by ladders, stairs, and passageways.

Grinst headed straight for roasters, a cheap and disreputable jumble of buildings clinging to a south-facing hillside that baked mercilessly in direct sunlight. No one stayed up at the surface during the day; everything in roasters happened underground. Grinst led them down narrow stairs and sloping tunnels to the Grubbers Supply. Inside he waited until the store was empty to speak to the clerk.

"Tell Crago," he said in a low voice, "Grinst wants to tally up some accounts." The clerk disappeared through a back door. The grubbers looked at the merchandise with little interest. 'Twas mostly shovels, ropes, and cook gear. The rack of used sun cloaks were ragged and patched. A display behind a counter held a variety of lock picking tools. The knives looked poorly made.

The clerk returned and ushered them through a different door to a ladder dropping down a dark shaft. A moment later a light was struck below and the steps of the ladder could be seen more clearly. They descended the ladder into a room where a large, muscular black man with thick silver earrings greeted them. Someone pulled up the ladder.

"Crago will be here shortly," he said with a bow. "May I offer you a drink?" The room had one door, a table with five chairs, and a small cupboard.

"Drinks all around," Grinst said with a grin.

The servant opened the cupboard and poured them each a small cup of alcohol. An even larger black man came into the room and gave Grinst an enthusiastic hug. "Grinst! My friend!" the man thundered. "Wants to tally up accounts. Welcome news indeed!" They slapped each other on the back with great fanfare.

Grinst introduced them all. "Crago and I go way back!" he told them. "He is one of the few people I trust in the city."

"Trust runs on short supply in Jchow Oasis," Crago nodded his head in agreement. "That is what makes it special." He pulled out an old scale from a wooden box in the cupboard, set it up, and tested the balance to make sure 'twas working properly. "So, what do you have?" he asked with a curious smile.

"Just a little taste," Grinst cackled with glee as each of the grubbers pulled out a handful of gold jewelry. "To get us some coin." It took an hour to weigh and price all the items and figure the money due. Then a long wait while Crago went to get the required coinage. Epoh felt dizzy when Crago returned and counted out a stack of silver and gold coins to each of them.

"We will each do another handful of gold jewelry when you get more coins," Grinst informed Crago with a sly smile. He nodded toward Epoh. "He seeks a small caravan to the Barrier Mountains. Not a regular guide," Grinst insisted. He never trusted anyone living in the oasis. "Find a herder, someone from the sand. And a cook."

"I can get more gold coins tomorrow," Crago grinned brightly. "A caravan herder will take a bit longer." He gave Epoh a thoughtful look. Epoh did not say anything. Although he had been practicing diligently, his Hool was stilted and foreign. He felt 'twas best to speak as little as possible.

The grubbers each returned to the street with a fat coin purse full of silver, which was safer and easier to spend, and a smaller purse of gold. They went straight to a nearby tavern and ordered everything on the menu for breakfast. Each item was bursting with flavor and aroma. Even though Grinst warned them not to eat too much, Epoh felt himself getting sick before the meal was even finished. The richness and spices were too strong for his stomach, which was long accustomed to much blander fare. Both he and Horton threw the meal back up. Harvig had to stop eating and looked peaked for a while but then recovered. Only Grinst, who ate slowly and very lightly, was able to finish and enjoy the meal.

Grinst led them through the city to Palace Heights in the center of town. Just across from the Palace, they entered into the swank Desert Night Inn. Rather than giving lavish tips and making a great show of checking in, as Grinst always dreamed he would do should he ever strike it rich, the old grubber found himself anxious and conflicted about spending three silvers a night for a deluxe suite and moon deck. The amount was a pittance to him now, but after a lifetime of scrimping and eking by, 'twas unsettling to hand over such a fee for a single night of sleep.

Horton, Harvig, and Epoh shared a similar suite together. Epoh's stomach had settled, and he was able to eat a few dates and fruit from a plate in their room. Then Grinst joined them, and they went together to a bathhouse. They were rinsed off, wrapped head to foot in piping hot towels, and laid out in steam rooms to bake on the stones. Harvig's skin was still tender and healing so his face and hands were left out and slathered will aloe. Next they were given massages, and their bodies were scrubbed with soft gritty mud, followed by a cold-water rinse and bath. Then 'twas back into the piping hot towels to repeat the whole process.

When they emerged from the baths, Epoh was ravenous and ready to eat again. He chose bland food, by Hool standards, ate modestly, and was able to keep it down. Horton and Harvig did as well. After final drinks and toasts on Grinst's moon deck, they all stumbled off to sleep in a real bed with silk sheets and a feather pillow.

ATTEMPT HIS ESCAPE

Jyg was sitting in the dark in the Mayor of Karvor's study, locked inside her liquor cabinet. The servant had turned off the lights and shut the main study door hours ago. Jyg sat fretting, hopefully waiting for everyone in the Mayor's household to go to bed. Then he would attempt his escape.

He had only one option. Break the door and climb out the window and down the side of the building before anyone knew what was happening. Then sneak up the terraced hill to climb a sun palm and get across the high wall without being seen and discovered. He rehearsed in his mind the climbing moves he would need to climb down the building quickly and safely in the dark shadows of night. He also pondered the most effective way of breaking the door and decided to use his feet rather than his shoulder.

When he could wait no longer, he gathered his courage and took a few deep breaths. He had his back against a sturdy shelf so he could kick out against the door with more power. He hoped to break the door with the first kick and be out the window and off the premises before the alarm was sounded. Jyg drew a leg back, wedged his body tight, and kicked with all his might.

Thump! The impact hurt Jyg's foot and shook the enclosure.

He kicked again. Thump! The sound was frighteningly loud yet had no effect on the door. He kicked harder. Thump! Still no damage to the door.

Jyg frantically rearranged himself in the dark so he could kick with both feet at once.

Thump!

Thump! He was convinced the sound must be heard throughout the house.

Again. Thump!

'Twas not working. He did not know what else to do.

Thump! The door felt different.

Thump! Yes, the door was starting to break.

Thump! Both feet, as hard as he could. The door banged open as Jyg fell to the ground. He scrambled out and shut the door behind him as he heard someone opening the study door. Jyg dived behind the Mayor's desk as the door swung open and the servant's lantern lit the room. Jyg closed his eyes to keep them adjusted for the darkness of climbing down the building.

"Hello?" the servant spoke. "Is someone here?" She walked into the room and showed her light around. When she saw the damaged door of the liquor cabinet, she gave a squeak of surprise, then turned for the door to call the guards.

When Jyg saw her lantern light shine the other way and heard her footsteps leaving the room, he bolted from the desk and opened the window before the servant was even out the door. Jyg slipped noiselessly out the window, closed it, and began traversing and down climbing the building mostly by feel.

He was near the bottom when he heard the guards sounding an alarm. He was in a dark corner not far from the study window, the first place the guards would look. He could see them racing toward him with their lanterns. Jyg dropped to the ground as they came closer, preparing what he might say when arrested.

"Blood and guts!" a voice roared out from behind the soldiers, who all turned to catch the perpetrator. But they were looking for a person, and none of them saw the black raven hidden in the shadows of an overhanging tree branch.

Jyg did not hesitate. With the guards turned the other direction, he slipped silently across the patio and around the backside of the house. While he scrambled frantically up a small terraced cliff to an upper patio, another group of guards were coming his way with lanterns.

"City guards!" Bones used a new voice to plead for help in the opposite direction. The guards turned to investigate. Jyg rapidly climbed up the shaggy bark of the sun palm beside the outside wall of the Mayor's estate. He held a palm branch to reach across to the rim of the wall and pulled himself over to lie on top. The alley appeared empty.

Jyg croaked like a night lizard. The Z's stepped out from the shadows. Jyg slipped over the edge and dropped to the other side to be spotted and assisted in the landing by the Z's, who had waited anxiously all night for him to reappear. They raced down an alley into the darkness without a word to each other.

Back at the apartment they joined Tyme, Wiir Waar, and Klew around the kitchen table. Everyone listened anxiously as Jyg told of being locked up, and how he broke his way out and made his escape.

"The guards were about to catch me at the bottom of the down climb below the study when Bones yelled out *blood and guts!* They all went the other direction."

"Bones!" the raven croaked in agreement.

"Then Bones called out *city guards*, to ward off the soldiers from the upper patio," Jyg continued, "so I could escape over the wall."

"You were saved by the bird," Zandero said in wonderment.

"Saved by the bird!" Bone repeated proudly. "Saved by the bird!"

Everyone cheered with merriment.

"So what did you hear?" Klew asked.

"Major Bayn Baya plots treason against the Czarzina," Jyg answered. "She believes the Czarzina is a disgrace to her title."

"We can all agree on that," Wiir Waar said with irony.

"The Major claims to speak for a group of patriots. When

the Mayor asked whom that might be, the Major inferred support from both the military and powerful Senasers. The Major believes they can stage a coup with minimal bloodshed."

"And what does the Mayor get if she joins them?" Klew asked.

"She becomes Queen of Tanis," Jyg answered.

"That would actually be a huge improvement," Wiir Waar had to admit. The current Queen was a weak and ineffective ruler.

"Major Bayn Baya wants a return to traditional teachings at the Womb, the cavort, and Mother's Milk," Jyg reported. "She would proclaim the new Queen to be like a Founding Mother."

"She is well on her way," Wiir Waar agreed. "The Mayor has already birthed three daughters."

"And two boys," Jyg added. No one ever counted the boys.

"Many women are not able to bear children without help from Womb," Klew noted. "The Major wants a fertile woman in power to encourage higher birth rates. The new Czarzina will claim 'tis a return to tradition, and mayhaps even believe it herself, as the results will give her just what she needs-- a dependable supply of workers and soldiers. That is the necessary first step for any long term plans of nation building."

A COSMOPOLITAN
EXPERIENCE

The grubbers met Cargo again the next day and exchanged a larger portion of their treasure. Cargo told Epoh he had not yet found a small caravan willing to go to the Barrier Mountains. "There is a great fear of traveling that direction," the big black man explained. "The Ambri are ruthless warriors who kill Hool on sight." He shook his head in distaste. "They tried to destroy Jchow!" The Ambri had killed all of the people and animals they had found in the Oasis. "Why do you wish to go there?"

Cargo had spoken quickly, and Epoh was not sure he understood some of his Hool words. But the meaning was clear enough. For generations Epoh's family had sworn blood oaths to protect the Barrier Mountains and stop any Hool from crossing. Now he wanted the Hool to help him return. He could not tell them who he was and could only think of one reason they might hopefully be enticed to make such a trip.

"Treasure," Epoh pointed to the gold jewelry they were selling. "I go for more treasure," he smiled slyly. "One quick trip to Valhal Oasis and back again."

'Twas Horton who had first thought of the danger in Epoh's original plan to hire a caravan to take him to the Barrier Mountains. If the guides thought he was carrying treasure, they might be tempted to rob him along the way. If they thought he was going to get treasure, they would wait until he was coming back to make their move. By which time Epoh would be in Valhal and have no more need of their services.

The ploy appeared to work. Cargo seemed less suspicious of Epoh's intent when he was told 'twas a round trip journey, and more hopeful of finding a willing camel herder. The grubbers divided their loot into smaller bags, which they tied around money belts hidden under their clothes. Then they spent a few hours eating and exploring the city. They got haircuts and shaves, and bought new clothes and sandals.

There was no Womb temple, of course, the Hool were heathen. Out of curiosity, Epoh stepped in to have a look at the temple to Bool. The building was gracefully designed with colorful blue tiles and high dome ceilings. He sat in a quiet side room with a simple altar and said his prayers to Divine, the Mother of All Life. Epoh was curious about the Hool's belief in a male god. He believed Divine had both characteristics--female and male. Yet it seemed odd to Epoh that anyone would choose the lesser qualities of the male when assigning attributes to their god. Power and might were certainly important, but nothing compared to the female role of creating and nurturing life itself, along with love and compassion.

Not to say the Hool did not have kindness or compassion. Epoh had been amazed by the friendly banter he witnessed on the streets. He had expected a more ruthless society. He was impressed to find there was a school and library. Epoh had never been out of Dayr Castle to see any of the old cities of the Empire. This was his first cosmopolitan experience. He felt an excitement and thrill at being someplace so exotic and different, and greatly enjoyed exploring and learning more about the oasis.

That evening they went to a rooftop tavern to eat, drink, and celebrate. Grinst cajoled the manager, with a friendly tip, to set up a private table with an awning in a corner where they had a wonderful view over the town. Grinst was getting more comfortable playing the role of a wealthy master, as the word manser was pronounced in Hool. Epoh thought he looked almost dignified in his new clothes.

They each wore one of the large clock bracelets, which continued to stay synchronized with the big and little arms moving and pointing in the same directions. Epoh now knew that the little pointer went around the dial twice each day. Two revolutions of 12 numbers. What was special about the number 12? Or 24? And the long thin jerky pointer had 60 quick segments. There were 30 hours in the Ambrian Day, 50 minutes in each hour, and 50 seconds in each minute.

Cargo had informed Epoh earlier that he had arranged a caravan to leave the next morning, which was the day before bright Moonday. A perfect time of the month for night travel. Now that his departure was imminent, Epoh found himself filled with sadness over the thought of leaving his companions. They had all been through so much together.

The same thought was in the minds of the other grubbers. While they toasted and celebrated the success of their adventures, laughing and slapping Epoh on the back, there were also frequent melancholy acknowledgments of their soon-to-be parting of ways. Although Epoh was leaving early, he stayed out most of the night with the grubbers, sitting in the moonlight around a firepot on the terraced rooftop patio, sipping flavored mescal, and looking out over the mysterious and beguiling Jchow Oasis, whose rooftops came alive each night with firepots, food, drink, music, and dance. The memory of that night would later change the direction of Epoh's life. But he did not know that yet.

WIIR WAAR

"Let's do something completely different," Wiir Waar said one afternoon as they lounged in the condition at the Ser Cus quarters at Skyline Stadium. She had the next day off and was eager to have some fun. "Let's go out tonight incognito."

"Like we did at the Feathered Plume?" Tyme asked. "In disguise?"

"I am thinking more like playing a part. Being someone else." Wiir Waar grinned. "We could dress as men. That is always fun."

"That is always fun?" Tyme repeated. "How often do you go out dressed as a man?"

"Occasionally," Wiir Waar chuckled. "My normal persona can draw a certain attention from both women and men." 'Twas true. All eyes noticed the striking Ser Cus star wherever she went, both on and off the stage. "'Tis interesting to take a break from that."

I do not think I would make a very convincing man," Tyme said doubtfully. "Have you ever gone as a different woman?"

"Mayhaps," Wiir Waar smirked.

"So who were you?"

"Guess."

Tyme looked at her friend shrewdly. "You would not play a noble because they are too boring. Nor a pauper, I don't think. An actor or dancer?" She could not think of anything else.

"A flaunt!" Wiir Waar cried.

"I should have guessed," Tyme chuckled.

"Much more fun to play a flaunt than a priest," Wiir Waar revealed sagely.

"A priest. A flaunt. Who else have you *played*?" Tyme said with amazement.

Wiir Waar giggled. "The best are fofar," she admitted with a sly grin. Born in a man's body, but with a feminine personality and appearance. "Fofar can be the most fun! That flamboyant movement." She jumped up and strutted dramatically in front of her friend. Her body moved in a whole new way. "And a change in voice as well," she said, with a new tone and texture.

Tyme marveled at Wiir Waar's transformation. She certainly projected at fofar-ness. "That is really good," Tyme enthused. "Where do you go?"

"When I am fofar, I go to the casinos and dance halls," she said vivaciously.

"I am afraid I would not be very convincing," Tyme said regrettably. "Nor does my coin purse like the idea of casinos and dance halls."

Wiir Waar's voice changed. Lower, slower, stronger. "If not fofar. How about fafor? You are close to my size now. We could be fafor mercenaries. Visit a few of the rougher places up the hill. We could go up to the Anvil Bar and have a look around."

"I could play fafor," Tyme agreed. "We could be soldier lovers."

"Perfect. Shall we be successful mercenaries out celebrating on the town, or newly arrived and seeking work?"

"Newly arrived sounds simpler and cheaper," Tyme replied. "We do not have to say from where."

Wiir Waar led the way to a Ser Cus wagon and got out an old trunk full of leather clothes and soldierly apparel, gauntlets, armbands, and chokers. They had fun trying on various items and assembling their wardrobes with each carrying a brace of throwing knives and a few other hidden knives as well.

After they darkened their eyes with kohl, Wiir Waar

prepared some powders on a leaf to chew. "Beetle is a cheap stimulant used by hill folk. It will stain our teeth and gums dark red."

"Sounds delightful," Tyme grimaced. "We don't have to act stern and serious all the time, do we?"

"Well, sort of. We're mercenaries. Tough bad-ass bitches!" Wiir Waar growled.

"Who recently met and are out to have fun!" Tyme countered. "You can be the experienced world traveler. I will be fresh from the mountains."

They left the Stadium and took back alley stairs up the hill to avoid the city guard, who would likely stop to question unsupervised mercenaries on High Street. They hiked discreetly up through the neighborhoods and were soon passing the Blue Moon.

"Mayhaps we should go inside," Tyme joked with a reddish smile. "See if Delgado would like a kiss."

"I don't think we could get in the door," Wiir Waar laughed. "Besides, I want something different tonight. Just you and me."

"Lovers," Tyme did a fake swoon.

"Not wimpy lovers," Wiir Waar grabbed her sternly.

"No," Tyme responded firmly. "Never wimpy." She flared her lips to expose her teeth and gums in a horrid, macabre smile. They both broke out laughing.

"I can see you are going to be a handful," Wiir Waar mockingly wagged her finger. "We should have names. I'll be Wiri Rawa," she said dramatically.

"I'll be Myte," Tyme proclaimed with a laugh.

They left the territory of the Jawbone Ridge gang and continued up the twisted stairs and narrow alleys into the heart of Old Town. On Cracken Street they descended the broken rock stairway to the Anvil, a dark basement bar with stone tables and benches tucked into a warren of alcoves. The bar itself was a once beautiful patterned stone, cracked and chipped from countless assaults and fights. The smell of meat pies emanated from a small kitchen.

"Can I get you a drink?" the barkeep asked, a large and formidable dark-skinned woman with a military bearing. "Something to eat?"

"Drinks," Wiir Waar said agreeably and leaned up against the bar. "Two gourds of cactus mash." When the barkeep served the milky liquid, Tyme made a toast.

"To Old Town." They tapped their gourds together. "May she bring me luck."

"New in Old Town?" the barkeep asked.

"One of us," Tyme admitted agreeably.

"I am going to teach her to play cards," Wiir Waar nodded toward two card tables.

"Good luck," the barkeep gave Tyme a smile.

The first table was full; the second had an open chair. Tyme joined the five others at the table playing poker. Wiir Waar pulled up a chair behind. She played each hand while Wiir Waar looked over her shoulder and explained how the game and the rules worked. To their delight, Tyme's small stack of coins began to grow, as did their joking banter.

They ordered two more gourds of cactus mash. Tyme liked the excitement of each new hand and the strategy of choosing which cards to give back for a redraw. How to bet, raise and call. She enjoyed watching the other players. She seemed to know instantly whenever anyone was bluffing. Her stack of coins continued to grow.

After another large pot went to Tyme, three of the players announced they were quitting and left the table grumbling about beginner's luck. Wiir Waar took one of the seats. She was ready to play, and Tyme now felt good enough to play on her own. They ordered two more gourds of mash.

Two light-skinned men loudly joined the table and sat next to Wiir Waar. The big one sniggered when he saw they were drinking cheap mash from a gourd. "We are toasting the Duke," he whispered to his buddy as if 'twas the funniest thing, "while the *girls* are drinking the milky white!" The other man hushed his friend while trying to choke off his own snickering.

Now that Wiir Waar was playing her own hand, she began winning more often than not. The two men stole occasional shots of liquor from their own corked bottle and voiced a few half-muffled and crude comments about fafors and untrained mercenaries. As they continued to lose at cards, their grumbling grew worse.

Tyme and Wiir Waar gave each other looks of tired disdain. The men were buffoons. Caricatures of drunken louts. From their comments 'twas obvious they were liquor smugglers who thought themselves clever. But now they were losing at cards. And they were growing in outrage.

Suddenly the big man jumped up from his chair and drew his sword partly from his scabbard. "You must be cheating," he accused Wiir Waar. His friend stood beside him, sword half drawn.

Wiir Waar signaled Tyme to stay seated, then rose nonchalantly with a knife in her hand. "That is a clumsy weapon for a small room," she dismissed the man critically. "Better to use something quicker." She spun her knife in the air. When she caught it, she had a knife in both hands. She turned and threw the knives, one from each arm, across the room to hit bull's-eyes on two targets, eliciting shouts of astonishment from those playing darts, and gasps from everyone around the card table.

Wiir Waar faced the big lout and his friend with new knives in both hands set to throw. "I suggest," her voice calm and hypnotic, "that you put your swords away before you get hurt."

The man's face quivered. He wobbled on his feet as he fumbled his sword back in its scabbard. "I apologize, ser," he stammered, "for my disrespect." His friend bowed his head in contrition.

A young mercenary who had been playing darts brought Wiir Waar's knives from the target and respectfully held them out to her. "You are awesome," she gushed.

"Thank you," Wiir Waar smiled warmly and sat down. "Now, are we back in good order?" she asked the man.

"Yes, ser," he bowed nervously.

"You may leave," Wiir Waar told him happily, "or stay if you wish. But no more whining or threats."

The men nodded silently in agreement as they headed out the door. Tyme was amazed by how easily Wiir Waar relaxed when she resumed playing cards. They were soon laughing again as if nothing had happened.

The next day when they told the others about their evening, they mentioned that the men were liquor smugglers.

"They had a small bottle of very expensive viruna," Wiir Waar said. "I got a glimpse of it. Labeled from the King of Sikes own distillery."

"When they first arrived, they said they were toasting a Duke," Tyme recalled. "Is there a Duke in Sikes that might be smuggling the liquor?"

"I do not know of any Duke in Sikes," Wiir Waar shook her head. "But there certainly could be."

"I will ask Delgado if he knows of any other Dukes," Tyme said, thinking of Duke Eddarko of the Siren. Delgado did not. He said he would look into it.

On the night before the Ser Cus was to leave town, there was a farewell gathering at the Blue Moon.

"Do not be sad," Wiir Waar told Tyme. The Ser Cus star was used to goodbyes. "We will be back to Karvor in just a few moons. We are going to Pintone next, then Dorgon and Ambrit. After that we will most likely come back to Karvor for the Pottery Festival."

"'Twas wonderful having you here," Tyme told her friend.

"I loved seeing you," Wiir Waar agreed with a hug. "Whatever happens after your stay in Karvor, know that you always have a home with the Ser Cus."

The next morning the three wagons of the Ser Cus, with half the troupe walking, left Skyline Stadium and took the

Royal Highway down the narrow Jintiga Canyon to Pintone.

PART VII

On that day the trumpets will sound,
the Bright One of prophecy is drawing near.
The world will never be the same.

> *Kabaal Prophecies*

Hope was raised of a new dawn.

> *Hope the Proclaimer*

RIIN RUEL'S REPORT

O n dark Moonday Riin Ruel had a visitor. She had been recovering for a few moons from the poison that helped her escape from prison. The former Blade and Point of the Daggers was at a secluded hermitage at Falcana Nunnery and was now strong enough to take short walks along a nearby beach of the Dead Sea. When she returned from her walk, she found a woman dressed as a nun sitting in prayer at her altar.

The woman rose and gestured the womb. She pulled back her scarf and introduced herself. "I am Major Gwen Gail of the Blades. I teach military herstory at the Ambrit Academy." She made a secret hand code to confirm her next words. "I am also the Hilt of the Daggers." She motioned for them to sit at the table.

"Anna Nana kept me informed of your mission to Dayr Castle in search of the Bright One," she told Riin Ruel. The Major said nothing more of the former Hilt or the unfortunate timing of her death, which had allowed a new Will of the Blades to alert the Czarzina of Riin Ruel's quest.

"I have long awaited your report," Major Gwen Gail nodded grimly. "And you have long suffered its burden." The Hilt assumed she had not found the girl. If she had she would have stayed with her or brought her back. But she had come back alone.

Riin Ruel told of her findings at Dayr Castle. The Major was impressed by her description of the soldier's dream--a Warrior Empress with a flaming sword and crystal shield, with armor of gold and jewels, leading a powerful host of mounted soldiers out of the clouds and into Dayr Castle.

"And the soldier who dreamed 'twas lookout on tower one of castle gate?" Gwen Gail wanted to make sure she had everything right.

"Yes," Riin Ruel confirmed. "But 'twas a boy who was born to the Barbarian King," she said sadly. She told the Hilt of her travels to Ezkia Nunnery at the edge of the Maze in the Endless Waste.

"I was shown an infant girl, but she was not the one we seek." Riin Ruel described the nunnery and the abbess before returning to her main concern. "The Bright One is linked the strongest to Dayr Castle. I must go back again to find her."

"Yes," the Hilt replied thoughtfully. "Even though the soldier's dream 'twas from a man, 'tis too powerful to ignore. It confirms what Anna Nana believed and dreamt herself."

"Let me be the Dagger's Point once again," Riin Ruel said with conviction. "I grow stronger with each day."

Gwen Gail nodded her head. "Yes. I believe Divine in Her wisdom has chosen you for this task." She nodded resolutely and added. "Lightning will be at the nunnery stables ready for you when you are strong enough to leave."

Riin Ruel gestured the womb. Reuniting with her horse would be healing as well. She felt a great flow of positive energy and hope. She had long believed it Divine Will for her to find and tutor the girl. But now she had new concerns and fears. What if the girl was grown? A tween? Without a Dagger to share the ancient teachings, how could the girl know all that was necessary to fulfill her destiny?

PART VIII

Destiny is the path we forge from our actions and deeds in response to life's joys and sorrows.

   Kabaal Prophecies

What is destiny? What is choice? What is free will without commitment?

   Hope the Proclaimer

THE FIRE IS GROWING

Gribono was playing cards at Red Peppers at his favorite table with Sergeant Etna Nate. She had been talking about the Fire and the red candles and altars in the refuge that kept getting taken down by the Womb authorities.

"The priests have to rely on the shaman to take them down," the sergeant noted, "since women are not to enter or use the refuge. Women worshiped in the sanctuary. "But the shaman and his workers do not always remove them fast enough. The priests now want the shaman to post a guard all hours of the day and night to find out who's doing it."

Everyone's doing it!" Gribono exclaimed. "I have lit countless candles and left a number of sun medallions myself!"

"The Fire is growing in Karvor," Etna Nate agreed. "The shaman, Tanfaro, does not have a clue as to what's happening."

"What is happening?" Gribono asked nonchalantly. He had spent hours playing cards with Tanfaro each week trying to find out what the shaman knew. Gribono believed he was a kind but clueless young man who had no idea of the anger building toward the strict theology of the Womb.

"The Fire is growing in the Heart Legion!" Etna Nate declared. "Even among the offisers."

"An offiser beside you?" Gribono appeared mildly skeptical.

"Captain Wirvimo has the Fire," the sergeant leaned forward and whispered with confidence.

Gribono had been asked to spy on Captain Wirvimo by Shamano, the shaman from Birjj who he had met at Dayr Castle. Since that time Gribono had only heard snippets of speculation about Captain Wirvimo's belief in the Fire. Now Etna Nate was confirming everything. Gribono felt the news important enough to report back to Captain Targono.

When he left Red Peppers that night, Gribono headed up the hill to Old Town. He wanted to make sure a horse would be made ready. Bright Moonday was just three nights away. This was a perfect time to set out for the eastern mountains of Vanttan and the back door to the Hammer Legion at Vrak Pass.

THE CARAVAN

Epoh left Jchow Oasis early in the morning. He was careful to say his final goodbyes to the other grubbers in their rooms, as the caravan driver had been led to believe Epoh was merely going to Valhal and then coming back.

"Thanks for teaching me about the desert," Epoh gave Grinst a back slapping hug. "And for saving my life." The old grubber had saved all their lives when the big sandstorm hit. And he had successfully led them safely across vast sections of harsh and desolate terrain.

"Thanks for believing in my book, even when I did not," Epoh gave Horton a warm embrace. *Dragons of the Endless Waste* had changed all their lives.

Epoh gave Harvig a long hug. "I will miss our practice together." Harvig had been diligent in joining Epoh during the heat when he did his prayer meditations. They had also frequently sung Divines and had theological discussions. "You have been like a brother to me. Keep strong in your devotions."

Harvig's eyes welled with tears. His face was only beginning to heal, and he still had no hair. The back of his hands would be horribly scarred for life.

Epoh left the grubbers in their rooms and carried his bags alone down to the street. Although he had used his sun cloak for an awning with the grubbers, he now carried a small tent and carpet for a floor and a few other camping conveniences.

He also carried a sword and dagger he had purchased from an armorer. Grinst had spread rumors about Epoh's skill with the sword, hoping to discourage any plans of trailside robbery.

The camel herder, whose name was Imir, bowed in awe at Epoh's appearance. The cook was too shy to look him in the eye. Imir walked in front, clearing the way through the streets and pulling the lead camel on a leash to a peg in its nose. Three other camels followed in line on leashes carrying water, food, and supplies with the cook walking behind trailing a goat.

Epoh felt like he was in a dream as he rode the lead camel through the city. For much of the trip he would walk, which allowed his camel to carry more water. But now he enjoyed riding with a good view above the crowded streets as they passed through town and headed out into the oasis countryside, a wide valley filled with rows of long walls and awnings that swung across the gardens for shade.

He thoughtfully ate a slice of melon. He had insisted the cook bring a variety of foods not normally eaten on caravan, including two chickens and the goat. Imir had to bring an extra camel for the extravagance and was relieved when Epoh paid him for it without complaint. Imir had assumed Epoh was too pampered to go a month without his favorite foods. But in reality Epoh was in caloric debt, and needed to build his strength back up. He also needed vegetables and fruits to heal the sores in his mouth and ease the pain in his swollen and bleeding gums.

It took less than a day for Imir to realize that Epoh was very at ease in the desert and had an excellent eye for following a trail. But, strangely, 'twas also apparent that Epoh had never been around camels before, which was completely baffling to Imir. How could a wealthy man of the desert know so little about camels?

Luckily for Epoh, Imir was not the type of person to ask many questions. Instead, he happily chatted with cook. Epoh was surprised by how much he understood of their banter. They spoke slower than many of the city folk and used simpler sentences. They addressed him in Hool as master. The more Epoh learned Hool, the more correlations he saw with his own language.

ON THE ROYAL HIGHWAY

E arly in the morning, Tyme called Klew and Jyg out onto the patio and pointed up the hill toward a ramshackle ridge of houses in Old Town.

"Gribono's getting ready to leave," she said with excitement. A yellow flag was flying on a pole above a small shack. That meant Gribono had requested a horse to be readied for a trip.

The plan had been to follow Gribono and find out to whom he was reporting. Tyme and Jyg had practiced tracking Klew through the mountains to insure they had the skills to trail Gribono, or one another, should they ever be separated. But now Klew questioned that plan.

"Our focus is no longer just on Gribono," he told them. "I think it equally important that the two of you stay in Karvor, follow what is happening with the message pigeons, and keep an eye on the network of suspects we have here." He brought his hand to his chest. "I can follow Gribono by myself and trail a spare horse to stay with him no matter his speed."

A big lizard skittered across the patio as Tyme and Jyg considered his words. What he said made sense. Klew quickly packed his saddlebags, food, and water skins. He gave them each an embrace and headed out the door.

Klew rode Veeda and trailed Zill up a steep, twisting back alley to Old Town. He had a spot between two sheds where he could stand and watch anyone leaving the stable. Klew figured Gribono would be going to Ambrit via the Scout trail to the west through the Tanis Hills.

As the sun was setting, Klew saw Gribono leave on a daya, packed for travel, heading the direction that Klew had expected. He waited a few moments and then mounted Veeda in pursuit, following Gribono through the night and into the next day. To his relief Gribono stopped for the heat. In the evening they rode down into the Iridi Valley. The hills and fire cactus glowed in the soft moonlight.

Klew was surprised when Gribono did not cross the dry riverbed to go westward on the Scout trail through the Hollow Hills to Ambrit. Instead, the spy turned left to follow the Royal Highway beside the dry Iridi riverbed south toward Tepu. Klew had thought Gribono was going to report to a superior, but now he was unsure what was happening. Surely the person behind his actions did not live in Tepu, or Thesson. He must be traveling to some other rendezvous.

A night with a short stop to rest and half a day later they came into Tepu. Gribono took a room at a men's tavern. Klew followed him inside at a distance. He used a small disguise kit from the Ser Cus to give himself a missing black tooth, gray hair and a tattered cloak. He could see the door to Gribono's upstairs room from his corner table. No one came to visit. Klew asked the waiter if the room was available to rent the following night. When the waiter said yes, Klew knew Gribono was stopping only for a night.

Klew noted that three other men at a table nearby seemed to be monitoring Gribono's door as well. They looked like trouble. The biggest one laughed and fiddled for a moment as if he had imaginary rings on his fingers. The same two fingers that Gribono wore his red stone and serpent rings.

When it grew late, Klew left the tavern for the road to Thesson. He camped on a hill beside the Royal Highway where he had a good view of Tepu, figuring Gribono would ride out of town at first light toward Thesson. If not, Klew would ride into town to see why Gribono was staying on.

In the moonlight Klew saw three riders leaving town. They rode only a short way up the Royal Highway before they turned off the road and into the hills toward him. They stopped on a hidden overlook not far below Klew's camp. Their horses nickered at the smell of Veeda and Zill. But Utuno had trained the daya horses to keep quiet while camping, and Klew was relieved that they did not respond.

Klew grabbed his sword and snuck down the hill to investigate. 'Twas the three men from the tavern. They were talking about Gribono.

"Anyone with expensive rings on his fingers will have a fat coin purse as well," the big one predicted. "When he leaves town tomorrow, we will follow behind. He will probably camp at the first caravansary on the Royal Highway. That is when we'll kill him. Tomorrow will be his last night."

The other two sniggered in agreement. "His last night."

Klew left them to get some sleep. He was not sure if the three could successfully ambush Gribono. He guessed the small whiny one would be worthless in the fight. The middle one might be of some assistance as long as the fighting was going his way, but more likely quick to run if things went sideways. Only the big guy looked like he might have some real fight in him.

Klew had a feeling that the rings on Gribono's fingers had lulled the robbers into thinking he was a soft noble. But Klew had seen the results of his expertise in killing Noot. Gribono could take care of himself in a fight. Klew decided to just follow behind the robbers and see what happened.

The next morning at first light, Gribono rode out of Tepu on the Royal Highway to Thesson. Klew watched the robbers on the hill below. They were slowly breaking camp and making excessive noise. Klew had already done his devotions, eaten, and packed everything on the horses. When the robbers finally rode out, he trailed behind them.

Klew knew that Gribono would be traveling quickly, but the robbers did not. They hung back to make sure they were not too close, and soon found that Gribono was out of sight when they came to a rise with a longer view. Klew was nearby behind a small clay butte and could hear the panicked tone of their voices as they realized their quarry was slipping away. They had to ride hard for over an hour to gain sight of him again.

Now the robbers followed erratically, nervous about being left behind, constantly pushing their horses, then slowing down. The effect on their horses was magnified by the rising temperature and Gribono's fast pace. Klew was glad he trailed the extra horse.

The robbers stopped for water at the Royal Highway caravan site for wagons. Klew knew that Gribono would get water and keep moving until the heat, which was still a good three hours away. The robbers wasted time ineffectually scouting the area trying to spot where Gribono was camped. Once they finally realized that he was not there, they had to push their horses under the growing fierceness of the sun to catch up.

Gribono stopped for the heat at a secondary caravan post for travelers riding faster between Tepu and Thessal. Built into the shade of a cliff was a row of rooms and conditions made with dry-stacked rock in pleasing and ornate patterns. Gribono's horse was tied in front of one of the smaller rooms. Two other rooms were also occupied. The robbers took a larger room to put their horses inside. Klew arrived last and took another chamber beside the robbers, who were exhausted from their efforts and did not see him.

As the heat was ending, Gribono resumed riding. This time the robbers were better prepared to follow. They realized now that Gribono was not a pampered noble but was on some urgent mission and guessed that he might be riding long into the night in the moonlight. They trailed him with more finesse, as if they knew this section of the road much better, and were careful whenever they might be seen if Gribono was looking back.

As a colorful sunset faded, a bright orange moon, just three days from being full, hung above the eastern sky, growing ever brighter and casting the desert landscape in a soft and marvelous glow. The temperature at last cooling down.

Klew started to wonder if the robbers might be more competent than he initially thought. They were able to get up close behind Gribono two or three times in the moonlight without alerting him to their presence. Gribono did not stop until early morning, when the moon was setting a few hours before dawn and the night was growing dark.

Gribono was exhausted. He was preoccupied with his thoughts and schemes and never considered that he might be followed. He rarely looked back. He picked a place to camp on a flat spot with a cool wind, without any thought of an ambush. He was sleeping next to a series of small, eroded gullies where the robbers could crawl up close on their stomachs. The direction of the wind kept the horses from smelling each other so none of them nickered and gave warning.

Klew left his horses and followed behind. When he could dimly see the layout of Gribono's campsite, and the robbers clear advantage, he began to fret. What if they did manage to kill Gribono? Klew would never find out to whom Gribono was reporting. Or the reasons.

Klew could not take that risk. He had sent messages to King Eyrico outlining Gribono's spying and possible treasonous intent against the King of Dayrstad himself. The King had ordered Klew to learn more about what might be happening. Now that mission was in serious jeopardy. He needed to think of something quick.

Klew snuck in closer and watched as the big one gave hand signals to the others. 'Twas a simple and lethal strategy. The smallest one would crawl up the shallowest gully toward Gribono's feet. Another eroded channel would bring the second henchman in close from the other direction.

The deepest trench would allow the leader to crawl up near Gribono's head.

Klew was behind a small butte. He watched the two accomplices shimmy on their stomachs to get into position. He had to make a decision fast. His first thought was to sneak up behind the leader, hit him hard on the head, and knock him out.

But, there was a small chance that one blow might not instantly render the man unconscious. He might cry out or groan. If Klew were discovered, that would ruin everything. Or, the robber could wake up from the blow before dawn with the same bad results and alert Gribono that someone else was following him.

Even if the brute did not wake until later, there was a possibility that he would seek revenge against whoever had hit him. What was to stop the villains from picking up their trail and trying another ambush? Klew could not track Gribono in secret if he had to worry about enraged bandits seeking revenge and attacking from behind.

There was also another consideration. Who might the bandits try to kill next? Did Klew have a responsibility to help protect any future victims?

If Klew was home in Dayrstad, he would arrest the robbers and have them brought to trial. He had no doubt they would be found guilty and hanged. But there was no court here, nor judge, nor executioner. If justice was to be served, 'twas up to Klew.

Should he be lenient and risk his task in following Gribono if things went wrong? Or should he be judge and executioner against a known killer and thief, and make sure that his mission for King Eyrico was a success?

Klew hardened his resolve. He was a soldier of Dayrstad and would not shirk his duty. He rapidly snuck forward in the darkness while pulling out his knife. When the outlaw leader dropped to crawl on his hands and knees, Klew darted from behind and sliced his neck, windpipe and vocal cords. The brute collapsed silently, hidden in the ravine.

Klew knew the two other robbers would not attack without their leader. They soon realized something was wrong and crawled back to find their leader dead. They made a quiet and hasty retreat. Klew let them go. There had been enough killing that night.

Gribono was still sleeping, oblivious to it all.

Klew sat watching in the darkness. He could not sleep. He was consumed with thoughts about what he had done. Klew had been raised at the Ambrit Military Academy, been a sergeant in the Heart Legion, and a trusted castle guard to a Barbarian King, but in all his years of service he had never killed anyone. Sure, he had been in fights, and stabbed and wounded offenders and brigands, but only to disarm them and throw them in jail. He had never deliberately ended someone's life.

And he had done it to defend Gribono, the man who had killed Noot. The thought made him sick. Had he done the right thing? None of it made sense.

GRIBONO'S REPORT

G ribono felt pleased with himself as he put on his old Hammer Legion uniform and changed to a Legion horse at Vadgan outpost, the eastern most checkpoint of the Hammer Legion in the mountains of Vanttan.. He was told that Captain Targono was with an engineering company north of Vrak Pass. It took a day to reach their camp in a narrow canyon.

Gribono could not imagine why the Captain would build a bridge in such a remote place. He could see the strange structure only from a distance, looking up at an odd angle to view the long, thin struts. It looked improbable and fragile.

Captain Targono did not return to camp until evening.

"The Fire is growing in the Heart Legion," Gribono reported. "Sergeant Etna Nate has definite confirmation that Captain Wirvimo is a follower of the Fire. I think Shamano believes so as well." The shaman had asked Gribono to spy on Captain Wirvimo. "On a number of occasions, Captain Wirvimo has given orders to ensure Fire gatherings were not disturbed."

"Interesting," Captain Targono said with faked sincerity. He had heard similar reports from others, but he did not believe it. He did not trust Captain Wirvimo. However, he kept such thoughts to himself. He nodded for Gribono to continue.

"Bokono, the rebel leader from Birjj was murdered," Gribono said. "Some say he was poisoned."

"Indeed?" Captain Targono said with mock surprise. His spies in Sikes had already told him. "Any idea who might have done it?"

"Most say the Queen of Birjj," Gribono answered. "But I have heard others say Duke Eddarko from the Siren in Dayrstad."

"The Duke!" the Captain replied with genuine interest. He had not considered that possibility. Lartso, his spy on the Duke, was late in reporting back to him. He shared none of that. When Gribono finished his account, Captain Targono pulled out a special bottle of viruna from the King of Sikes that Lartso had acquired through the Duke.

"This is from King Gorijo's personal distillery," the Captain said as he filled two small metal cups. They toasted to Gribono's news.

"Now it grows increasingly important to keep an eye on everybody and everything," Captain Targono told his spy. "You are still living at the same apartment?" He read from his notes the street location.

"Yes," Gribono said. "'Tis comfortable and well located."

"Good," Captain Targono said cryptically. "Do not move anywhere." He opened a satchel with two coin purses and gave the fat one to Gribono. "Keep up your good work."

RETURN TO
THE SIREN

The journey from Jchow Oasis to the Barrier Mountains passed slowly for Epoh. The days seemed to last forever. The camels plodded along at a slower pace than the grubbers had marched to the dragon. Even weighted with treasure, Epoh could have kept up with the beasts. After the initial novelty of riding a camel grew old, Epoh preferred to spend most of his time walking. It felt better to stretch his legs and hum Praises.

By the time they reached Jou Oasis, their halfway point, the moon had faded and they were able to travel only during the day. The temperature was hot, but nothing like Epoh had experienced with the grubbers, traveling at a much faster pace and carrying all their water and meager food rations.

Now Epoh feasted constantly on dates, figs, dried fruits, and nuts. Each afternoon during the heat, the cook baked corn bread in a sun oven, which they ate with honey and camel milk tea. Most mornings Epoh enjoyed one or two eggs from the chickens. They killed the goat, which gave them fresh meat for a few days, and dried meat for the remainder of their journey.

A week later they began to see the hulking mass of the Barrier Mountains coming into view through the dust. Epoh thought about how the first Hool must have felt crossing the

Endless Waste to see such a huge imposing wall rise up from the horizon. Two days later they began to see the details of possible canyons. Another two days and he got his first glimpse of the Siren. Long before Valhal Oasis came into view, they could see the shiny roofs of the castle built by the Ambri as a beacon and a trap to lure enemies and invaders.

Epoh remembered the steep hidden trail he had ridden from the Barrier Mountains down into the Siren on his 100th moon. And riding with his uncle to camp in the desert. It felt like two lifetimes ago. What Epoh had remembered as a faint desert track now appeared like a highway to his nuanced eye. As they drew closer, the Siren became especially stunning and beautiful. He had hoped and prayed for this moment for such a long time! He gave thanks for it now coming true.

They began to see the lush green valley of the Bait beneath the Siren, and then emerging from the haze at the base of the mountains, the small, dusty village of Valhal. The small oasis was mostly narrow rows of black stone fences and covered gardens among a scattered collection of hovels. The only sizable building was the crumbling Prospector Inn beside some dilapidated stables and corrals for mules and camels.

No matter how Epoh tried to cajole Imir and the cook to enter Valhal, they chose instead to camp beside an old well in an area away from the oasis near the tents of some other desert nomads. Epoh had tried to explain to his companions that although the Ambri were sworn enemies of the Hool, they accepted the presence of salt traders, miners, and even occasional grubbers at the oasis. "Just do not call yourself Hool," he told them. "You are nomads."

Epoh rode by himself on one of the camels into Valhal. At the stables he bought all the supplies Imir would need for the return trip to Jchow Oasis, and also a Daya horse and saddle for himself. With the heat coming on, he took a room at the Prospector Inn, ate a simple meal of familiar and wonderful Dayrstad food, then did his practice. His mind would not be still from all his excitement so he sang Hallelujahs quietly to himself. Nor was he able to nap afterward. He could only think of getting home.

When the burn of the sun began to fade, Epoh returned to the stables to load up the camel, then trailed his horse behind as he rode back out to the nomad camp. He paid the stunned Imir and the cook their full wages to return to Jchow without him, along with a bonus and all the supplies on the camel. Then he mounted his horse and rode like the wind up through the gorgeous terraced fields of the Bait to arrive at the Siren just before dark.

At the Siren stables, a boy took his horse to feed and groom without question while Epoh carried his few but heavy bags and his sword to the castle. A guard at the door noticed his foreign clothes and snapped to attention.

"I have come to see my uncle, Duke Eddarko," Epoh told him.

The guard looked confused.

"Just escort me to him and I will explain everything."

There was little moon so the Duke was inside his banquet hall. As Epoh approached the room grew quiet. He set down his bags and sword and drew closer. The Duke did not recognize him and was eyeing the foreign style and weave of his clothes. A few of the guards were also taking notice.

"I greet you at last Duke Eddarko!" he said with emotion, "I am your nephew, Crown Prince Epohco."

The Duke's face turned white. "Are you a ghost?" He shrank back as the soldiers drew their swords.

"I am as alive as you are. I was swept in an underground river to the Maze and rescued by nuns. Then I traveled with grubbers across the Sea of Dunes to Jchow Oasis." When he dreamt of this moment, he imagined his uncle jumping up to embrace him with a hug.

Instead Duke Eddarko sat shocked and nervous, uncertain what to believe. "You are alive?" he asked again with bewilderment. He was plotting the overthrow of King Eyrico. The last thing he wanted was the reappearance of the first

Crown Prince.

"Twice I thought I had drowned," Epoh said. "The first time I woke inside a deep cave under the mountains. The second time I was found floating in a sacred pool by the nuns who nursed me back to health."

The Duke looked at him like he had come back to life through some sorcery or witchcraft. "You speak Hool?" he asked with distaste.

"The nuns and grubbers spoke Ambri," Epoh said, trying to mitigate his uncle's concerns. "But I did learn some Hool," he added unapologetically. "How else was I to find my way home?"

TRAVELING CLOAKS

When Singer and his four followers left the red agave farms of the King of Sikes, Manser Shelodo outfitted them with old traveling cloaks and sun capes, pots and pans, basic camping supplies and food.

They avoided the capitol and went down the Sikes River Valley toward Jintiga Bridge and Karvor. They sang as they walked, which created surprised smiles and gestures of approval on those they met coming up the canyon.

It took them six days of walking to reach Jintiga Bridge. They crossed and turned east to bypass Karvor and go up into the mountains on the old road to Birjj. They had heard about an old kiva there.

When they drew near, they sent Grodoro, the former would-be assassin, ahead to check for any of Bokono's supporters. He came back shaking his head.

"I did not get to the kiva, only to the tavern at Perich. Everyone was in an uproar about a Womb spy that sliced the leg out from under a local Fire agitator named Otovo. A tween girl. She went in the kiva. They are stirred up like hornets. And they all have swords. They call themselves the burners."

Singer shook his head. This was not the place for them. Without a word he turned around and resumed singing as they headed back toward Karvor, taking the trail to Old Town. They were mesmerized by the brightly painted buildings and the spectacular views.

"I never imagined anything so big!" Swindovo marveled. "And so colorful!"

They kept walking through town toward the Painted Hills.

THE PAINTED HILLS

The Painted Hills near Karvor were a kaleidoscope of brightly colored clay mounds, buttes, and eroded valleys with hardly a plant or tree to be seen. The colorful clay mined from the barren, inhospitable landscape was used to make the famous pottery and artwork for which Karvor was known.

Some colors were plentiful and easy to find, but others were very rare and highly prized. The Potters Guild owned the best mines and pits. Other valuable family and individual claims were scattered throughout the arid countryside. There were also remote areas where miners could still lay claim to their own workings. Those regions were hard to reach with no wagon access; the clay soil had to be carried out on foot. In one such isolated region at an intersection of trails along a drop-off into a narrow, twisting gulley was the Dusted Man tavern.

Early one evening Tyme was out riding Cadie through the Painted Hills. The daya horse excelled at tight winding corners and had raced up a narrow, twisting gulley to arrive breathing heavily at the colorful Dusted Man. Tyme jumped off to stretch her legs. A man whose body and clothing was covered with yellow powder came around a far corner with a heavy backboard and tumpline. He eased his load backwards onto a waist high bench lined with similar yellow loads and went through a yellow door at the other end of the tavern. The middle door was red, matching an outside bench with red backboards of clay. A closer door and bench were bluish green. Intrigued, Tyme went inside.

The tables were colored by the dust of the workers who sat according to the color of their mine and not mixing with others. Most of the patrons were covered with bright yellow dust and took up the middle and the far end of the room. Set apart from the yellow tables, and each other, were tables for red and orange workers in one corner, and tables for two shades of green and one of blue in the other.

In the aisle in front of Tyme, a young woman in dark red brushed past a man in yellow.

"You got your red on me!" the man shrieked and held out his arm to display a broad swatch of her color across his sleeve.

"I am sorry," the woman appeared startled out of some other thought.

"Red is the worst!" he spat. "You know how long it will take to get this off?"

The woman looked at him helplessly, saying nothing.

"You must be stupid to be working here," the yellow man sneered accusingly. Women had a monopoly on all the good jobs. Jobs they claimed he was not qualified to do. Now women were taking jobs even here. Women did not belong in the Dusted Man.

"Just because I am working the clay hills does not mean I am stupid," she answered. She was so tired of men thinking her dumb. "I have a reason for being here." My family disowned me, she wanted to tell him but didn't. She did not have any money. Or any friends.

"You are taking jobs from men," he hissed threateningly.

"She said she was sorry," Tyme repeated apologetically and stepped forward to make sure he was not going to strike the woman. "Give her a break."

The yellow man sneered at Tyme. "Noble born women like you get all the breaks, horse girl!" He said the name in a derogatory tone, as if riding a horse affirmed that she was spoiled and pampered.

Rather than make her mad, the name gave Tyme a grin. Horse girl. 'Twas better than being called noble born. "Horse girl I am," she agreed.

Her lightheartedness only made him angrier. He followed her outside. "A princess on her horse, a fine animal indeed," he said with vitriol. "That animal is worth more than I will make in my life. You pay more to feed and board your horse than what us Canaries have for living," he scolded her.

"What do you want from me?" Tyme asked earnestly.

"I want your respect!" he thundered and walked over to the yellow shelf of backboards. He gathered pinches of yellow dust from the ledge, and dabbed and smudged the yellow over the red mark on his sleeve. After fussing a while, he slipped the tumpline over his head, hoisted his backboard with sacks of yellow clay, and set off down a gulley trail too steep and narrow for a daya horse.

Tyme took another path. Making her way toward the outskirts of town, she joined an empty wagon track and let Cadie run one last time along a curvy ridge of cliff bluffs. Rounding a corner she saw a clay wagon that had been driven slightly off the inside of the track up against the bluff. The driver appeared to just be getting his hands back onto the reins, while a big worker was punching and fighting with another smaller worker.

Tyme pulled up just behind the wagon. "Are you alright?" She asked.

The driver's eyes bulged when he turned to see her. He looked rattled.

"No problem, ser!" he said unconvincingly. "Just having a bit of personal argument." The big guy hit the other a final time, knocking him into the back of the wagon onto the load of clay sacks.

Tyme had just seen how the workers abhorred mixing the colors of the clay. She knew no worker would so risk damaging the bags. Something was not right.

The driver waved for Tyme to pass. "Go ahead. We will just

roll along behind." He glanced nervously down into an eroded gulley. Tyme looked down to the same spot. Was that a body?

"What is going on?" Tyme asked with suspicion.

"Lady," the big man gave her a menacing look, "just ride on by and don't get involved with something you do not understand."

"I understand your actions appear less than honorable," Tyme told him, "Shall we fetch the man down in the gulley to see what he has to say?"

When they gave no reply, she knew the truth of it. "I am not going to let you steal this wagon," she told them, and rode Cadie in front of their horses to block the way.

"What in the seven hells!" the big man swore in exasperation. He pulled a long staff from the back of the wagon and jumped to the ground as Tyme dismounted and took out her sword. The man came at her confidently assuming the reach of his staff would keep her sword away from him. He swung and jabbed aggressively in her direction. But she was quick and surprisingly hard to hit.

Klew had taught Tyme how to fight against staffs, poles, and spears. Compared to sparring against Klew, the man before her was nothing but a clumsy brute. She danced around enticingly close, letting him swing and flail until one of his forceful efforts tipped him slightly off balance. Then she darted forward with one quick flick of her sword and sliced deeply across the muscle of his right arm rendering it useless.

"Blood and guts!" he screamed as he dropped the pole. He looked at her with hatred then quickly turned to scramble up the hillside of clay and loose rock. The driver jumped from the wagon to join him scampering up the steep bank to disappear over the top of the butte.

Tyme sheathed her sword and went down the gulley to help the shaken man lying below get back up on the road as the younger man who had been beaten climbed out from the back of the wagon.

"You should have seen her fight!" he whispered to his

companion. "I never saw anyone so fast!"

They explained how the robbers had surprised them on a rock ledge, as they came around the corner, and used the pole to knock the driver off the wagon and down into the gulley. They jumped onto the wagon, one grabbing the reins while the other attacked the young man. Tyme had arrived so suddenly, the robbers had not seen her approach.

"I would have liked to see you cut that brute," the driver grimaced as he gently probed his broken ribs. He eyed her shrewdly. "You come out here riding often?"

"Often enough," she smiled and patted her horse. "Cadie and I love riding through the Painted Hills."

"Ever ride past the Dusted Man?" he asked.

"I stopped there just today," Tyme told him.

"Next time you stop, tell Dari Riad that you saved her pigment wagon," he advised. "I reckon she will want to buy you a drink."

KNIFE HER IN
THE BACK

Rocozo listened in growing outrage as he heard the report.

"Twas a tween girl on a horse," Cutono told him. The big man's arm hung useless in a bloodied sling. They had been stealing a wagon of clay pigment when the girl had suddenly come upon them and foiled their plans.

"Blood and guts!" Cutono swore. "I tried to hit her and crack her skull with a pole. Suddenly she darts straight at me and slices my arm worthless!" He still could not believe how fast she was. Like a blink.

Rocozo knew from the description that 'twas the same tween girl who had beaten him at the Blue Moon with the Jawbone Ridge gang. "Her name is Tyme," he said vehemently, stunned that she was causing him still more problems. "'Tis time that *we* deal with *her*."

Cutono looked at his gang leader skeptically. "With your leg and my arm?" he snorted. Rocozo still limped with a cane.

"We are not going to fight her!" Rocozo sneered. "At least not fairly. We are going to trap and ambush her!" He ground his remaining teeth. "Then we will all knife her in the back."

RETURN TO DAYR CASTLE

After his unsettling audience with Duke Eddarko, Epoh went to bathe and clean up. His uncle insisted he change into "proper Dayrstad clothes." When he returned to the hall, a large table had been set with food and drink. The Duke greeted and hugged him stiffly. His smile lacked all warmth. Epoh felt hesitant to tell Eddarko about the grubbers or the treasure, and oddly, the Duke did not ask. All of his questions concerned the Crown Prince's survival of the underground river and pools.

Epoh excused himself as soon as he could. He wanted some quiet time to pray alone at the Womb. Inside the temple he was surprised to see part of the screened wall between the refuge and the sanctuary had been taken out. There was a large shrine to the Fire with the thick, burned red wax of many votive candles and offerings. Epoh kneeled in a corner and did his own prayers of thankfulness for his return.

He slept fitfully and woke early the next morning. The Duke insisted on sending three soldiers to accompany him back to Dayr Castle. Epoh had earlier considered doing the ride alone in just two days. But after his strange welcome at the Siren, he now felt a slight foreboding about his return to the castle. Mayhaps it would be better to go slower and take the extra day, and send one of the guards ahead with news of his return. He went to the Womb to do his practice, said goodbye to his uncle, and left the Siren with the guards, hoping their company would help him ease back into the role of being Crown Prince.

Epoh was fine as he walked his horse up through the caves and cracks of the Scout trail leaving the Siren. But when the soldiers were able to mount, Epoh found himself terrified and shaking inside with fear. The last time he rode on a narrow trail, a rock viper had bitten and killed Merrylegs. He had been thrown into the river and swept into the Endless Waste!

He saw the soldiers watching him as he stiffly swung up into the saddle. He had to force himself to keep from closing his eyes. The trail had been exhilarating on his first trip to the Siren. Now 'twas dizzying and frightful.

He thought of Tyme riding Spike in the high mountains and tried to channel her fearlessness. But instead doubts began to fill his mind. What if she had changed? What if she had other suitors?

That afternoon during the heat, which seemed like nothing to Epoh as the mountain temperatures were much cooler than the low desert, they relaxed in comfort in a trailside condition. At first the soldiers seemed wary and afraid of talking with him, but as he made an effort to chat, he realized they were just shy and intimidated. He felt strange being called Epohco again. They asked mostly about Jchow Oasis and were amazed at his descriptions of the legendary town. He asked for news of the castle.

"Crown Prince Dracoro had a tournament," the younger guard began to say, and then realized his mistake. "I mean, prince Dracoro," he corrected himself. Now that Epohco was back and alive he was the Crown Prince.

"That is okay," Epoh excused him. The foreboding returned. "A tournament you say?" As Crown Prince, Epohco would never have considered hosting a fighting championship. He would have been more inclined to invite a gathering of scholars. He listened with growing unease about the success of the festival and the obvious popularity of Prince Dracoro with the soldiers and military offisers.

The next day the riding was more relaxed, not so close to cliffs and more enjoyable winding through the cactus-filled mountains and valleys of Dayrstad. After the stark barrenness of the Endless Waste, Dayrstad appeared bursting with growth and life. He never remembered home being so green.

The last day Epoh was filled with anxiousness. At last he came out into Dayr Valley and could see the castle. Only then did he urge his horse to gallop. Drawing closer he could hear the castle bells ringing. He was glad he had sent a soldier ahead with the news of his return.

With his horse slowing to trot up the switchbacks to the castle, Epoh could see Krugero standing and waving at him from the top of tower one. The old guard, his first Hand as a boy, whooped and shouted in greeting. Anda Dana, the big, black, tattooed guard, saluted him as he passed through castle gate. "Praise Divine!" she said in awe. The two other guards cheered.

A small, shocked, and confused crowd had gathered in the commons and also stood outside of the Grinding Stone tavern to greet him and nervously wave as he rode past and up the switchback hill of the Grand Way. Small bands of people stood beside the road. More than a few gave him apprehensive looks. He did not appear at all like the young man who had left Dayr Castle so long ago. He planned to stop at the stables to greet Tyme, but as he approached he saw she was not standing beside Utuno and the other cheering workers. He guessed she was in the mountains with Tao Tau. He continued to ride up into the keep, to the courtyard where he had begun his ill-fated ride of the Ambri Scout trail. Like before, a crowd was gathered with the King and Queen, and his brother and sister.

With stunned expressions they welcomed him home.

THE DUSTED MAN

The next chance Tyme got she rode Cadie back into the Painted Hills. The multi-colored clay mounds, valleys, and buttes offered spectacular riding. Though desolate and barren of plants, the landscape felt alive from the vivid hues and tints woven like patchwork across hillsides, or splashed and intermixed in the soil and rock of steep valleys and arroyos.

Again Tyme raced Cadie up the narrow, twisting gulley that led to the Dusted Man tavern. When Tyme dismounted and tied her horse, three yellow men went through the door on the far end. She entered the closest door and headed for a discolored section of the bar where it looked safe to sit. The bartender had shiny ebony skin. Her teeth were a dazzling white, her hair frizzy and black. She had numerous smears of color on her arms, a dash of yellow on her neck, smudges on her cheek.

"You must be the defender of my pigment wagon," the bartender said with a big smile. "I am Dari Riad." The wagon driver had relayed Tyme's description along with the story of the ambush.

Tyme gestured the womb and introduced herself.

Dari Riad returned the gesture. "Would you like a drink?" she asked. "'Tis on the house."

"Watered wine if you have it," Tyme answered.

"I only have pulque," the owner of the Dusted Man laughed.

"Poor man's liquor, but I will water that." They talked about the attacks and robberies that had been occurring with pigment wagons being stolen.

"The thieves must be taking the loads to somewhere other than the normal collecting points," Dari Riad shook her head. "The appraisers and guild collectors all know who regularly sells those colors. They would remember and know if a different wagon driver came in with those loads."

"You haul the clay into Karvor to sell," Tyme mused. "Why don't the workers just sell their loads at the collection point down the valley at Vermillion Cliffs?"

"The price is lower," Dari Riad answered. "The Guild charges the workers dearly for hauling the loads to town."

"So a few enterprising business women from the Painted Hills have bought wagons and started hauling loads to Karvor," Tyme nodded approvingly. She had also done a little investigating.

"I can give the workers a better price and still make a tidy profit," the tall, thin, black woman replied. "If I don't get robbed." She took a few minutes to serve some other drinks. A small, red lizard skittered across the wall, stopping frequently to do a series of rapid pushups on its front legs.

"Any of the Guild wagons getting robbed?" Tyme asked when she returned. "Or any of the wagons from the larger mines?"

"No. Not a one that I have heard."

"Do you think the independent wagon owners are being targeted specifically?"

"Seems that way, doesn't it." Dari Raid's bright smile disappeared.

"Who runs the outpost collection points and the wagon shipments?" Tyme asked.

"The Potters Guild owns everything," Dari Raid told her. "Whoever is profiting from the current system does not want any competition."

"Well, I don't know anything about the Potters Guild, but I

will keep my ears out." Tyme drank the last swallow of pulque. "When I was here the other day," she changed the subject, "I got a scolding by a bright yellow worker. An older man with a sharp nose and sharper tongue."

"Most likely Ozono," Dari Raid guessed. "His name fits him." Boys from the Milk with a third o in their name were said to be especially aggressive. A name starting with O was the worst. "He is the leader of the Canaries. You do not want to cross him."

"He does not seem to care much for women," Tyme observed.

"No, he does not," Dari Raid shook her head sadly. "I don't think that man has ever known any tenderness in his life. He is so angry he would not recognize love if she appeared naked before him and kissed him on the lips!"

Tyme could not help but smile at the thought.

"Still," Dari Raid continued, "He is the one who convinced the other workers to use my wagon and try to sell their clay in town."

"Mayhaps if we meet again we can get off on a better foot," Tyme stood to leave.

"Hopefully, when he hears you saved our wagon," Dari Raid speculated, "that will calm his attitude toward you."

"I have enjoyed our drink together," Tyme told her. "I will keep a watch out for your wagons whenever I am riding in the Painted Hills. I will also keep an ear out for any word about who controls the wagons owned by the Potters Guild."

Dari Raid reached across the bar and shook Tyme's hand Barbarian style. "Come back anytime. You drink for free at the Dusted Man."

OZONO

Word spread quickly through the Painted Hills. A fierce young ser warrior on a fine horse had stopped an attack on a clay wagon, sword cut and disarmed a large brute of a man with a long staff, and driven the robbers off. 'Twas said she had vowed to patrol the Painted Hills to insure the attacks did not happen again.

When Ozono heard a group of young Canaries talking about the news, he thought back to the young woman on horseback he had met at the Dusted Man. She fit the description of the ser. A strong, formidable older tween with dark olive skin, black hair and golden-green eyes on a prize horse.

He had been so enraged by the witless red woman who smeared him, he had not looked closely at the ser who defended her. He had been sidetracked by the breeding of her horse and not truly taken stock of the girl who rode the horse. He had called her a princess.

What do you want from me? she had asked, as if she might actually care.

The whole thing made Ozono uncomfortable and agitated. He did not like being rescued and beholden to a young woman.

KLEW'S DECISION

After three weeks of tracking and following Gribono through the mountains, Klew followed the spy back to Karvor. Klew was now sitting on the apartment patio. A shimmering and bloody red sun was sinking into a sunset of crimson haze on the far horizon. From the way Klew acted, Tyme and Jyg could tell that something unsettling had happened.

"I thought Gribono would go to Ambrit," he reported. "Instead he went up the Iridi Valley to Tepu." Klew told of seeing three roguish characters watching Gribono's room at a men's tavern, and how the three had camped near him.

"I snuck down and overheard their plans to rob and kill Gribono at his next campsite," he continued. "They did not seem organized or formidable. I figured Gribono could take care of himself. I trailed behind as they followed him up the Royal Highway. They seemed amateurs at first, but after the heat and through the night, instead of dropping off, they grew more stealthful. I started thinking they might be dangerous after all."

"You helped him," Tyme guessed, sensing Klew's discomfort. "You helped Gribono."

"He camped in a spot where they could easily crawl up some shallow ravines unseen and ambush him," Klew shook his head. "When I saw his vulnerability, I knew I had to make a decision."

"If they killed him," Jyg said, "we would never find out who he was reporting to."

"I kept hoping Gribono would realize what was happening and scare them off on his own. When he did not, I felt I had to act," Klew said remorsefully. "When the robbers split up to attack, I snuck in and killed their leader."

"What did you do?" Jyg asked.

"I slit his throat," Klew replied.

"Like Gribono slit Noot's?" Tyme asked.

"Yes. Except he was a highway bandit about to commit murder," Klew replied. "Not an innocent boy."

"You had to do it," Jyg was quick to justify. "You had no choice."

"That is what I tell myself," Klew said. "But that does not make me feel any better. I have never killed anyone before." Klew shook his head with disbelief. "And I did it to save Gribono, a man who I would prefer dead."

The sun had set and the sky was now dark. A cold breeze came down off the mountains. No one said anything as Klew started a firepot.

"Was it worth it?" Jyg asked at last. "Did you find out about his superiors?"

"Gribono continued traveling, unaware of what happened," Klew said. "A few days later, south of Thesson, he left the Royal Highway and headed southwest on an old mining trail into Vanttan. I followed him to Vadgan outpost, which is the back door to Vrak Pass and Vargo Garrison. He changed to an army horse and put on a uniform. Gribono is reporting to someone in the Hammer Legion."

"What a mess," Tyme riled. "Plots of treason in both the Heart and the Hammer Legions."

"Treasonous!" Bones agreed dramatically in Klew's voice.

"Gribono returned five days later," Klew reported. "Which means he didn't have enough time to travel to the garrison headquarters. Only enough time to reach the barracks at Vrak Pass or the mine itself."

"Do you have a guess who he might be meeting?" Tyme asked.

"Because of the timing, there are two likely possibilities," Klew answered. "Captain Nard Rand is in charge of guarding the mines. They say she spends more time making sure the workers are not stealing ore from the mine, than she does guarding against rebel attacks. However," Klew added, "she does have access to great wealth. 'Tis always better to have a full purse when starting a coup. Troops need to be paid, fed, and supplied. She is a strong possibility."

"Captain Targono guards the supply lines and protects the shipments of gold and silver from bandits and Vanttan rebels. They say his aggressive targeting of rebels has stopped all losses from robbers on the route from the mine to the garrison camp." Klew raised his eyebrows. "'Tis said he's obsessed with chasing rebels and rarely spends time in his office."

"A man of action," Tyme observed.

"Who also has access to great wealth if he's guarding the supply lines," Jyg added.

"Treasonous!" Bones exclaimed again.

"And he is a man," Klew said pointedly. "Men are more aggressive and willing to take risks in a fight. I think he is the one." Klew added a few more sticks to the firepot. The dried branches of mesquite gave off a pleasant smell as they burned.

"There is one other thing," Klew told them. "My best friend at the Military Academy was named Targono. 'Tis a common name. The last I heard from him he had been unfairly court marshaled and demoted to private in the Hammer Legion. Rising from a private to a Captain is a tall order." Klew shook his head. "That would be unthinkable for a man in the Heart Legion."

"But in the Hammer, it might be possible to rise through the ranks to become Captain, especially in guarding the supply lines. 'Tis the hardest job of all. A job most offisers don't want." Klew gave a knowing look. "My friend Targono was one of those rare cadets who had the skills and the drive to become such a man."

HIS TRUTH

Epohco dismounted his horse and stood in the courtyard in front of his father, King Eyrico, who held him stiffly at arms length to get a good look at his face. For a few tense moments no one spoke or moved until finally King Eyrico pulled him close in a warm embrace.

"My son, Crown Prince Epohco, has returned!" King Eyrico announced as Epohco hugged his crying mother, Queen Lina Lara. His brother, Prince Dracoro, was nearly as tall as he was and hugged him apprehensively. His little sister, Princess Lona Lina, looked and acted surprisingly grown up.

"We will have a gathering of the small court to rejoice and hear of your story," King Eyrico proclaimed. "This evening we shall have a grand welcoming banquet with food, drink, and song!"

"My King," Epohco said, "I beg you. Let me first go to the Womb to say prayers of thanks for my return. I have long promised Divine to do so should I ever find my way home."

King Eyrico looked surprised. "As you wish," he said without much enthusiasm. "Your family and court will wait upon your oath to Divine."

Epohco hurried across the plaza to the Womb refuge and sat where he could look down without obstruction to the Sanctuary. He gave thanks for his return and prayed for strength to do whatever came next, trying to let go of all his previous expectations.

Epohco strode back to the audience hall and rejoined with his family and the small court. Everyone sat intently watching him. He now realized that parts of his story would not be well received. So he did not plan on saying everything just yet. He told them about falling into the river and how he had thought he had drowned, only to wake in a cave with glowworms that looked like stars. How he had drowned a second time, and been found floating in a sacred pool by nuns who nursed him back to health.

"They spoke Ambri," he said without further explanation. "But some of them could also speak Hool, which I learned in order to find my way back home."

There was an instant murmuring. Epohco was sun baked and blistered and looked like he was Hool as well. But 'twas his truth and he would not deny it.

He omitted the details of Riin Ruel's visit to Ezkia Nunnery, and of the belief by the abbess, and himself, that Tyme was the Bright One, prophesized as Empress to bring back the Ambri Empire. Epohco needed to share with Tyme all the details of the story before he told it to anyone else.

Instead, he told about the grubbers, and going to the Sea of Dunes, and what they found. The audience looked at him with disbelief until he held out his wrist to reveal the heavy metal clock bracelet with the magical little wands that rotated in precise fashion around the dial. He spent the rest of the evening showing it to people. He said nothing of the dragon exploding.

The next morning, Epohco went straight to the stables. Utuno sadly told him the story of Noot's death, of their suspicions about the fancy ring man, and of Tyme, Klew, and Jyg following the murderer all the way to Karvor in Tanis.

Epohco gravely shook his head. Noot was dead! "Why would anyone kill Noot?" he asked in shock. What kind of a man kills an innocent stable boy?

"Klew guessed he might have thought that Noot overheard him talking to someone." Utuno lowered his voice. "They believe Noot's murderer is plotting treason against King Eyrico, and the Czarzina as well. They have been gone over a decade," Utuno continued. "Klew has sent a few reports back."

Epohco was speechless. What could possibly link King Eyrico with Ambrit political intrigue? "So they are still watching the man?" Epohco asked for clarification.

"Trying to learn his motives and find out his leaders," Utuno nodded. He did not know much else.

That afternoon during the heat Epohco had a chance to speak with King Eyrico about the matter. "I gave Klew authority to investigate the stable boy's death," the King confirmed. "And he has found an infestation of snakes."

"You also sent Tyme and Jyg," Epohco said. "Have they given any word about when they might return?"

The Queen, who was sitting nearby, gave the King a look. She remembered the crush and fixation her son had on the girl. Thank goodness she was far away from the castle.

"They vowed not to return until they get to the bottom of this whole sordid business," the King replied.

"So, they are still in Karvor?" Epohco asked.

The King nodded his head.

That night there was another banquet in Crown Prince Epohco's honor where he answered more questions about the Ancient Ones and let people examine his clock bracelet.

Later he sat alone, exhausted in his room, thinking about the one thing he had been contemplating all day, yet hardly spoken about to anyone. Tyme was not here at Dayr Castle! She was in Karvor. He realized the castle held no appeal to him if she was not in it. All the thoughts he had in the desert of returning to Dayr Castle, of being home again, was a yearning to be with Tyme. He did not want to stay here if she was someplace else.

And then it struck him like a thunderbolt. Of course, she would not be here. She was destined for much more than Dayr Castle. She was already following that path without him. If he was going to be included, he had best hurry and catch up!

SCOOP

Scoop sat tucked into a dark, recessed, and shuttered upper window of an alley across from the building where Tyme stayed. He had found the spot the first night he followed her from the Blue Moon to see where she slept. The lookout was perfect, tucked away and hidden with a wide view of the street and door to her room, and the alley as well.

The girl who passed as a boy sat contentedly, comfortable with an abundance of time required for the job of spy, through all hours of the day and night. The passage of time did not bother or overwhelm Scoop, but filled him with a satisfying completeness.

The steady yet imperceptible movement of the moon and stars arcing across the heavens at night was something to be savored and never rushed.

One evening Scoop saw a large shadow, a big man with his head and face covered in scarves, slowly working his way up and down the alley, looking and snooping in each doorway and cubicle, each corner and alcove. The man went back and forth the length of the alleyway before finally disappearing into the night.

Four nights later Scoop saw the same shadowed figure lead a small group into the alley. He motioned where a man and a

315

woman should stand a short way down the center of the alley, then directed two men to hide in the shadows on each side nearby. He placed another figure closer to the front of the alley, then stood lookout at the alley corner to the street.

Scoop slowly eased his slingshot out of his back pocket.

The leader hissed a warning and hobbled briskly to his own hiding place in the shadows nearby. The man and woman in the middle of the alley positioned themselves as if arguing, with the man raising one hand in the air to strike the woman, who posed in a cowering manner.

A few moments later, Tyme walked into view on the sidewalk. The man slapped the woman to her knees.

"Don't hurt me!" the woman whined, shocked at how hard the man had hit her. She fumbled to keep hidden the dagger she was to use on her supposed rescuer.

"'Tis a trap!" Scoop yelled out. "An ambush! Others are hidden in the alley!" He fired his slingshot and scored a direct hit to the temple of the fake mugger who dropped to the ground.

The woman whom the supposed mugger had struck, now shook his body to rouse him. "Get up! Get up!" she shrieked in distress. When he did not respond, she gave Tyme a venomous look and ran off down the alley.

"City guard! City guard!" Bones called loudly from the eve of a roof. She had been alerted by Scoop's cry, and had flown down to investigate. At the sound of her alarm, two large shadows jumped out from the darkness below the raven to run away.

Bones flew across the alley to a closer roof. "Blood and guts!" she swore. Another large shadow broke and ran from the darkness beneath her. Then the last shadow, Rocozo, limped rapidly away down the alley.

"That is all of them!" Scoop reported as he climbed down from a dark corner of the recessed and shuttered window nearby. "There was six." He looked around. "Who yelled for the city guard? And cursed?"

"That was Bones," Tyme replied. "A raven." She reached out

to shake his hand. "Who are you?"

"Scoop," the boy said proudly. "With the Jawbone Ridge gang." He explained why he had been hiding in the alley. "Delgado sent me to watch and guard where you live."

"How long have you been here?" Tyme asked in amazement.

"Since you first joined the gang," Scoop explained cheerfully. He felt honored to be chosen for the job.

"You have been out here watching all those nights since then?" Tyme could hardly believe it.

"Days and nights. Sometimes I follow you around town," he shrugged. "Sometimes I just wait here and watch to see if anyone else follows you. I saw one of them scout out their positions for the ambush a few nights ago."

Tyme bowed to the boy. "I am in your debt," she said. "You are my guardian angel."

Five of the assailants had run off down the ally. One was still lying on the ground.

"I hit him with my slingshot," Scoop explained as they examined the man.

Tyme felt for his pulse like Tao Tau had taught her. "He is dead," she said solemnly.

"I killed him?" Scoop was taken aback.

Tyme showed him the gash on the side of the head where the rock hit.

"Good riddance!" the boy said fiercely, acting tough. But Tyme could see the shock of what he had done revealed in his eyes. "I had to do something," Scoop said with nervous justification. "They were going to kill you!"

FOR YOUR BLESSING

"What do you mean, you are leaving?" Queen Lina Lara cried out in a shocked voice.

Epoh stood before the King and Queen in their private chambers. He could not be Crown Prince Epohco. Now he was trying to explain it all to them. He turned to his mother and sighed unhappily.

"I have no choice," he shook his head. "I must." He hated breaking her heart again.

"You are serious about following these so-called signs and visions of the stable girl?" the King demanded incredulously.

"Yes!" Epoh repeated. "You know as well as I there were dreams and omens about her since she first came to the castle."

"That is only because you babbled on about it," the King hissed. "Not that I, nor anyone else, ever put stock in it."

Epoh sighed. What could he say that would help convince the King? That a Blade in a secret group thought the same thing? Or a group of nuns believed it in the desert? Those arguments would only make his father angrier.

"All I can say is that I have to leave," Epoh painfully continued. "I am afraid I may never come back." His eyes welled with tears. "I beg for your blessing that I may leave with your good graces." He bowed his head.

"You refuse your duty as Crown Prince?" King Eyrico was scandalized. "The oath of your own family?"

"The family oath will survive without me," Epoh shook his

head regrettably. "Dracoro has already proven his abilities as Crown Prince."

"Give your heritage to Dracoro and you will never get it back!" the King thundered. "Never!"

"I have no choice," Epohco apologized.

"There is *always* choice!" the King roared. "You have just made it now!"

"When do you leave?" the Queen asked in bewilderment. "There was to be another banquet tonight!"

"I will attend," Epoh offered meagerly, "But I must leave tomorrow at first light. I feel my return has only brought you pain. I am so sorry. I never imagined this."

"Then tonight I will announce for the second time," the King vowed, "That Crown Prince *Dracoro* will follow me to become King of Dayrstad. And I will declare my eldest son, Prince Epohco, as dead to us." He gave Epoh an angry look. "But this time, *no mourning bells* will be rung."

That day a lone rider approached Dayr Castle on a shiny silver-gray horse. Riin Ruel wore a sun cape and had two curved swords. She learned from the guard at castle gate there was to be a big celebration that night.

"Crown Prince Epohco has returned," the big black tattooed woman told her. "He was swept into an underground river that drained into the Maze." She loosely held her hands together in the sign of the womb. "Then rescued and saved by nuns."

Riin Ruel thought immediately of Ezkia, the only nunnery near the Maze. She gestured her hands in prayer as well. "Divine Grace is all powerful," she said with conviction. "And all knowing."

This was a momentous occurrence! He was the boy who was born when Riin Ruell first visited Dayr Castle more than two centuries ago in search of the Bright One. The boy born of a King, instead of the hoped for girl of prophecy. Then he had appeared at Ezkia Nunnery. He had turned up unexpectedly in both places that Riin Ruel had searched for the Bright One. And now, he had returned to Dayr Castle, just as she had come back herself. Riin Ruel did not believe in coincidences. She was meant to meet Crown Prince Epohco. He was somehow important.

Riin Ruel rode up the Grand Way and greeted the stable manser, who remembered her from her beautiful horse. When he called a groom to take Lightning to her stall, Riin Ruel asked about Noot.

"Where is the stable boy?"

"He is no longer here," Utuno shook his head sadly. "He is now with us in spirit."

"I will pray for his spirit," the former Blade replied, gesturing the womb. She followed the groom into the stables. When she came back out with her bags and swords over her shoulder, Utuno was standing and talking with a weather-beaten, dark, muscular, and sinewy young man who was buying a horse.

He turned and gasped upon seeing the curved scabbards of her twin swords. She had the weaponry of a Blade. Could she possibly be the mystic warrior who had come to Dayr Castle in search of the Bright One so long ago? The one who had traveled to Ezkia Nunnery? She looked so much older than he would have expected. Her braided dreadlocks were white and wrapped in a bun on her head. Her black skin dried and wrinkled. Her body less than robust.

"Are you Riin Ruel?" he guessed uncertainly.

"I am," she bowed in respect. "You must be Crown Prince Epohco." He looked totally burnt and fried by the sun with blisters on his lips and nose. He had obviously spent most of his time away from the nunnery and out in the Waste itself.

"I am no longer that person," he brought his hands together in the sign of the womb. "Please call me Epoh."

"We have much to discuss!" Riin Ruel exclaimed.

"Yes," Epoh stopped her before she could say more. "But little time now. The girl you seek, the Bright One, she has gone to Karvor. She is the foundling from these stables."

Utuno gave a startled look of surprise. What did they mean, the Bright One?

"Her name is Tyme," Epoh continued. "She is trailing the man who killed Noot, the stable boy. I leave in the morning to find her. I assume you will come with me."

"I will be ready at first light," Riin Ruel agreed. They were obviously meant to travel together. She stepped forward and gave Epoh a heartfelt embrace. He hugged her firmly in return, and then strode resolutely back up to the keep to spend his last night with his family.

Tomorrow, he would ride out of Dayr Castle with the mystical warrior in search of his childhood friend, the young woman he loved, who was also the Bright One of prophecy heralded to bring back the return of the Ambri Empire.

A Bright One

The Making of a True Warrior

B. Burgess Junek

Book 4

A Bright One

A wild ride to a final conclusion of the remarkable 4-book series will lure the reader into an exhilarating and utterly gripping finale.

Tyme and Epoh reunite at last in the colorful, artistic, gambling city of Karvor. Both are apprehensive about their relationship after so long apart and nervous of adjusting to their dramatically changed roles—Epoh no longer a Crown Prince, and Tyme now heralded as the Bright One, with Riin Ruel proposing to train her as the Divine Dagger.

The intrigue and suspense grows along with the threat of coups and civil war as the characters strive to control their destinies in the gritty, evocative, and fascinating world of Ambra.

Coming out in November 2022

The Road of Dreams
A Two-year Hiking and Bicycling Adventure Around the World

Bruce B. Junek

Follow the unforgettable exploits of seasoned travelers Bruce Burgess Junek and Tass Thacker on their 26-month around-the-world bicycle trip.

They crossed four continents through sweltering temperatures and winter snowstorms--punctuated by 42 flats.

This deeply personal travel book is also the story of an inner journey with a compelling message: Recognize what you value most in life, and pursue it.

Available from the author at imagesoftheworld.com

Andes to the Amazon
Seven Journeys in Mexico, Central, and South America

Bruce B. Junek

Join Bruce and Tass on seven wild and
exotic trips south of the border.

Bicycling through Central and South America

Kayaking and swimming with whales in Baja

Hiking through cloud forests in Costa Rica

Snorkeling with penguins in the Galapagos Islands

Traveling by dugout canoe in the Amazon Basin

Available from the author at imagesoftheworld.com

GLOSSARY

Adept's pose - for sitting meditation, similar to sitting cross-legged, but with left ankle tight under groin area, and right outer ankle comfortable over left inner ankle or calf, hands relaxed on thigh or knees, palms open or up, which holds the back straight and erect

agavr – worker harvesting agave to make viruna liquor

Ambra - all countries and lands west of the Endless Waste

Ambri - people of the Ambri Empire

Ambri Empire - the great matriarchal civilization that arose from the chaos of the Dark Ages and lasted over six millennium (486 years), but broke apart two and a half millennium ago (200 years)

Attributes - the seven aspects or Attributes of Divine are Spirit, Womb, Love, Compassion, Truth, Justice, and Forgiveness

Beast - the devil, also excessive and uncontrolled male energy

Beatifics - choir songs, prayers, and praises of Divine

billy - a male ibex or goat

Blade - former personal guardians of the Empress now protecting the Czarzina

Book of Elders - the sanctioned holy word and writings about Divine

burner - a rebel follower of the Fire

castle gate - the main entrance into a castle

cavort - the back section of Womb temple for sexual love and fertility

centurion - a person who is 100 moons in age

condition - a thick walled and protected room to escape the heat with cool stone couches or beds to sit and lie upon, can also be any shelter from the afternoon heat, even just a hole dug in the ground to reach cool dirt

Czarzina - woman ruler of Ambrit replacing the Empress after the collapse of the Ambri Empire

Dagger - or Divine Dagger, secret warrior group seeking the Bright One to become Empress of a new Holy Ambri Empire

daya - type of horse bred in Dayrstad for mountain travel

decade - 10 moons or months

Divine - the Ambri name for God, who is female and gave birth to Creation

Divine Council - the women elders who establish and protect the holy doctrines of the faithful

Divine Daggers - secret warrior group seeking the Bright One to become Empress of a new Holy Ambri Empire

Divine Essence - Holy Spirit

Divine Fire - originally considered an Attribute of Divine, but much later banned by Divine Council and labeled a heretical men's cult or sun cult

Divine Fist - men's warrior group in the Barbarian kingdoms and old cities but not sanctioned in Ambrit

Divine Hand - a politically and religiously sanctioned warrior group for both women and men

Divine practice - a person's spiritual devotions, prayers, meditations, disciplines

Divine Womb - the temple, or the Mother temple

Divines - hymns and liturgical songs, Beatifics, Praises, Glorias, Hallelujahs

eyass - an unfledged (no flight feathers) bird of prey taken from the nest for training by a falconer

familiar - an animal that has an extra-ordinary and special bond with a person

fifir - queer or gender blend sexuality and behavior, with further defined terms:

   fafar - queer or transgender woman tending toward feminine

   fafor - queer or transgender woman tending toward masculine

   fe - intersex between she/he

   fer - intersex between her/him

   fers - intersex between hers/his

   fofar - queer or transgender man tending toward feminine.

   fofor - queer or transgender man tending toward masculine.

Fire - formerly Divine Fire, accused of being a sun cult, often for men only, some shamans believe only the Fire can purify the grievous   taint in men's souls

flaunt - teacher of sexual love and fertility expert who works at the cavort in the Womb temple

gate - entry way or tunnel through a fortified wall

gender terms - see fifir

gesture the womb - a greeting of peace with both hands prayerfully held loosely in front of the chest, forming a womb shape with the hands.

Glorias - traditional choir hymns used in worship glorifying Divine

grubber - a scavenger for lost treasure in the Endless Waste

hall of Attributes - entrance into Womb temple for both women and men

Hand - a protector, mentor, errand runner and guardian for nobility, also an enforcer

Hallelujahs - exuberant and ecstatic hymns of joy toward Divine

herselves - a group of women

herstory - history

herstorical - historical

herstorian - historian

Hilt of the Dagger - the leader of the Daggers, who seek the Bright One to become Empress of a new Holy Ambri Empire

keep - the walled inner most protected area of a castle

kookerboom - a sparse desert tree, no leaves but fleshy fingers at end of a few thick branches after rains

manser - master, male head of trade, or male title of respect

mantle(d) - a climbing term, the move made to get out of a swimming pool or pull up to get on top of a wall if there is no ladder

mark - a person targeted to swindle

marked - someone seen and noticed

mayhaps - maybe, perhaps

meda powder - from medaar plant, used as energy and sustenance when fasting

mew - a building for training birds of prey and keeping them while they molt and shed feathers

Milk - slang for Mother's Milk, the orphanage in the Womb temple

milker - a lactating woman, a woman who works at the Mother's Milk

mis - young woman

missin - loose woman, mistress

moon - one month, 29-30 days

moon blood - menstruation

moonboy - young male prostitute, also a starry-eyed man who thinks he's in love

Moonday - first day of the week as follows:

    dark Moonday or Divine Night begins the first day of each month

    bright Moonday starts the second week with evening socializing

    full Moonday begins third week with celebrations and festivals

    dim Moonday starts last week of month with dwindling moonlight

moon patio - a east facing patio for maximum enjoyment of early evening moonlight during bright and full moon, and also for receiving the healthy early morning rays of sun just after sunrise

Mother(s) – workers at the Mother's Milk

Mother's Milk - the mostly boys orphanage that is an integral part of every Womb temple

Mother Womb - largest or 1st Womb temple built in a town or city

mun - derogatory term for an adult male

Noble Path - a code of ethical combat behavior espoused by True Warriors

offiser - officer

old cities - cities formerly part of the Ambri Empire that are now all capitols of new countries

penat cactus - notoriously bland tasting and fibrous plant growing everywhere in the low mountains

philomanser - a male philosopher

philoser - philosopher

Point of the Dagger - the leading enforcer of the secretive Daggers, who seek the Bright One to become Empress of a new Holy Ambri Empire

practice - a person's spiritual devotions, prayers, meditations, disciplines

Praises - simple short, repetitive, and catchy songs praising Divine

precurser - precursor

priest - an ordained woman minister of Divine

professer - professor

prophet - a woman who makes Divine predictions and pronouncements

refuge - outermost section of Womb temple for men only

remembrance - the recalling of a dream sparked by seeing someone who is gifted to trigger such events

sanctuary - inner section of Womb temple for women only

sanctum - most holy inner section of Womb temple for menstruating women only

ser - title of respect for women

seremony - ceremony

seremonies - ceremonies

senasers - senators

shaman - a male clergy for men's rites, in the Womb refuge and subordinate to women priests

Siren - fortified decoy castle built by Ambri to delay Hool attacks from the Endless Waste

smear(ed) - climbing term, using surface area friction to stick against the rock when no holds are available

soothser - woman who makes daily life predictions and forecasts

stretching postures – hatha yoga

surge - another name for the power of moon blood, or menstruation

tanche - a loose muslin shirt and baggy pant with tight cuffs around the wrists and ankles

'tis - it is

True Warrior - men who follow Tatano's vows to serve the Women's Clans, protect the weak and innocent, and be morally strong in the way of Divine, which led to the end of the Dark Ages and the birth of the Ambri Empire

'twas - it was

tween - ages between 150 moons (coming of age/12 years) and 200 moons (full adulthood/16 years)

unfledged - a young bird without the strong feathers to sustain flight

viruna - a fiery and expensive golden liquor from Sikes, known throughout the Ambri Empire

Voice - originally called Peoples Voice, an area for open public forum and discussions on all topics

wait - the period between the first darkness of each night until the rising of the moon, which after the full moon increases nightly by nearly an hour

Will of the Blades - the leader of the Blades, the personal guardians of the Empress who now protected the Czarzina

Womb - a round and domed temple built to honor Divine, also the creative power of Divine

womb - a greeting of peace in a gesture of holding hands prayerful and lightly together in front of the chest

xerophyte - a plant that needs very little water

Yoke - ceremony and bone prayer bead connecting a Divine Warrior, who ritually slays an evil person, to take on their sin, and the demon behind the sin

Cast of Characters

Bayn Baya - Major in Heart Legion with spies and plans for a coop

Bokono - rebel leader of the Fire, originally from Birjj

Bones - clever and talkative raven raised by Jyg

Cata Cara - Heart Legion General who plans treason with Major Bayn Baya

Dari Riad - owner of the Dusted Man tavern in the Painted Hills near Karvor

Dracaro - brother to Crown Prince Epohco

Draktono - leader of the apprentices to the Singer

Duke - see below

Eddarko - Duke of the Siren, brother to King Eyrico, uncle to Crown Prince Epohco

Epoh - name Epohco calls himself after near drowning, former Crown Prince of Dayrstad

Etna Nate - sergeant in Heart Legion, plays cards with Gribono

Eyrico - King of Dayrstad and father of Crown Prince Epohco

Frisato - one of the apprentices to the Singer

Gambler – nickname for Gribono

Gribono - the gambler, spy for Captain Targono

Grinst - a tough, old grubber, desert survivalist and scavenger for lost treasure

Grodoro - sent by rebel leader Bokono to infiltrate and kill Singer

Gwen Gail - major at Ambrit Military Academy, covertly new Hilt of the Daggers, the leader of a secret mystical warrior society

Hana Hama Hala - Czarzina that imprisoned Riin Ruel

Harvig - apprentice grubber for lost treasure and former trail worker at Ezkia Nunnery, brother to Horton

Horton - a real grubber, older brother to Harvig, scavenger for lost treasures

Jakiko - set fire to Panr's dovecote and stole her pigeons

Jartlono - a boy from the choir of the Sikes Womb, becomes Singer

Jyg – Tyme's friend, manser of birds, companion of Bones the raven, climber extraordinaire

Klew - soldier of King's Guard who teaches Tyme the sword, full name Klewono

Lana Pana - acrobat, juggler, and bossy tween Ser Cus performer

Lartso - spy for Captain Targono to watch Duke Eddarko of the Siren

Mams - matriarch and leader of the Ser Cus

Narvago - coach and trainer for the Ser Cus

Noot - stable boy at Dayr Castle who is murdered by Gribono

Otovo - rebel from kiva on old trail to Birjj from Karvor

Ozono - leader of Canaries, the yellow powdered miners at Dusted Man tavern

Panr - pigeon breeder, partner with Pio (Jyg's uncle) whose birds are stolen

Pio - uncle to Jyg, owner of Pio's Pigeons and Chickens

Pranamo - Panr's son,

Riin Ruel - Blade to the Czarzina, covertly in the Daggers, a secret, mystical, warrior society

Shamano - an influential shaman and Fire devotee from the mountains of Birjj

Shelodo - Manser of Viruna to the King of Sikes, organizes Singer and the apprentices

Singer - Jartlono's new name after a mental breakdown and series of visions compels him to sing

Starai - baby girl Riin Ruel tested, later found Epoh near drowned and brought him to Ezkia Nunnery

Swindovo - youngest apprentice to the Singer who knows tavern songs

Tana Pana - young acrobat, juggler, and contortionist Ser Cus performer

Tao Tau - wise old herb woman who mentors Tyme on trips to Lost Valley

Targono - captain in Hammer Legion who plots a coup and send out spies, boyhood friend of Klew from Military Academy in Ambrit

Tatano - the first True Warrior, ended the Dark Ages when he convinced his soldiers to stop fighting for leadership amongst themselves and submit to the will of the Women's Clans, wrote Book of Tatano, only book by a man in the Book of Elders

Telapo - smuggler and brother to Shamano (the shaman from Birjj)

Tyme - the foundling of Dayr Castle and possible Bright One

Utuno - Manser of King's Stables where Tyme is raised

Vela Vara - Will of the Blades, the leader of the personal guards to the Czarzina who arrests and imprisons Riin Ruell

Weethee Wona - youngest and smallest female Ser Cus performer

Wera Wahn - naturalist, philosopher and survivor of failed Ambri expedition who becomes Saint of the Desert and founds Ezkia Nunnery

Wiir Waar - sword juggler and knife thrower in the Ser Cus

Xacano - philosopher and teacher at keep school, counselor to King Eyrico

Zandero - acrobat, tumbler, and juggler for the Ser Cus

Zintowo - finest male acrobat in the Ser Cus and all of Ambra

Z's - nickname for the cousins Zintowo and Zandero of the Ser Cus

ABOUT THE AUTHOR

B. Burgess Junek

Bruce Burgess Junek has traveled and bicycled with his wife, Tass Thacker, through more than 50 countries. In 1987 the two photographers created Images of the World to share the stories of their continuing adventures. To date nearly two million students have seen their educational school assembly slide presentations, along with adult audiences at festivals and cultural events.

A Bright One Chronicles is rich with influences from their journeys, including bicycling through the Kalahari, Sahara and Gobi deserts. Their pilgrimages to sacred shrines and temples around the world celebrates the universal longing to find meaning in life through personal practice, spiritual beliefs, and mystical teachings.

Bruce has written two travel narratives, The Road of Dreams and Andes to the Amazon, a rock climbing guidebook, and created the feature length documentary film Bruce & Tass Bicycle China. They still travel and are now enthralled with salsa dancing and cha cha. For more info visit :

www.imagesoftheworld.com   iow@hills.net
Instagram and TikTok @bbjunek / Facebook - Bruce Junek

www.ingramcontent.com/pod-product-compliance
Lightning Source LLC
Chambersburg PA
CBHW020227180626
46810CB00006B/2070